NORCREST GARDENS

To: [signature]

From: Isaac Winters

Norcrest Gardens

A Novel

Isaac Winters

Copyright © 2012 by Isaac Winters.

Library of Congress Control Number: 2012914655
ISBN: Hardcover   978-1-4771-5854-8
              Softcover   978-1-4771-5853-1
              Ebook   978-1-4771-5855-5

All rights reserved. No part of this book may be reproduced or transmitted in any form or by any means, electronic or mechanical, including photocopying, recording, or by any information storage and retrieval system, without permission in writing from the copyright owner.

This is a work of fiction. Names, characters, places and incidents either are the product of the author's imagination or are used fictitiously, and any resemblance to any actual persons, living or dead, events, or locales is entirely coincidental.

This book was printed in the United States of America.

To order additional copies of this book, contact:
Xlibris Corporation
1-888-795-4274
www.Xlibris.com
Orders@Xlibris.com

CONTENTS

Introduction		9
Chapter 1	In My World of Ruins	11
Chapter 2	All Strange Happenings To More Curious Questions	21
Chapter 3	Morbidity Becoming an Understatement	31
Chapter 4	Sordid Trials Faced For Answers	40
Chapter 5	The Rotting Man	48
Chapter 6	Is It Coincidence or Is It Fate?	59
Chapter 7	Leaving the Last Remnants	67
Chapter 8	Long Roads and Lacking Explanations	73
Chapter 9	All Roads and Nightmares to Meet	86
Chapter 10	Lovely Scenery and Devious Secrets	103
Chapter 11	In the Darkest Places the True Histories Hide	117
Chapter 12	Vicious Traditions and the Hell That They Bring	138
Chapter 13	Every Story Has an Ending, Be it for Better or for Worse	153
Epilogue		161
The End	The World in Ruins and the Aftermath	163

This book is dedicated to

Jennifer Winters, the love of my life
Sam
Dave
Austin "Cheese"
Mikey
Theresa
Kale
Matt "The Starr"
Kevin "The Action Man"
Dean
Steve "Mr. West"
Greg "The Heppster"
Parker
Johnny Ray "Opossum"
Scott "Nancy"
Mr. L Adams
And to anyone and everyone who believed in me and helped and supported me, through this endeavor. You all know who you are.

Sincerely,

Isaac Winters

INTRODUCTION

I've found that life has its odd ways of showing us how small we are in the grand scheme of things. So desperately we climb that mountain only for it to erupt into a volcano beneath us once we reach the summit. Maybe it doesn't happen to everyone; falling victim to metaphoric forces of nature, unfortunately, I was not lucky enough to escape it. Before I continue, I suppose that it would be fitting to explain some of the background and some of the events that acted as a catalyst for what got me to where I am now. For starters, my name is Evan Clarke, and before all this, I was a journalist and had published a few novels. I married my high school sweetheart Savannah Burke, who was the reason I went to college where I did my graduation. Shortly after our graduation, we moved back to our hometown and settled down. I started working for the local newspaper and had just published my first book, and all seemed right and good in the world, at least for a time.

Six years, three novels, and the purchasing of a few assets later, I began to notice a change in things. My wife was becoming more and more distanced from me, my last book stopped selling, and I lost my job at the paper. The job loss, though bad for obvious reasons, was really more of what I would count as a mixed blessing; frankly, I was never a good journalist.

Bad things happen. That much I understand, and it was simply my turn to draw the shit card out of the deck of cards we call life. What I didn't know was that the next hand would be the "coup de grâce," the royal flush of terrible things to lead me to the place I am now. I had just reached a point where I had decided to start pulling things together, and by "things," I mean my life. Starting the change was the thought of beginning a new book, something that had been a long time coming. The next came in the form of a lead on a new story; I may have lost my job, but I could still sell a news story. However, just as I began to think that it all was going to start the uphill climb again, a landslide crashed down on me—I was getting divorced. Now, disregard any precognitions that she had asked for it; I was the one who said the word first. She simply thought that it was a good idea.

As horrible as it all may seem, none of it nearly compared to what was to come, and what this story is all about. The loss of the job, the books dropping in sales, and even the divorce—they were all things that were foreseeable. Though no one ever wants to admit it and, sure as hell, don't ever see it, they are all horrors kept in those dark recesses of the mind: the "what ifs" and the "could it happen" that we all keep and refuse to acknowledge as things that might come to pass. All of them are events that would be considered realistic and very possible . . . But what about the things that never cross our minds? You would be blindsided, or at least I was.

The things that have happened, the things I have seen, I'll try to keep accurately to the way they have transpired. Even now I can see and hear them scratching at the windows and jostling the doors, just waiting for the moment. There's still so much that I don't understand and probably never will. Even if I survive this, I don't think anything or anyone short of God could explain this. I was looking for a story, and I got one.

Chapter 1

In My World of Ruins

A terrible electronic beeping filled the room and pulled me from my coma-like sleep. At first, I couldn't recognize the sound. I only knew that it was maddening and had to be stopped. The span of a few moments passed with the god-awful noise still chiming before I gained the perception enough to figure out that it was the phone on the nightstand ringing off the hook. I groaned and rolled over to pick up the receiver; I had forgotten that I had asked for a wake-up call, and hell forbid that I be late for that day of days.

"Yeah?" I asked as I picked up the phone. I didn't mean to sound so perturbed, but the hangover was running strong, and I honestly didn't want to face that day's dealings.

"Good afternoon, Mr. Clarke! This is the wake-up call you had asked for." The desk clerk's enthusiasm was far too much for me to deal with. I suppose that was my punishment for going cheap on a long-term room for rent; most corporate chains used synthetic and automated room calls, but the "Mom & Pop" I went for used real service.

"Oh, yes, good, good . . . Mission accomplished and all that, thanks." I heard his voice on the other end saying good-bye as I sat the receiver back on the base. Although it wasn't my general pattern of behavior to wake up in the afternoon, the light binge of drinking I was on had changed my normal time frames—late nights and late mornings.

For the last three months, I had been living in that hotel room. My wife had more or less asked me to leave after what I came to realize was our last argument. That day was the day I had worked so hard to prolong, the day that I got to see her again.

Sitting up in the bed, I rubbed my face in some strange gesture of waking up. I sat there for a while until I knew that time was running short, delaying the inevitable. Throwing the covers off and standing up to stretch out happened in one motion, I had held off long enough. There was a sudden consumption of a bad feeling, a sadness that I could not shake away, despite that, I continued on to the bathroom.

I took a long, cold shower and then took the towel off the rack to dry off. There in the mirror, I saw my reflection as I was about to shave.

Who are you trying to impress? I thought to myself as I lowered the razor back down to the sink. The truth was that it was nobody; my battle was lost, and the fight in me had gone. All that there was left was to follow through with the conclusion of the events that had unfolded before me. I went to my suitcase, pulled out some clothes, and put them on: a faded pair of jeans, a maroon T-shirt, and a brown with white pinstripe button-up shirt. One last look in the mirror showed me my short and slightly messy light brown hair, and I had not the slightest intention of combing it. For a moment, I knew that I was all that I had and that I was all that was left. **I looked into my reflection's Topaz blue eyes and said,

"You can do this . . . You have to do this."

With that, I made for the front door of the hotel room.

Down the stairs and to my Jeep I went, and it was sitting there in the dull noontime glare shining off its metallic olive-green hood. That jeep, my vehicle, was the only thing that had been a constant in my life; like a modern day horse to its knight or lone ranger, it was always there. I got in and turned the ignition to fire up the eight cylinders of American-made power and drove off to my inevitable horizon.

The short drive over and the parking lot itself seemed barren; there were very few cars, pedestrians, or even signs of life on the way there. Another overcast September day in Colorado; although it was unusually rainy for the time of year, I figured that it was the reason for the town seeming so dead. I sat there in the parking space smoking a cigarette for a moment before I pulled the e-brake and turned off the motor. A number of things were crossing my mind, and not a good thought among them; my stomach began to knot up, and my hands were shaking a bit. I knew that I couldn't sit there sulking any longer, though I personally would rather have done that than opening the door and stepping out into the cold rain as I did. There was only one step left to take, and no matter how badly it hurt me to admit it to myself, I started my walk across the parking lot to the courthouse where, it all would end.

Gripping the cold metal door handle, I entered the building, and it was more or less how I would have expected it to be. It reeked of that "dentist's office" smell and fake foliage—that very unmistakable and sinister scent of a strange cleanliness. In front of me, there was a large plate glass divider between the entryway and the rest of the building, and to my right was a rather fat security guard and his equally fat counterpart standing watch over the metal detector. I walked over to the conveyor and x-ray system and placed my pocketed items in the tray: cell phone, keys, wallet, those sorts of things. As I walked up to the metal-detecting corridor, the guard put his hand up as if to say stop.

"Your shoes," he said in a plain and monotone voice.

I looked at him confusedly for a moment and then complied with his wishes and was about to walk through when he put his hand up again.

"Your belt too." His bland voice and pointless demands were starting to get on my nerves.

"Really? Am I flying somewhere?" I shut up and did as I was directed to.

I finally got to walk through the checkpoint, but they weren't quite done with me yet. As soon as I walked through, the other guard, who was silent the whole time, got up and waved the handheld detector over me.

"Enjoy what you do?" I asked sarcastically as he finished up.

"Yep. Get your items from the tray," he said, pointing over to it.

I gathered my belongings and returned them to their rightful places and proceeded down the hall. Before me was a large digital board directing all cases to various rooms and times, I found my allotted place and realized that I was ten minutes late. On that discovery, I hurried down the hall as quickly as I could without running. Swinging open the door revealed a very empty courtroom; the only people in there were the judge, the bailiff, the lawyer, and her. I was never the one to make grand entrances, and most certainly not the one who liked all eyes on him, but that was the moment for both.

"Evan, you're late!" The judge's voice thundered out from across the courtroom.

"Sorry, Henry . . . I mean, Your Honor." Oddly enough, I knew the judge very well; he was my neighbor growing up, and a very good neighbor at that, not to mention, the various speeding tickets that kept me in his professional presence throughout my life. I made my way down the aisle and took my seat at the table to the left and waited for it all to begin, or end, depending on how you look at it. Everything that carried on was like a dream, a bad one at that, and it all felt extremely surreal. The words went on without me as everyone spoke their piece while I was barely there, and then it was my turn.

"Mr. Clarke . . . Mr. Clarke!" The judge yelled out.

His voice brought me from the distance that I had found and back into the matter at hand.

"Yes?" I asked completely unaware of his reason for calling my name.

"I asked if both parties are 100 percent in agreement for dissolution of this marriage, and if you had anything to add before we conclude this matter." He looked at me expectantly when he was done speaking. I looked back at him with a confused expression on my face and unsure of what to say, still in a bit of a haze.

"Uhhh . . . Yeah, that was fun . . . Can I sign whatever I need to and go?" Why I said that, I still have no idea. At least on the upside, it drew some pretty interesting reactions. After a few more minutes of formalities and all that junk, I signed the paperwork and made my way to the outside.

Just out of the building, I stopped and lit up a cigarette, took a long slow drag, and blew the smoke up into the sky.

"Hey, Evan . . ." I knew that soft, sweet voice anywhere, and I turned around to see my as-of-moments-ago ex-wife. I looked at her for a moment trying to figure out what to say, but I could only decide that there was nothing to say at all.

"Why did you say that back in the courtroom? I don't want any hard feelings out of this. We're just two people who didn't work out," she said it in way that was so matter of fact.

"Yes, says the one who kept everything and left me with nothing." I could see that it hurt her, and there were very mixed feelings in me about what I had just said.

"That was what you agreed to, and the only way around alimony payments, Mr. Clarke." Her smarmy bastard of a lawyer walked out of nowhere and crammed in his unwanted two cents, causing me to lean toward very violent tenancies.

"Shut your fucking mouth! I am not at all above hitting you, especially now! Hitting you right in your shit-spewing face, you dirty bastard!" I clenched my fists tight and walked over to him with my cigarette hanging out of my mouth.

"And after I'm done kicking your worthless ass, I'm going to walk back into that courthouse and proudly turn myself in." His beady eyes widened at the idea of actual confrontation, and I could tell that he knew that his worm-like physique wouldn't fare well with such an ordeal. He looked around nervously for a moment and then hurriedly walked away. The sickening attorney looked back one last time from the middle of the parking lot, and I raised up my forearm and flipped him off.

"Evan . . . I'm sorry, but . . ." I cut her off before she could finish.

"No, don't say it. I got my jeep, the cabin, and a few other things that I need. So really, there's nothing, and I mean *nothing*, left to discuss. Have a nice life." I turned from her and briskly walked away.

"Evan, please . . . ," she pleaded as I strode away.

"If there's anything else, have your dick-weed lawyer contact me!" I shouted over the distance of the parking lot as I was returning to my jeep. There really wasn't anything left to say, and all there was left was to wait for the divorce decree to come in the mail.

Satisfied with my performance, I covered the rest of the parking lot to where I left my jeep. As I made my way, I couldn't help but notice again the dark gray overcast weather. I couldn't say that it was unusual for autumn, but there was a strange sense looming in the air. Some combination of nausea and light-headedness came on for a brief moment. Perhaps that was the reality of things setting in. I couldn't be sure. I was sure that there was a possibility that it was how all men feel after leaving the place that finalized their divorce. With all the thoughts racing through my head, I was too preoccupied to pay attention to where I was going. At least until I ran into *him*. He was a strange man, about a foot shorter than my 5'10", and clad in a black trench coat and a hooded sweater underneath. He had the hood pulled down enough to shroud his face and hands buried deep in his pockets, and looking down at the ground and mumbling incoherent gibberish.

"Oh shit. I'm sorry. I wasn't looking where I was going." I apologetically backed up from him, hoping to get some sort of reply. He walked a little further past me and then stopped; a horrific scent trailed behind him much like rancid meat. He slowly turned and looked up at me. His face was incredibly pale, sickly white-gray in color, and his shaggy and mangy looking gray-white hair could be seen in a few places coming down around his face. His eyes were probably the most unsettling feature as they had an odd glaze to them reminiscent of cataracts. I stood there staring back at him for a moment unable to move. I felt locked in place for some unexplainable reason as he stared back.

"Are you okay, man?" I asked knowing that he might not need help in any conventional sense of the word. He tilted his head to the side in a twitching motion and raised his hand out of his pocket to point at me. I began to walk away backward as not to take my eyes from him, unsure of what might do. He continued with his unfathomable chanting as he stood there pointing. It seemed as though his murmuring was directed at me. However, he didn't seem angry or insulted; the look he gave me was fear. It was about that time he began to muster an intelligible sentence.

"Go . . . They want . . . you . . . Run . . . they come . . . for . . . you . . . It came . . . to . . . me. came to me . . . first . . . meant for you . . . They want . . . you . . ." The more he said, the more violently his arm began to quiver. The scene had become too much for me to handle. It was the last thing I needed to have happen after just leaving that terrible courthouse. The need to flee came quickly to mind as the disturbed man continued the same chanting and rambling of those same words. I turned and began power walking to my jeep. I looked back to see the man still standing there pointing. My quick walking turned into a dead on sprint to my vehicle as I felt chased by an unknown terror. As I came to the door, the keys could not be retrieved from my pocket fast enough.

The cold cloth of the driver seat came as a surprising relief. Whatever the hell that was about, it was most definitely not normal, at least not to my daily routines. The jeep started as it normally did, then I popped the clutch and burned rubber as I tore hell out of that parking lot. My escape was well justified as I drove up the highway out of town toward the deep forest and cabin that awaited my return. The drive was about an hour and a half away, which was too much time for me to be alone and sober. I needed a strong drink and a peaceful setting. I reached over to the knob on the radio and cranked the tunes that would get me there in one piece, at least mentally anyway. The ever-darkening curvy mountain road led me to hope that good things were soon to come.

Getting to the driveway, I could see nothing more than a silhouette of my woodland refuge. The sun was making its final descent behind the mountain side, bringing the blanket of twilight behind it. I grabbed a couple of suitcases from the back of the jeep, intending to come back for the rest of my belongings later. It was an odd feeling walking upto that entrance for the first time in about six months or so. Upon unlocking it, the door made an eerie and forlorn creek as it was slowly opened.

The cabin had the feeling of neglect and being unused. I bought it at the peak of my performance, when there was something to get away from. Was that why it was all that I wanted? A place to run away to? Back to a place that I thought I was the happiest? I wasn't sure. There was, however, a comfort in the solitude. The small mountain cabin in the middle of nowhere Colorado was my retreat from the madness prior. I thought for a moment that there was at least one thing to be thankful for. I had put the cabin on the market through a realtor when I lost my job; lucky for me that it hadn't sold yet, and the utilities were left on for showing the place. I figured that I should probably give the agent a call to inform him of the situation, but that was something that could be left for another day; I really didn't want to talk to anyone.

Naturally, I've always been a solitary person; such a quality is very fitting of a writer or so I'm told. Although I was very alone, I was lacking something; in all actuality, it was someone. Solitude I could deal with, loneliness I could not; believe it or not, there is a big difference between the two. I beat back the sad feelings the best that I could and began to look around what would be my new home. The cabin had little to offer, just the basics and just enough to survive, and a telephone in case I needed it. The mostly barren walls and empty floor made an excellent retreat for uninterrupted seclusion. The ill lit living room though for the most part empty, offered understanding and open arms. It seemed that the cabin itself knew everything that I was feeling, and why I was running. I set my bags by the couch and sat for a moment to collect myself. My sight jumped around the room looking at the unvarying wooden walls and the creaky hardwood floor. So that was home.

Though it had little to offer in the guise of entertainment and the like, it did house an impressive stock of my favorite spirits. The kitchen acted as my storeroom for the liquid of perdition. Walking in, I was almost shocked at how little there actually was as far as kitchen devices go: a small refrigerator and small stove opposite an even smaller sink nestled in the counter top. I opened up the cabinet to reveal a rather puny collection of dusty plates, glasses, and bowls. Two varieties of the before-mentioned kitchenries did not interest me; I needed a glass. After rinsing away the evidence of time's passing from the glass, I made my way into the pantry that hid my immaculate collection. Opening the door, I revealed to myself the long untouched gallery of whiskies, bourbons, and varieties of scotch. No matter what I would decide, there was no bad choice. I opted for the tried and true: The Glenlivet twelve years old. It was time to get reacquainted with my surroundings; that meant breaking the ice, and that beverage was the "ice breaker."

The clear golden liquid made a comforting sound as it splashed against the bottom of the glass. It was the sound that somehow vindication would soon be reached. I raised the glass to my lips and began the process. The persey liquid stung as it moved down my throat, a feeling I had recently grown accustomed to. I made my way back to the living room bottle and glass in hand. I sat at the hardwood table for two at the far end, staring into the darkness outside of my window. With each passing drink, I became more numb to the emotions that clouded me from rational thought, trading one dream for another. That was the way it was supposed to go and the way that I wanted it.

It didn't seem too much later that my thoughts began to overtake my mind. What was supposed to help me to get rid of the maddening emotions began to amplify them. I could scarcely beat back the memories of brighter days. I dwelled back to times with my ex, when we were still happily married. Nostalgic flood gates opened more and more as I drank. Every glass I filled augmented my far-gone days and recollected times. All those things that previously would not be acknowledged came as a formidable terror as I sat in the dim room. I felt like something in me had died, and I was becoming all too obvious that the new void was not soon to be filled. I was just coming to realize what it meant to lose a best friend, and it was killing me. There was only one thing I could think to do, so I sat there and I cried.

I was snapped out of my pathetic sobbing state that I was in by the sound of a loud ringing. For a confused moment, I stared at the wall that the phone was hanging on. The phone was ringing? Another loud ring followed confirming that the source was, in fact, the phone. Much to my dismay, I looked at my watch as the phone continued its terrible banter. The time read one o'clock in the morning, too late or early, depending on how you looked at it, for someone to be calling. Aside from the time, there were very few people who knew the cabin's phone number: close family, my ex, the nearest post office, and emergency services. Far be it for me to question, but why would any of the before mentioned be calling?

I wiped my eyes and got up from the table. Cautiously, I made my way over to the phone's location. Too many thoughts and questions burned though my scotch-soaked brain to pick just one. The phone continued its annoying song as I reached for the receiver.

"Hello?" I uttered in an almost frightened voice. It was to my surprise that I was met with no voice on the other end.

"Hello?" Again I asked expecting to hear the same from someone. After a moment, I could hear what sounded like a distorted and echoing static.

"I said hello!" saying what I wanted to be the last time. Just as I was about to hang up, a voice came through on the other end.

"I . . . will . . . be . . . waiting . . . there . . . Norcrest . . ." The voice that came through was soft but severely distorted. The chills that it sent down my spine were unbearable; whatever was on the other end of the conversation was causing immense stress to ensue.

"What?" Confusion and some form of anger took my speech.

"I know you . . ." The voice returned in a nearly inaudible whisper, it was said quickly and not as distorted as it was before.

"You know me? What?" The call ended with a slow click, followed by the sharp buzzing of being hanged up on. What the hell was that? I could barely wrap my mind around what just happened. Not to mention, the other terrible events of that day. Was it a prank? Did someone get hold of my number by accident? Whatever it was, I thought of a familiar number to see if everything was all right.

I dialed faster than I ever had before.

"Hello?" I was met by a well-known and soft-spoken voice.

"Savannah?" I asked just to be certain. Given the day's track record, I wasn't sure what to be sure of; yet I was confident about that one.

"Evan? Evan, is that you?" she answered. Just the sound of her voice put me at a slight ease. My heart rate stayed elevated, however, as I still was unsure of why was calling her and really didn't know what her reaction would be to my doing so.

"Yeah, it's me." I could hear in my own voice the distraught tone. I was shaken, and the odd part of it was that there wasn't much of a reason to be, not just then anyway. Though all of it was really quite unexplainable, my feelings about that day shouldn't have been lumped into the category of fear. I just needed to make sense of it all, and I was hoping that the phone call would clear the air that sat heavy over and all around me.

"Why are you calling so late?" The fact of the matter was that I had no good answer. All I could do was mutter out the first words that came to mind.

"Did . . . Did you try calling?" In the back of my mind, I knew she didn't. I suppose I asked merely out of sheepish hope.

"No, it's one thirty in the morning. Is everything okay?" Her concern was genuine, and I once again felt a little peace of mind. Clearly, it wasn't her who called. Any doubt I had in my mind was confirmed, which still left the question about who the hell it was.

"No reason. I'm at the cabin, and I missed a phone call. I just thought it might have been you . . . Not many people have this number." It was the best excuse I could make for my erratic behavior.

"Evan, are you sure everything is okay? You sound . . . different." I didn't want to tell her that it wasn't; that everything was pretty damn far from being okay.

"I'm sorry. I know we really shouldn't keep talking like this . . . ." Retreating was the only option I felt that I had. Besides, just hearing her voice was enough to rip out my heart all over again.

"It's all right, Evan, really. Are you sure everything's fine?"

"Yeah . . . Yeah . . . Well, I should go now." It was about all I could manage to say.

After getting off the phone, I realized that I was acting like I should have been institutionalized. I needed to just sit down and relax; the stresses of the day had become too much, and I had negated the whole purpose of my being there. By then, the self-help I was treating myself to was in full effect. My mind and body became numb and void of the feelings that tormented me. The final act of my drunken nirvana I had found was to put my tired body to rest. I was confident that by the time that I came around the next day, all would have returned to some form of normalcy. I swaggered my way to the bedroom to find my resting place. I last remember slumping on the bed, and a deep sleep came soon after.

Still sleeping, I felt some warmth come over me. My mind, felt as if I were awake.

"Evan . . . wake up, dear . . . ." I fought hard to open my eyes, but when I finally did, I saw her. It was her voice that brought me from my poisoned slumber that I had entered what seemed like an eternity before. How long was I asleep? Was everything just a bad dream, a nightmare? No, that was not the voice of my ex-wife. As I looked up at the woman in a dazed stare, I was filled with a euphoric feeling. The beautiful woman stood before me surrounded by what seemed to be a soft white blue light. She was wearing a light blue, long cotton gown, with her golden hair stopping at her shoulders. The petite figure moved closer to me in sort of a blurred motion. I got a better look at her face as she came over. Her slender face was soft and kind, with a very light complexion. She had some trace of a smile on her faintly pink lips, and her eyes were green to the likes I had never seen before, a brilliant bright emerald green. As my eyes met her, I saw a look that held much familiarity. There was a look of longing and happiness and filled with a feeling I once was looked at with . . . Love? It wasn't in a romantic sense though, there was something of a maternal quality that I couldn't quite understand.

"Who . . . who are . . . you?" My words came as a struggle. I knew that I was drunk, but there was something else. It was not the average slurring and trouble finding words common with intoxication. I had to force the words out. She moved closer to my face then and placed her hand on my cheek. There was a sensation of warm and cool at the same time, coupled with a heart racing lift in my chest.

"Don't be silly . . ." she whispered softly. The softness of her voice and beauty of her smile caused everything that punished me from hours before fade. Somewhere in the back of my mind, I had the inclination that I should be alarmed that some woman I didn't know was in my room, yet I had no alarming thoughts or emotions. Her presence brought some sense of divinity all around me in a way I had never felt before. Despite all those wonderful feelings, I still couldn't stop my inquisitive mind.

"You . . . kn . . . know . . . me?" Why were my words so hard to mutter? It was as if I was just learning to speak. It strained me to talk in every way it could, ridiculously difficult.

"Of course, I do. Why else would I be here?" Her words echoed in my mind as I tried to put it altogether. For some reason, in the state of mind I was in, what she said made sense to me. I looked around the room to see if my settings had changed. It came as a shock to me when I could move nothing more than my eyes, and even that was troublesome. Straining my gaze about me, I could tell that everything was the same. The only difference that I could see was that there was a haze over everything, and the room looked to have a soft brightness or glow to it, much like the girl.

"Here . . . Wh. why . . . here . . . ?" I knew in my mind what I wanted to say, but there was something breaking the connection to my voice. What was it?

"You will know why . . . soon." After she spoke, she began to pull away. As she did, a sharp and terrible ringing began to overtake my sense of hearing. It was like my ears were ringing after a loud noise but amplified beyond all reason. As if someone turned the volume of a speaker up beyond its capability. Simultaneously, the room's soft glow had gone from subtle to unbearable. The intense white light enveloped the room to the point that I could hardly make out the woman's figure. The torment of the blinding light and ringing distorted my thoughts as I struggled to bear all of it.

"If you go there . . . I will be waiting." Her whispered words were narrowly heard over the horrible ringing. The sensory overload made my head feel like it was about to explode. If there ever was a time I thought that I was dying, that was it. As much as my body ached and trembled, I was able to muster up enough strength and will to cover my ears and tightly close my eyes. The intensity was too much though, and my efforts were futile as the hell continued.

"St . . . sto . . . p . . . stop!" I yelled at the top of my lungs in a last desperate attempt to end all the madness.

I awoke sitting straight up in my bed, still covering my ears with my hands. I lowered my arms and looked around the room. Once again, or even still, I was surrounded by the night. The most obvious difference was that the extreme ringing had subsided. As easy as it would be to discredit all what had just happened to being a very stress induced dream, I couldn't allow that conclusion so easily; it was all too real. Again, for that to have been real would be more troubling than just some vivid fantasy. My head was still splitting, and I could recall every little detail of the experience, not a characteristic of any dream I've ever had. Weary of the toiling thoughts, I looked over to the nightstand and grabbed my pack of cigarettes. Another odd realization hit me; I didn't recall leaving my smokes there. Weird as it might have been, it didn't stop me from opening the pack and enjoying its contents. The need to sooth my rattled nerves was the immediate thought as I lit my nicotine therapy.

"It had to have been a dream . . ." I whispered aloud between drags. Sitting there at the edge of the bed, I tried to piece everything from that moment together. A better question, who was that girl? I've had dreams, including people other than myself, sure, but that was different. There was somehow a familiarity to her presence; it was like I'd known her from long ago, but I can honestly say that I had never seen her before. If ever I had seen or met her, I know I would have remembered; there was something very different about her. My scattered thoughts ran in too many directions, and all the spinning had left me drained. I reached to the ashtray and put out the smoke, then promptly slumped back down on the bed. Although there was some degree of fear for falling back to sleep, there was also a twisted curiosity as well. Either way, sleep was inescapable; I was tired, so tired.

Chapter 2

All Strange Happenings To More Curious Questions

The telephone was not the first thing I wanted to hear after a long night of heavy drinking and disturbing dreams, but it's god-awful ringing acted as my alarm clock. I glanced over to the nightstand in my hardly awake daze to see the time: 12:46 p.m.

"Jesus . . ." I groaned in very perturbed tone. It was very evident that I had a rough night. I slowly moved out of bed, the calling of that terrible device on the wall still chiming for my attention. As I made my way over to the persistent phone, I couldn't help but feel like I was hit by a car the night before. My body hurt, my head pounding, and it felt like every tiny strand of muscle fiber I had got an intense workout. I carefully grabbed the receiver and put it to my ear.

"Hello?" I asked, halfway expecting it to be the voice from the night before. Although I had no reason to believe that it would be, or that any of those events had even taken place, I couldn't stop my curiosity from wondering.

"Good afternoon, Mr. Clarke. I've got something here for you. It came in yesterday." The voice sounded like Thomas, the man who worked at the small forgotten post office in town. It had been some time since I had talked to him, mainly because it had been some time since I had been at the cabin. Back when I was still getting mail from fans, publishers, and the like, I'd always ask him to call me if anything came for me. More specifically, anything that might seem important enough to drive all the way down for. The post office in that small rocky mountain setting was about a thirty-minute drive from here; one could well imagine that it would be a huge pain in the ass to check daily. There was only one thing that didn't make sense about the call. How did he know I was there at the cabin?

"I see. Just out of curiosity, what made you think to call me here?" A valid question I thought. With so few people knowing where I was, there had been a lot of calls to that location. On top of that, it struck me as odd that he would call me "Mr. Clarke." He only ever called me that when I first bought the place years ago.

You can't talk to someone frequently over a few years and not get a little personal. Point and case, we were generally on a first-name basis.

"It will be waiting for you . . . ." That wasn't the first time I had heard some semblance of those words, and it brought back the same bone-chilling feeling that I had before. Apart from his choice of words, there was something off about him, and I couldn't quite put my finger on it. Granted, I knew I had been rattled over the last couple of days, so maybe that was it. I was just being overly inquisitive.

"Okay . . . What is it by the way?" There was long silence from the other side of the phone. After a moment, there was a kind of static in resemblance of the call from the night before.

"Hello?" I asked in an almost frantic tone. I'd never been one for repeat history, especially repeating unpleasant ones. Perhaps the phone line was damaged or possibly even the phone itself; the Rocky Mountains did have their fair share of lightning storms. It had been a long time since either had been serviced or even touched for that matter. That could've been the root of all the strange phone occurrences. Despite the more immediate happenings, it was something that needed looking into. There was a familiar sound of the other phone hanging up. Confused and slightly upset, I set the receiver back on the base. None of it was making any sense; the pieces just weren't fitting. That led to say that there were in fact pieces, and to that point, I wasn't sure that there were pieces of anything. It all seemed like a collage of shitty and random events.

I thought back for a moment, over everything that had taken place in the last twenty-four-hour time frame. Sure there were some unusual happenings, but there was one in particular that sat on top of the hellish pile of brain activity I had suffered then, the divorce. Not even the divorce per say, but maybe the final act of signing the papers that made it so real. So real to the point that I had just slipped into a bad state of mind. All the stress, unresolved thoughts, and emotions were getting to me. I just needed to remember why I came to the mountain retreat and to fulfill that very reason. Besides, everything can be taken the wrong way, depending on how it's looked at.

After a moment, I walked away from the phone and into the kitchen. With the thought of collecting myself, I reached to the cold water handle of the sink and turned it on. The sound of the rushing water hitting the basin was uniquely soothing. As I bent down and began splashing the cold water on my face, many of the plaguing thoughts I had over the last day or so ceased for a time. A few moments of that went by before I cranked off the water valve and stood up for a deep sigh of release. I reached for a nearby dish towel to dry off with and a glass that I promptly filled with water. I stood there for a time, staring out of the window above the sink. As I admired the view of an overcast sky floating above the rocky mountain forest, I was calmed enough to see that I was ready for whatever was to come next.

There were two things that I needed to accomplish that day as I saw it: first, the post office. I had to see what the hell that call was about and what was waiting for me. Second, I needed to head back to a town with a decent enough shopping center to buy a new phone. Trivial as the tasks might have seemed, I felt that they needed to be fulfilled. At least reaching those small goals would be a good start. I reached the glass of water I had filled to my lips and drank down the clear refreshing waves as I went over the simple plan of action I laid out in my head.

I walked out of the cabin to be met with the crisp and cool embrace of the season's air. My jeep seemed to be as ready as I was when I jumped into the driver seat and started it up, we were off to make some sense of all of it. First gear was winding high as I took it from the driveway and out to the main road. Traversing the path, I couldn't help but crack the window to let in the scent of the fall season. The all-too-familiar smell of the early afternoon mist reminded me of my childhood; it brought back one memory, in particular. Though faded and incomplete, I could see myself as a little boy stepping out of the classroom onto the playground. If memory served me correctly, I had feelings of being alone and insecure. I thought deeper on the memory as I drove along the road; I had time to dwell. As I dove deeper into the past thoughts, I remembered why I felt the way that I did. The little boy that was me felt the way he did because he really was alone. It came to me that the time I was reminiscing about was the year I had started at a new school, and I didn't know a single person. I was naturally a shy kid early on, and it was hard for me to make friends because of it. This sudden travel down memory road was peculiar, as I hadn't thought back like that for a very long time.

The ongoing air of the autumn sky flowed into my jeep, sparking further exploration into this odd spur of memory. I was brought back to that child version of myself standing bundled up in my coat and hat, standing alone on the playground. Though there were other kids, I was the new one and the odd one out. Perhaps that was close to the way I was feeling about the current predicament. How old was I? I really couldn't pinpoint my age. Then it came to me: I was twelve. Twelve, it seemed a significant age as if there was something important lost in the complex maze that was time. I could remember more with each passing breath, but there seemed to be something missing. I could see a man walking across the playground along with my mom, and they were coming to me. I drove down the ever-twisting road replaying that same memory over and over, but I couldn't remember passed that. Nothing beyond being approached by my mother and that man came to mind. For some reason, though I couldn't remember, I felt some unsavory event had transpired. Twenty-four years had gone by since that point in time had come and gone, and I wasn't sure why it had surfaced then.

My being lost in thought was evident by me reaching the post office in what seemed like record time. I was too deep within my memories to realize that I had come to my destination. I turned the wheel and pulled into the gravel driveway to reveal a much more weathered building than I remembered. Pulling into the anyone's guess parking spot, I couldn't help but examine the structure. The once sea foam green siding had faded into a very light green-white color, and the wood shingle roof was in dire need of repair. As I parked my jeep and stepped out, I could see that the windows had not been washed in quite some time, and the screen door was on it last literal hinges of life. The overcast sky and degraded building made for a very unsettling scene as I got out of my jeep and approached the entrance. My feelings of discomfort were enhanced as I stepped onto the creaky low-sitting deck and opened the door, only being greeted by the bell above. I looked upon the surroundings well; though the outside seemed a bit tarnished, the interior had not changed at all since the last time I was in it. The PO boxes still lined the walls and gave a soft shine at me as if no time had gone by. Over to my left was still the hardwood counter with a nice dark cherry finish that looked ageless, along with all the office supplies one would expect to see on a desk. Then in the center of the room, there was the small kiosk that held envelopes of various shapes and sizes. Given the state of the external look of the building, I was rather shocked to see everything inside exactly the way I remembered it. I walked toward the counter over the beautiful picture frame wooden floor to see if I could get the attention of Thomas who was most likely in the backroom.

"Hello?" My voice was slightly raised. Thomas was an older gent, and I wanted to be sure he heard me. There was a sound of someone slowly getting out of a chair from the back; I could almost see him already. If nothing in there had changed, I was sure he hadn't either. I imagined the short and round man coming about the corner, still wearing his denim overalls and plaid button-up flannel shirt. His gray hair combed to the side, of course, and thick handlebar mustache. Possibly one of the most memorable features was his room-lighting smile. No one could make you feel more at home than he did. Admittedly, over the years of my going there, he became much like the grandfather figure that I never had. The reality of the situation, however, was a lot different than what I had built up in my head. From around the door frame of the back room came a man that I knew was not Thomas. He was taller than me and held a very muscular build, wearing a red flannel shirt with the sleeves rolled up. The only two resembling features were his mustache, and the fact that he looked like a much younger Thomas in the face.

"What can I do for you, sir?" He came across as very friendly and polite. Though I wasn't sure of it, I imagined that he was somehow related to Thomas.

"Yes, I have a post office box here, and I got a call that there was something waiting for me." I choked on my own words. I didn't quite ask exactly what I wanted.

"A call, huh?" His puzzlement was obvious. It would make sense that he wouldn't know of it if he didn't place the call himself. "I'm pretty sure I'd remember calling someone to pick up their mail if I did. When did you get the call?" The statement he made caused my confusion of the situation to increase. I was sure that it was Thomas who called, though he sounded a little off. It had to have been him.

"It was about forty-five minutes ago. I live in a cabin just up the hill from here." I thought if I explained a little more that it might jar a thought.

"I've been here by myself all morning. Are you sure it was this post office?" I could see that he really had no idea what I was going on about. At the risk of sounding crazy, I asked what I meant to all along.

"Well, the man on the phone was Thomas. I used to come by here all the time when he'd call and tell me I had mail. I've just been away for a while. Is Thomas here?"

"Thomas? He's my uncle. I took over for him here about a month ago when he started getting sick. He just had a stroke about two days ago."

As he said those words, I could feel my eyes widen and heart rate start to increase. None of it made sense at all and was in many ways peculiar to the point of nearly being frightening. I thought that I had put some of the pieces I had together, yet there seemed to be an ever-growing puzzle before me. Though, the situation had become that much more bizarre, I decided to keep that man's involvement to a minimum. Not to mention anything that would have kept any suspicions of weirdness off me. There was no need to talk about that call any further as I saw it. So I played it off as something else.

"I'm sorry. I must be mistaken then. You have a good one." As I turned to leave, he said something that stopped me dead in my tracks.

"I did get two things in for an Evan Clarke. Is that you by chance?" Though that man had never called me or even met me for that matter, whoever did wasn't lying.

"Uhhh . . . Yeah, that would be me. When did they come in exactly?" I tried to hide whatever perplexity might have been in my voice.

"The package is dated for about a month ago, but the other has been here for just a day or two. I think that the package was delivered to the wrong addresses . . . a few times. There are a lot of 'return to senders' and 'wrong addresses' written on it. I haven't gotten around to putting them in your box yet. For some reason, Thomas had the package at his house. You can take 'em now if you want." He reached down behind the counter and pulled out a package about the size of a CD case and about six inches tall, wrapped in standard brown packaging paper. On top of the package sat what looked like a postcard.

"I see," I said, very unsure of either items origin.

"All right, I just need you to sign here for the package, and if you could show me the key to your PO box that'd be proof enough that it's you." After his prompt, I signed the paper that sat on the counter before me and flashed him the key to my box, number 117.

"All right, Mr. Clarke, here's your mail. Now you have yourself a fine day." The apple didn't fall far from that family tree; he was just as pleasant as his uncle in many aspects.

"Thank you . . ." I paused and held out my hand to shake his and hopefully get a name for the new face.

"Oh, I apologize, my name's Keith." He returned a firm handshake and gave what I suspected to be the family smile.

"All right, Keith. Nice to meet you, and you take care." It had always been those kind of people who brought the best out in me. While generally, and as of that time especially, I kept to myself and carried a fairly quiet demeanor; there were certain people who could bring out how I really was upon meeting them. Thomas was definitely one of them. Deep down I still couldn't shake off the most recent news of his condition. Luckily, I could hide my distress, and any other emotions for that matter, very well.

"You do the same. Come back soon," he said as I headed for the door.

Clambering into my jeep, I couldn't help but dwell on the news about Thomas. We were close enough to where I would have thought he or his wife would've have called me or something, especially if he was that bad off. In a daze, I slowly turned the ignition and put the transmission in gear. I was too tied up on Thomas's situation to think of the mail I just picked up. I nonchalantly tossed the package and postcard to the passenger seat and began the trek to town. The road seemed longer than it was to the post office, not only because it actually was, but also because I was disturbed about all that I had learned there just minutes before. Not only was it not Thomas on the other end of that haunting phone call, but the idea that he was not in the best of conditions at that moment and I didn't have the slightest idea. I pondered on those thoughts for a good long while down the road until a turn shifted the mail in the seat beside me. I glanced over a few times before the wording on the front of the postcard registered in my brain. I promptly pulled over to the side of the road to further examine the mystery parcel closer.

As I held the postcard up to closer view what I was sure I had seen, my jeep's radio began to blare loud static. Startled by the noise, I frantically fumbled to turn the radio off. I was far too intrigued by the unusual piece to stop and think of how bizarre it was that my stereo would have done that at that very moment.

The front of the card had a picture of what looked like an old-stone fortress or castle on a grassy hill, with many flower gardens all surrounded by a large stone wall coupled with a heavy wrought-iron-looking gate. At the top of it, there was text that simply said: "Come Lose Yourself in the Beautiful Norcrest Gardens of Upstate New York." Norcrest? If I remembered right, that was what whoever was on the other line of that freak ass phone call said. There was a large part of me that hoped that it wasn't, but in the same respect, if it was, perhaps it would have explained some things. Regardless of the outcome of that topic, I flipped the card over to see if there was any writing on it or at least a return address. For some reason, I found it surprising that there were some words scribed on it, but for the letter mentioned return address, there was none. There was but a couple of sentences on it, and what was written chilled me beyond the bone and into the marrow: "In the night, they sing, and that is where I'll be waiting for you. When you get here, you'll find me."

I wasn't sure what set me more uneasy; the fact that I didn't know anyone in New York, or that I somehow knew that the Norcrest mentioned in that phone call was the same as this one. A sudden feeling of a slight dizziness and nausea took me. Whatever it was about the whole thing didn't sit well with me. At the point I had reached with the postcard, I couldn't bring myself to even acknowledge the package. I quickly tossed the postcard back onto that package in passenger seat and resumed driving. In the passing moments down the trail I followed, I didn't allow myself to be drawn to thoughts of that postcard. As much as I wanted to drive along and tear my thoughts and ideas a metaphoric "new one," I instead lit up a cigarette and turned up the volume of my stereo. I had my mp3 player plugged into it, and I almost perpetually set it to randomize the songs; I liked to keep myself guessing. Although I put the music at a volume at such a rate that it drowned out any hope of thought more than to sing along as loudly as I could, I couldn't help but feel that there was some premonition with the song my mp3 player had chosen; it was called "Set it Off." I drove down the road singing at the top of my lungs with the song. Yet every time it ended, instead of letting it progress to the next song, I was compelled to replay that one and belt out the lyrics as loud as I could. Maybe it was because it took me back to my rebellious youth, or even just back to simpler times. Whatever it was, it helped.

Again I was drowned in thought having reached my next destination and not really realizing that I had; as I pulled into town, I snapped out of the song-soaked trance I was in upon entry. The place was familiar; it was the town I grew up in. Ironically, the same town I was divorced in, where life began and ended as I knew it. I drove to the best and most convenient electronics store that I could think of. As my jeep and I made our way down the highway to the store, more memories emerged to act as a harpy to my mind. I was taken back to a time long passed as I drove by a French restaurant that I knew too well. It was a place a boy took his high school girlfriend, and years later proposed to her at the very same place, and she said yes. I drove past the place we first met; the event center that the town held the fall masquerade. So many memories were tied to the fall, and I didn't even have to roll the window down for that set of memories to come forth. It seemed that for some reason, all those recollections I had longed to forget were surfacing to punish me.

I drove into the electronics store parking lot and turned the ignition off. I got out and began walking for what I thought I needed. The automatic double doors that opened before me triggered a thought about how robotic that place was. Funny how the simple act of opening a door myself felt more personal to me. The discomfort of the establishment made me blow through the aisles until I found the one that I needed, the kingdom of the phones. I found a nice technological masterpiece to take home and replace the old one I had at the cabin. Or at least the most advanced corded phone that I could find. Though I knew that corded phones were going the way of the dinosaur, it was the personal versus the impersonal with me. A cordless phone gives either party of a phone call too much freedom. If you have a cord keeping you put, you tend to find less distractions while engaged in conversation. Having picked the phone I wanted, I moved on to the checking line.

It was about time too, the general ambience of that fluorescent-lit warehouse of consumer electronics was getting to be sickening.

The sound of my quick footsteps across the insidious carpet tiles glued to the concrete floor beneath was even beginning to annoy me. I had always had my aversion to department stores such as those for as long as I could remember. Even as a kid I always hated going. When my brothers and I were forced to go as children, we would embarrass our mother with our witless jackassery and public disturbances that usually ensured our safety and refuge from such family trips for at least a month. Unfortunately, that wouldn't work for me in my later life or the moment at hand; I would most likely just get kicked out if I acted the way I used to when I was a kid, and I laughed quietly to myself at the thought. I finally made it to the counter that was being run by a girl who looked way too young to be working. Not that I had a problem with employing the younger generations, I just remembered sacrificing much of my youth to dead end employment myself, and I sympathized. She couldn't have been much taller than 5'3" with a skinny build and had long light brown hair. As I came up to the register and set down the phone that I intended buy, I was met by big green eyes behind thin round glasses and a braces wearing smile. Seeing that, I couldn't help but smile myself; she reminded me exactly of what my daughter might have looked like if I ever had one. That, and the green of her eyes sparked a brief memory of the woman from that dream.

"Hello, How are you?" she said as she ran the phone over the laser-operated price-reading device.

"I'm fine. And you?" Though I was sure that the store was pure evil, I had no animosity toward the employees, just trying to get by like the rest of us.

"I'm doing good, thanks. So just the phone today?" It seemed that she asked me more out of programming instilled by the corporate nightmare than actual care.

"Yep, that'll do it." Though her and my responses were nothing more than fake pleasantries, the only real part of it was her smile. She seemed happy, and that simple fact for some reason or another made me feel a little removed from the traumas I had been dealing with. As she bagged up my newly purchased item, my eyes wandered to her name tag; her name was Jill, and somehow it just fit.

"Okay, the total is $37.86," she said still smiling. In all actuality, I was less than happy about the total. It seemed quite steep for what I was buying, but I kept the smile on my face anyway. I must have been in such a hurry that I missed looking at the price tag. There were cordless models with more options at a better price.

"Wow . . . The price we pay to keep our old ways, huh?" She giggled at my comment as I slid my card through the money-snatching reader.

"I guess so. I just need you to sign there on the screen, and you're good to go." She gestured to the same device that just read a magnetic strip to take my cash.

I signed the electronic pad in an awkward manner; the cord came out of the right side of the machine. Being left-handed makes the whole procedure difficult.

"Thank you, sir. Have a great day." Even though the mundanity of her statement was evident, her smile made for a better situation.

"You too," I said as I grabbed the bag and began my travel toward the door.

The outside world beyond the storefront was almost blinding as I exited the building. My jeep was parked at the far end of the parking lot as I always did. I didn't mind the walk as long as my vehicle was removed from the others. I walked cross the highway side shopping outlet to my automobile waiting at the other end of the lot. Upon my approach to the jeep, I couldn't help but notice something across the highway from me. It was the man I had seen in the parking lot of the courthouse. I stood and stared for a moment at the man standing at the opposite end of the street from me. I watched as he appeared and disappeared between the gaps of passing cars. I saw him pointing at me as he did before. Then the more unexpected happened; he jumped in front of the moving traffic. The spaces between did not matter. The man was pulverized by the oncoming cars, trucks, and vans.

I was there to bear witness to the travesty. I looked on in horror as it happened, completely helpless to do anything. Some sick version of human pinball took place causing a sizable automobile accident. I ran over as fast as I could to see what I could do to help, full knowing that the scene would be hellacious. The worst part of thinking that it would be was that I was right. I made my way through the mess and metal unsure of what I could possibly do to make any good impression on the situation. I couldn't quite believe what had just transpired. The few seconds that slipped by seemed like hours of shock and fright as people began to emerge from their broken, battered cars. By the look of everything, no one was worse for the ware besides the obvious misfortune of the pointing man. The surrounding vehicles, though damaged, all seemed to be in about moderately torn-up condition, and the drivers and passengers beginning to mingle about among one another.

"Hey, buddy! Did you see what the hell happened?" One of the drivers approached from my right.

"Yeah, the guy just jumped in front of all the damn traffic!" I didn't mean to come across so harsh, but I couldn't help the tone. At the time, I wasn't too worried about that anyway; my mind was still stuck on having seen exactly what caused and happened in the whole event.

The blaring sound of approaching sirens brought me out of the staring gaze that I was in as I looked in on that scene of destruction. The man's lifeless body laid mangled in the middle of the street. I gazed at it knowing that the image would most likely be burned into my memory forever. Not to mention it filled me with the strong need for an even stronger drink.

"Sir, are you injured in any way?" I turned around to meet the voice from behind me to find a police officer standing there.

"No no. I just saw what happened and ran over to see what I could do to help." Really, there wasn't much more to say than that.

"You saw the accident happen? Well, I'm gonna need you to step over to my car with me for a moment and give a statement." He pulled a notebook from his pocket and led me in the direction of his squad car. I stood there giving him all the information he needed as I looked into his still spinning lights on top of the car. I negated to tell him that I had encountered the man before and that he was pointing at me just before he committed his final act; that was all information that I would keep for myself. After my spilling of details, he cut me loose to find my way back to the jeep.

Images of the most recent unsavory events blitzed my brain as I pounded my way over the cold black asphalt. I reached into my pocket to find the rectangular box that housed an unknown number of burnable inhalants of a small slice salvation, also to find the device to set the fire. The joyous sound of the cigarette's subtle cracking as it was lit was the closest thing to a beautiful symphony that I could've hoped for at that moment. The metallic olive-green of my jeep was a beautiful sight that told me that soon a drink was to be had. Another lovely series of noises took place as I fired up the engine and heard all the parts working together for a common goal: to get me the hell home and away from that place. Though the day had brought a couple of fucked-up happenings, I did manage to accomplish all that I set out to. With that small victory in mind, I began my way to the cabin. The road home was going to be a particularly long one that time, and I knew it.

Over the winding pathway, I couldn't help but once again crack the window and surrender to the autumn air. I released control of my mind and set the helm to autopilot for it to find its own way. The way that it found was once again to a distant plane in the back of my memories and surfaced events long past. The unearthed relic of time was one of more tragic topics, as well the tone of that particular day. I could see a child form of myself standing on a hill under overcast skies. That young boy in suit and tie was there for a time of mourning, a final farewell to someone of significant importance. As the road continued its twisting way, I looked back to find a view of my mother taking my small hand and leading me down the hill. The grass and trees were dead around me in that hallowed field of stones. I could see us walking together hand in hand. In her other hand she held an urn, the contents self-explanatory. We were there on the grave mission to spread someone's ashes, my father's ashes—a task that should not be appointed to a child so young. It then dawned on me what was happening in the previous memory of me in the playground of the school. It was the day I got the news, and my mother did as well. I would like to have said that I was close to my father, whereas, in fact, it was the opposite. He left my mother and me shortly after I was born, around the age of one or so. I couldn't help but not feel much, even though the times we did have together were held in fond regards. I was distanced from a lot of people, as was my personality. There never was any real reason I could think of or find for explaining my detached behaviors, but it was the way it was.

CHAPTER 3

Morbidity Becoming an Understatement

The lonely cabin once again welcomed me as I pulled into the driveway. The time to find exposure to my booze born medicine was long since passed. I was ready for the Glenlivet twelve years old that I'd been so longing for. About halfway to my door, I turned back to the jeep. I had forgotten the package, postcard, and new telephone. Retrieving the items from the passenger side, I couldn't help but take notice of the real estate office's for-sale sign at the end of the driveway and made the mental note to call the agent in the morning. I once more made my way for the cabin door. The creaky welcome was the only one I had to look forward to as I entered the empty cabin. After placing my mail on the table, I went to the kitchen in pursuit of the scotch that I so desperately needed. On my way back to the table to drink all my problems into submission, I accidentally bumped a picture off the wall. I picked it up and caught a glimpse of what the frame held inside of it. It was a picture of my ex and me that we had taken on a trip we once took to Astoria. The picture came with me back to the table for further examination. A tear welled up as I looked upon all that the photograph encompassed. Her beauty still radiated from even a picture with the bay bridge in the background. We were so close. What happened? Toiling over the many possible answers to that qualm, I took a drink of scotch and set the picture aside. It was time to solve the mystery of the package that came in the mail earlier that day. Squarely in front of me sat the box of unknown contents. I pulled it closer to me and saw that it was, in fact, addressed to me at the cabin. Seeing that ruled out any doubts about it finding me—that was no accident. What was peculiar about the package was the many different colors of ink and handwriting, all stating that it had reached either the wrong address or person and the fact that it was addressed to the cabin in the first place. There was one scribe, in particular, that caught my attention, it simply said, "Wrong Evan Clark!" My eyes crept up the wrapping to find the return address. What I had found was deeply disturbing; it read that it was from Lucas Clarke, my father.

After reading it over and over, the evidence was indisputable. There were no mistakes in the writing, and no flaws in my reading; it said that it was from him. As impossible as I thought it was, it didn't change the fact that the package remained in front of me unopened. Without hesitation, I began to unravel the brown paper surrounding the box. As I did, there was a subtle scent that I vaguely knew; it smelled of my father, sort of a blend of Old Spice and pipe tobacco. I carefully opened the small box to find a piece of paper; upon removing it, I saw something in the bottom mostly hidden by the newspaper padding in place. I reached into the box to pull out some form of medallion. It was silver and disk-shaped with a strange blue gem set in the middle. Around the outside were characters of a language I did not know. Hoping that the paper I found on top of all of it would explain, I unfolded it and began to read the text that it offered.

> *Dear Evan, October 1, 1989*
>
> *If you're reading this, then you're old enough to have the contents of this box. I waited a long time before I would send it to you, hoping that now you'd understand. You will be ready soon, and this is one of the last shreds of your heritage that is left. This item has been passed down through generation after generation to all the men in our family, a legend that has existed since the colonial times. Your great-grandfather had it, your grandfather had it, I did, and now you will. They all said that there is a secret held within it, so keep it close because I know they were very right, just not in the way I could have ever imagined.*
>
> *I hope you will forgive me one day for everything that happened, but if you had known, you would have understood. Even now, I can hear them coming for me.*
>
> *I love you, son, and I always will. Just remember me like that.*
>
> *I hope that you will finish what I couldn't and succeed where I failed.*
>
> *Evan, some things in this world are beyond explanation, and I can only hope that you are strong enough to survive it and not give in to the madness. I hate to leave you. Be a good boy.*
>
> *Love always,*
> *Your father, Lucas Clarke*

I felt my hands began to tremble, and I resisted every urge to have a complete meltdown. One's initial thought might have been that it was some kind of hoax or sham, a sick prank that some depraved asshole would have concocted, but I knew the handwriting. The letter was undoubtedly from my very dead father, but how did it get there? Why, of all the times, was it then that it decided to surface? I felt it to be rather fitting given the strange air that had blanketed everything about those days. Somehow, out of all the things, that one made vague and unexplainable sense. There was something at work; I didn't know what exactly, but it appeared that all the seemingly random nightmares taking place all around me would somehow fit together if I looked at it all in just the right way.

Then again, maybe not. I pulled my mind back from the clouds and began to think of it all rationally. The package's address was my father's last address; that was true. What I didn't know, given the date of the letter, was how long it had been there. I rifled through the mess of torn brown paper on the table in the hope of finding some clue to its origin, and there it was. I brought the postmark up to eye level with me to get a closer look at what it had to tell me; the postmark was current, even though it had been stamped over countless times. That led me to believe that there were only a couple of options. There was a chance that my stepmother, my father's widow, had found it buried somewhere in the confines of the house and decided to send it, even though it was much later than was initially intended. There was also the case that it simply might have been lost, floundering around in the US Postal system almost never to be seen or found again. As far-fetched as the latter was, it didn't seem too far out there considering recent events. I knew that there was one way to check one of my theories against fact and fabrication; I was going to call my stepmother.

Grabbing the new phone and strange medallion, I traveled over to where the old phone was located. I set the odd disk down and began tearing into the box that housed my glorious new communications device. I had always hated buying new electronics, not because I didn't like them, but I just never did feel compelled to fight them out of the box. That one I had purchased was a fighter. Pulling and maneuvering, it finally broke free from its confines along with an explosion of small plastic bags and instruction manuals. Pain in my ass as it was, the phone was ready to serve its purpose. Promptly unhooking the old one, I put the plugs in the new one and watched in almost child-like amusement as it illuminated to greet me. I picked up the receiver to be met with a dial tone; it worked. Not that I doubted it, but I couldn't be too sure of much of anything then. It took me a moment to dial the number that was estranged from me, but the sound of a ringing assured me that it was the correct combination of numerals.

"Hello?" I knew the voice. Though our interactions over the years had not been as close as they should've, I could never have forgotten her soft southern accent.

"Hi, Sherry. It's Evan." I tried to sound as normal as possible, full knowing that there was probably something to my speech that could've been taken as distress.

"Oh, Hi, Evan! It's so good to hear from you! How have you been?" Her excitement was welcoming.

"I'm doing well. This might sound a little strange, but did you by chance send me anything. Like a package or anything?" There was a short silence from the other end of the phone. I was hoping deep down that she had sent it.

"Hmmm. Not lately. The last thing I sent was that little gift basket last Christmas." After she said that, I knew that there was something beyond all what I initially thought. A deep sinking feeling started tugging in my chest. If it wasn't from her, who sent it apart from my deceased father?

We talked for a long while catching up on each other's lives and how my siblings from her and my father were doing. It was nice to have a normal conversation through all the bullshit that had been going on. There was a lot of comfort in hearing how well everyone was doing there in Oklahoma. My stepmother had just started a great new job, my younger sister was well on her way through law school, and my little brother started a chain of his own body shops. There was a thought in my head that was geared toward hoping that they would never have to suffer my situation.

Granted it did already happen to one of the two brothers I grew up with there in Colorado, divorce I mean, and he seemed to do all right. Dwelling on all those thoughts and feelings, I had almost forgotten what I still had yet to accomplish, my drink.

I stepped back over to the table where my drink sat. Putting glass to lips, I finished one after another. The bottle and glass my only company, I relished in that fact. In all my loneliness, those simple comforts kept me in some sort of balance. The unbearable anguish I had felt became more bearable with each passing drink and every fill of the glass. In that at least I found peace. The bottle became emptier and emptier as we crept through the passage of time. The slow burning of cigarettes permeated the air around me as the evening fell over the cabin. As I once again glanced about the interior, it pleaded solitude and uninvolvement. The very feel I gathered from my surroundings made for a realization of loneliness. More specifically, how much of it I had done to myself.

With the publication of my first book and landing the journalism position those many years ago, a rift grew between my friends, family, and me. Shortly after, I married the woman who would become my ex-wife. Soon after we got married, my world revolved around her, furthering the gap between me and the world I once knew. Alone in the dark, my thoughts escaped my mind like smoke fleeing a fire. Too many memories to mention flashed before me in a disruptive and regret filled sort of nostalgic collage; however, it all halted on one in particular. Another memory provided an image of the young boy that once was me. The only difference was that the kid was younger. I could see me grabbing someone's hand and being led to a swing in the park; the hand I was holding was that of my father. No sooner than the cerebral movie had started, it ended; just a brief flash of stored information set free to wreak havoc on an already troubled man.

The silence was broken by a horrific electronic sound from across the room; it was the new phone. I hadn't heard the sound of the ringer before, and it was a startling new experience. In a half-drunk stupor, I walked over to the chiming creature. I was hesitant to answer in fear of what I would be met with when I did.

"Hello?" My voice sounded quiet and sad as I answered. I waited for a moment, but there was nothing there. I returned the phone to its base, confused and slightly pissed off at the noise it made to indicate an incoming call. No sooner than my turning around to return to my chair of dark musing, the phone began another barrage of that god-awful chirping.

I slowly turned back and picked up the phone again, more hesitant than I was before. I said nothing as I carefully brought it up to my ear and just waited. Met by what sounded like a faint raspy and strained breathing, an uneasy feeling crawled over me.

"You . . . you . . . don't . . . believe." The voice came across just as raspy and strained as the breathing before it, and it caused for an untold level of discomfort to manifest in me. It was clear that I was rattled; I swallowed hard and began to speak.

"What do you want from me?" My voice was about the same quiet tone as before but more demanding that time. There was no immediate answer, just more of the heavy and strained wheezing.

"Never . . . never before . . . You . . . you know nothing of . . . in the night, they sing . . ." The voice was more electronically distorted than before but still had the other menacing qualities. I felt my blood run cold and my heart sink into the deepest recesses of my rib cage; whatever was on the other line felt it to be, in a word, evil.

"Who the hell is this, and what kind of sick angle are you playing? *Tell me!*" As it usually does with some people, my fear conveyed as anger as I yelled at who or whatever was at the other end of the call.

"When light . . . goes dim . . . all . . . left is . . . black . . . they sing . . . they sing . . ." The words became more distorted as they were spoken. It was echoed and twisted in a way that words could not describe, but the audio was a terrifying reality.

"All right, I'm done with this shit! You tell me now why you're doing this!" My frustration with the situation had become clear, and I projected it loudly. Yet I was met again by that same familiar sound of the call ending. As I set the phone down on the hook, I couldn't help but think of why those calls were happening. My way back to the table was filled with troublesome thoughts and a disturbed mind. By the time I came to the table, I was under the impression that there could be a very real threat looming in the shadows. There was only one option and comfort I could go for at that point in time, and it was not just the good 'ol beverage.

I knew exactly what I was going for as I quickly made my way through the cabin to my gun safe in the closet. The dull green metal was tucked in the back left corner, propped against the front was the "For Sale" sign that prompted me to buy the cabin those years ago; Why I kept it? I had no idea. It seemed to be impeding me more at that moment than anything. I removed the obstructing sign to reveal the much desired combination dial of the safe, and I made no hesitation to begin madly turning the dial. After a few twists and a click, it opened to reveal my minimal collection. There were three guns left over from my once great amount of weaponry. The rest of them long since migrated to my former home to the apparent care of my ex. Of the three remaining, two of them would properly serve as home defense items. One was my prized piece that I could never have parted with, the one that I hid from the world and the divorce for that matter. I pulled the handle of the case to reveal its dull silver glory. The other remaining gun that was well suited for my need was a nice Mossberg 500 twelve gauge shotgun; another one I couldn't bring myself to part with. Grabbing the guns and all the ammunition I could handle, I made for the table I had been at before.

The wonderful display of armament laid spread out on the table before me. If there was anything out there that would have tried to get in, the event wouldn't end well for the malicious party. I reached to the shotgun and pulled it to me; it still needed to be loaded. The brass-ended red cylinder felt comforting to the touch as I loaded it and its friends from the box of shells into the shotgun. Upon completion of getting it loaded, I pumped the forward grip to be greeted by the sound of the action cocking, and I clicked the safety off; it, as well as myself, was ready for whatever might have come next. The time came to reveal the other piece as I set the Mossberg back down on the table. I carefully slid the dull silver case squarely in front of me. Placing my thumbs on the locks on either side of the handle, I pressed down and watched the latches jump open. I could feel a slight grin come over my face as I slowly raised the lid to expose what I considered to be my secret weapon. As strange as it might have seemed as far as my character was involved, being a man of aesthetics, I was also, in fact, a bit of a gun nut. Even growing up, I had always had a great appreciation for firearms. Needless to say, there was always that drive to fulfill some sort of manliness through weaponry. With the case fully opened, I gazed down at my beautiful marvel. Its sleek black color was complemented nicely by its ivory grip. That .45 Caliber Colt was a very beautiful thing to me, and the light scent of 3-in-One oil was a glory to me as I gently lifted it from its confines.

As far as your standard semi-automatic handgun is concerned, to me it was the Cadillac of them. Anything that could've been lurking in the night, I was confidently prepared for.

Every hour crept sluggishly by as I sat at the table: Marlboro, Glenlivet, my shotgun, and my pistol as my companions on guard. Waiting—waiting for the next terrible event to surface from nowhere. Feelings of being completely threatened had passed some time before, my level of extreme alert reduced to one of caution. I stared over to the postcard that had been shoved to the far end of the table and taunting me.

"Who sent you?" I whispered to myself almost hoping that it would somehow answer. Why all those things were happening, especially then, I did not understand. It all in some way felt orchestrated. Through all the thoughts of theories and possibilities that raced through my mind, they seemed to orbit around the thought of that girl from the dream. Who was she, and why the familiarity associated with her presence? No sooner than my reaching that point of my thought process on the matter, the electronic chime that I had quickly learned to loath broke the barriers of silence. In some mad and curious, I almost thought that it would be that girl.

I approached the screaming phone with utmost caution. Rather quickly, I snatched the receiver from the base and said nothing. If that was the way it had to be, then I'd play into it. However, there was no answer from the other side either, just heavy wheezing . . . and gurgling? My alert level heightened once more, and my hands began to tremble with a mix of fear and anger. The sound of the hang up soon followed. Something strange had begun to happen to me as I dropped the phone from my hand. The room started to get distorted and hazy as a sick feeling and dizziness invaded my body. I painstakingly tried to make my way to the table, but each step I took felt as though I was wearing lead boots. My goal was within reach, but I stopped and directed the little focus I could to something that didn't make sense. It was the medallion on the table; it seemed to be vibrating, and the gem in the middle was illuminated with a soft blue glow. I stared for a moment and then dropped to the floor next to the table; whatever it was that ailed me was winning. All went black around me, and all I could hear was a faint sound of a pulsating humming comparative to some sort of energy flow. Sometime later, I must have passed out because a dream was soon to follow.

"Evan . . . I'm here . . . I'm here for you . . ." The familiar soft voice filled my ears as she spoke. I slowly opened my eyes to find her standing there over me, such beauty and immaculate grace. Where did she come from, and why did she come to me?

"Why . . . why me . . . wh. why now?" My words, much like the last time, came with great difficulty. Why was it so hard to speak? It was impeded by something, much like my own vocal cords were fighting my very will. I knew all that I wanted to say, and all the questions I had to ask, but the words weren't finding their way to my mouth. Could it have simply been the sheer intoxication of her overwhelming presence or something more? I couldn't be sure of anything at that moment. All I knew was that I had never had a dream like that.

"I've always been here for you. Why wouldn't I be now when you need me most?" Her question that shouldn't have made sense somehow did and, for some reason, stirred up emotions that *I* didn't even know I had. In some strange twist of feelings, I wanted to laugh, cry, and scream, anything to express the swelling of my consciousness that was happening, but I could do nothing.

"But . . . I . . . I don't . . . even kn . . . know . . . you . . ." My voice was still not functioning properly, and it was maddening. I could scarcely begin to understand the reasoning for that terrible impediment.

"Of course, you do not, but I know you . . . and I need you . . ." Yet another statement that shouldn't have even come close to making sense somehow registered perfectly in my subconsciously twisted brain.

"You . . . do? . . . you do . . ." My mind was in a bend as to why I would have said that. I didn't know the woman; there was no possible way of familiarity existing between us. As all of it went on, it made less and less sense to my seemingly conscious mind.

"No . . . there is . . . no way . . ." I fought against whatever held me and expressed my thoughts on the impossibility of a connection between us.

"I do, Evan . . . believe." She moved close and nearly put her lips to my ear. The sensations were far more real than any dream I had ever experienced. The touch, the feelings, and the very scent of her were all too vivid for anyone to have ever imagined; in some way, it felt more real than the real world itself. She began to whisper.

"I'll be waiting there . . . ."

With a deep gasp and my eyelids snapping open, I came to on the floor. It seemed like I had only blinked rather than passed out. The insanity all of it was almost too much for me to handle. I sat up from the hardwood floor and looked around to see that I was in the same place that I was before. I rationalized as everything came rushing to my mind; I had been under a shit load of stress, and I had been drinking in about that same measurement—that was all that it was; but who would've known better than myself that I was a terrible liar. I sat for a moment trying to collect myself, but an odd and faint scent caught the attention of my nose. The soft smell of lilac floated in the air around me. Was it perfume? If ever there was a time that I had questioned my sanity, it didn't hold a candle to the wind of what was happening. I picked myself up off the floor and took one last confused look around before sitting back down at the table. I needed to drink the pain away from myself. As I put the glass to my lips, I looked at the postcard across the table from me. I thought my eyes had deceived me, but it looked like there was something else there that wasn't before. I reached across the table and grabbed the postcard. I brought it up to my face and studied it. Upon my examination, terror and paranoia took me, and I dropped my glass to the floor. There was something else on it.

"I am waiting, dearest Evan," were the words newly written onto the postcard.

Gripped in utter despair, I quickly picked the shotgun up from the table.

"Who the fuck is doing this? Where are you?" I began yelling into the apparent nothingness. The fact that there was no answer didn't mean I was alone. I slowly and quietly made my way to the front door. The usually soft creaks in the floor seemed to echo loudly through the room with each step I took. It was still locked; the door had not been opened since I had last went through it. Puzzled and feeling that threats loomed around any given corner, I walked by each window on the way to the kitchen, only to find that they too were firmly shut and locked. I turned the corner into the kitchen, the shotguns butt snugly in my shoulder, ready to smite anything that might have been lurking. To my shock, there was nothing but what should've been there. I couldn't fathom any possibilities as to what or who could've written the extended text on my postage, short of breaking and entering. However, there were no signs that anyone other than myself had been there. I made my way back into the living room and toward the bedroom to check there for any invaders. As I traversed the silent rooms, a cold and sinking feeling consumed me.

I reached over to the light switch to illuminate the pitch black room, never removing my finger from trigger. As all became visible, it was evident that there were no entries in there nor any signs of violence. The more I searched, the less I found, and it only compounded my confusion and fear. My bedroom was untouched; the bed still made, the curtains still set nicely to either side of the unopened window, and the closet doors still opened from my gathering of weaponry. Nothing menacing had reached that room either. I didn't know what was more troubling: the fact that no one was there, and the additional words on the postcard were, or the thought that someone might have actually been hiding somewhere in my cabin. Satisfied to only a loose meaning of the word, I knew that there was only one room left to examine—the bathroom. I hit the light switch off as I exited my sleeping chamber and made my way to the final stop of my examination route. There was an unexplainable feeling in the air, one reminiscent of the feeling of being lost, yet it was different somehow. Too many questions burned in my mind to allow any rationalizing or thought exploration. The once subtle squeaks in the floor were once again amplified as I treaded over them on my way to the bathroom. I let the shotgun point the way through the short distance between the bedroom and bathroom. Just like the last room, I flicked the light switch to better reveal the surroundings, ever ready to blast any anomaly to kingdom come. Yet much like the bedroom, there was nothing to be seen that wasn't there before. All amenities of the room were in perfect place, undisturbed, and left all alone.

The simple fact that there were no abnormalities was offsetting and disturbing. I casually made my way back to the table with all the terrible thoughts running circles around anything that could be taken as normal thought. I ached from the possibilities that surrounded me and was drained by all the emotional trauma up to then. Returning to the table, the processes of my mind haunted every moment of my solitude. It again seemed that the drink, the smokes, and the guns were my only companions in the terrible loneliness. Sitting down in the chair once again, I reached down to the postcard staring at me from the table. I looked at the newest part of the text that comprised the writing on it. No matter how much I studied it, it still made no sense. How did it get there, and better yet, who put it there? There was no rhyme or reason to any of the questions I asked myself, and the same could be said about having to ask the questions themselves. I took a strong drink of the scotch and began to formulate a plan for the day following. I needed to answer something, anything that was on my mind. The first stop of tomorrow would be the post office. I needed to know exactly what happened to Thomas. Another thing was the strange man who approached me before, and then later jumped into oncoming traffic. Who was he, and why did he say what he did to me that day? If there was an answer to be found, I would find it. After all, I was a journalist; my job was to find the truth. Nothing would drive me more than my own need for answers to my questions, and I was going to find them.

Chapter 4

Sordid Trials Faced For Answers

By the time I woke up, it was already midday, yet another mark against my usual times of awakening for the past years. I rolled out of the bed to my feet and reminded myself of the task list for the day. In realization of what was needed to be accomplished, I walked toward the bathroom to begin the morning ritual of showering, grooming, and dental health treatment. A nice cool shower was just what I needed; the slightly warm water cascading over me washed away all the night before, and it gave me the sense of renewal and the energy to follow through with my goals that I had set out for that day. I exited the shower and dried off. Clothing myself, I was hit by a recollection of the events that had transpired the night before. All the events that flooded my mind drove me to discover everything that I could about the tangible questions asked. As soon as I was dressed and ready to go, I grabbed my essentials and headed out the door. All I really needed were my cigarettes, a lighter, my wallet, and my keys. My walk to my jeep was particularly eerie. For the first time since I got that vehicle, I felt like I was not its owner. It was such a strange feeling to climb into an automobile that for some reason didn't feel like my own. Regardless of the feeling of my jeep, I started it up and put it in gear toward the end of the driveway.

Driving down the road, I couldn't help but notice my surroundings of aspen and pine trees beautifully scattered along the side of the road. The aspens were in the full effect of the fall; they displayed their colors of yellow, orange, and gold proudly. Like before, I couldn't help but crack the window to let the familiar scent of autumn in. Through all of my being lost in thought, it seemed as though my jeep knew exactly where to go as we pulled into the parking lot. The post office seemed more solemn and stoic than before. It standing alone against the mountain backdrop was almost like a painting. It cried sadness and a sort of satire of its situation. As my jeep and I pulled closer, it all seemed to fall into perspective.

It was time to part ways with my beloved vehicle; having shaken the lack of familiarity I had with it earlier, I parked it and pulled the handle to open the door. It was déjà vu situation as I made my approach to the weather-worn door. For some reason or another, that same cold feeling once again took me as I reached my hand to the door knob. It seemed as though the feeling had become some sort of indicator of weird situations. The familiar sound of the bell on the door sounded upon my entry into the PO box-filled room. I turned to the counter to see that Keith was already standing there.

"Hello, Mr. Clarke." He gave me a warm welcome as I walked over to the counter area.

"Hello, Keith." I kept my reply short. For reasons that seemed appropriate to me at the time, I assumed that anyone and everyone could be behind the happenings that I was evidently the target of. That having been the case, I had no desire for drawn out pleasantries with the man. I got to the counter and rested my elbows on it.

"Keith, I have to say, Thomas and I had become pretty close friends over the years. Frankly, I'm shocked that I hadn't heard what happened to him sooner. I knew his wife Carol as well. I'm sure she would have called me. What happened exactly?" I expressed my concern clearly. There were too many gaps to be comfortable with—too much of the story missing. I thought that if I could get a better picture of the situation, I could, at least, put that one worry to rest.

"Well, Carol died shortly before he had the stroke. We all kind of thought that it was her passing that did it. Right after she did, he started rambling about crazy things and spending most of his time in the library in the city. They found him in the spiritual section on the floor." Upon his statement, that cold feeling from before came on stronger and the sinking feeling returned with a hard swallow. I was almost afraid to ask what I needed to.

"How . . . How did Carol die?" Asking that simple question was a task all in its own, dreading what the answer might be.

"Well, as hard as it is to say, she took her own life, Mr. Clarke. I'm sorry you hadn't heard anything until now." I could feel my eyes get wider as he said what I somehow already knew. It was all in the feeling I had, some grim feeling that happened to be correct.

"Where is Thomas now?" The questions I had became increasingly difficult for me to ask. It was as if I didn't even want to know the answers at that point. The news was terrible and very troubling to say the least.

"He's at the Rocky Mountain Pines home. He doesn't respond too well anymore, but he's there if you'd like to see him." Though all of the information seemed to be about a fist-sized pill to swallow, I took it in the best stride I could.

"Thank you, Keith. I'll have to pay him a visit." With that, I knew what was next on my roster of things to do. I was headed for town anyway, and I knew the place he was talking about.

The way to the door felt incredibly distanced, much more so than it really was. All the information was too much to handle. I couldn't help but ask myself how all those events came to fruition, yet my questions would go unanswered as there was no one there who could answer them. I reached for the door knob and turned to bid farewell to Keith, but he beat me to speech.

"I'm sorry you had to hear all that from me. But do you want to know something really strange?" He asked as I was just about to leave. I wasn't sure that I wanted to, but I turned to face him, despite my unwillingness to hear more weird news.

"Sure." I could only speculate what he was about to tell me. At that point, he could have told me he had been to the moon, and I might have believed him.

"When I first found that package of yours at their house, I got a bad feeling. Then I started having all kinds of terrible nightmares, so bad, and they almost seemed real." The look he wore on his face was stone serious and almost frightened.

"Was there a woman in those dreams?" What he was saying immediately called for my attention.

"No, sir, they had things in them that I would never repeat. Things that for the first time in my life made me fear for my soul. But as soon as you picked up that box, they all stopped. That's why I might have seemed on edge and leery when you came here last." I did notice that he seemed a bit different from our last meeting, but I couldn't say that it meant much to me as I was trying to comprehend everything that he told me.

"That . . . That sounds terrible." I could barely think of the words to say; it was all too much.

"Did anything strange like that happen to you after you picked up that box?" He asked with a pleading look in his eyes. Not that I wanted to be dishonest, but I felt that everything I had been through up until then was best played close to my chest.

"No, nothing out of the norm for me," I said quietly.

"Well, be careful, Mr. Clarke. It seems like there's a strange air about lately," he said, and I wasn't entirely sure that he believed me.

My jeep might as well have been parked a mile away with the amount of shit that I mentally carried out with me. The automobile sat with open arms once again, beckoning me with an offer to be taken away from that place as fast as it could take me. Some feeling resembling comfort held me as I climbed into the driver's seat. I sat for a minute to collect myself before sparking the ignition. My view from the jeep could've been taken as one of beauty with the mountains and pines standing tall against the gray-canvas-like sky, but the image was sullied by feelings that I was battling then. I turned the key over and shifted gears to begin my way back to town.

Winding asphalt would once again lead me to where I needed to go. The first stop would be the nursing home where Thomas resided. Unpleasant memories surfaced from the thought of the home. I recalled a time in which I had to frequent that very establishment; my business there was not one of happier themes. It was about ten years back, when my grandmother had fallen too ill to be self-sustaining. She was placed in the care of the home, and over the two-year period of her stay, she recognized me less and less with each visit. By the end of it all, she had not the slightest clue as to who I was. Thinking of that begged the question of the same event happening upon that visit. Would he even know who I was when I came to see him? I didn't know. The road continued on, leading me to answers unknown. Twisting and winding down the autumn-covered mountain side, I decided that it was high time to put those problems on hold. I reached to the mp3 player that was patiently waiting for use. Music filled the inner sanctum of my jeep as I cruised down the road. As the usual goes, I could not keep myself from singing with the tunes as loudly as I could. If there was anything keeping me sane, it was moments like that. A moment in which I could just let go of all that surrounded me and troubled me. That was as close to any kind of salvation that I could reach.

The town seemed vacant as I entered into it. There were scarcely any other cars on the highway and a major lacking in pedestrian activity. All was quiet around me, save for the stereo blaring in my jeep. Pulling up to a red light, I couldn't help but adjust my view to the one car I saw, and it happened to be next to me. Not only because it was one of few traveling the road as I was, but it was what the car's interior had to display. It was a young man and what I presumed to be his significant other. I watched as they laughed, kissed, and carried on. All in that instant, I couldn't help but feel a very profound disdain. The feeling wasn't toward them in any right but more toward the idea. With the realization of that particular emotion, I couldn't help but wonder how long I would feel that way. I knew the root of the feeling, the relationship trauma that I had recently experienced. The car began to move forward indicating to me that it was time for me to do the same. Passing under the green light signaling safe passage through the crossroads, I could hardly keep my thoughts from my ex-wife. My mind drifted to questions of the nature of what I did wrong, and why things turned out the way they did. What deity did I piss off to deserve all of it? Another question that I was sure would go unanswered.

Turning onto Orchard street, I could see my next destination in the distance. It stood in a sad way against the surrounding residential backdrop. A dread befell me as my jeep and I pulled into the mournful place of parking. How many people had spent their last days in such a place? The last days of existence on the earth wasted in some veritable theater of hell with its cast of emotionless drones. I would rather have been shot before meeting an end like that. A cold breeze blew as I left the vehicle and made way for the entrance of the highly uncomfortable establishment. The dead leaves scuttled across the ground before me as I walked the distance to the door. The familiar feeling of the autumn air comforted me as I made my way. But all comforts brought through the fall breeze were taken by the automated doors that opened to consume me. I found myself surrounded by the scent that is shared by all hospital-type environments as I came into the lobby. There was a receptionist behind the desk with a look of extreme boredom on her face. It was clear that she had a bad day or just didn't give a damn about the job. In either respect, her appearance indicated evidence of both scenarios being possible. She had her long blondish hair pulled tightly back into a ponytail, and there was no indication of makeup on her face. It was a large possibility that the scrubs she wore added to her very plain look; they were maroon in color with her pink baseball-style T-shirt underneath. She seemed in no aspect approachable, but conversation had to be made to achieve my goal. I got to the counter behind which she sat and was met by beady brown eyes.

"Hi, I'm looking for Thomas Watson's room." It was almost painful to ask, but it was necessary. The very look on her face was one of disbelief that I was troubling her with my query. She typed a couple of things on the computer and then looked up at me with an expression of apathy.

"He's in room 202." It was simply stated as she went back to the magazine that she didn't hide very well under the manila folder. I didn't feel the need to convey pleasantries as I was extended none, so thanking her for the service seemed inconsequential to me. On the desk, I happened to catch a glance at a layout of the home; 202 was to my left.

I lightly stepped down the silent corridors of the wing, drifting back to the memories of my visitations to my grandmother. Though her room was in the wing to the right of where I was at the desk, there was little to distinguish differences between any of the wings. I came to the room and stopped outside the door. I had to stop and go over all possibilities of what I might face upon my entry into the room. Would he know who I was? Would he even have the ability of rational thought? All these thoughts brewed as I stood outside the door. The moment of truth was there, and courage had to be strong as I reached out to the handle on the door. The handle made no sound other than the latch unhooking as I turned it. Opening the door revealed a room with a familiar placement of furnishings. Two beds on either side of the room, two nightstands to the side of each bed and pictures of loved ones strewn about. That was the end zone. As I walked further into the room, a feeling of despair was gained. I knew that whatever state I would find that man in wouldn't be good.

He was sitting in a wheelchair parked in front of the window as I walked up to him. The stare he wore on his face was one of a vacant loneliness with an overtone of sorrow. His portly figure was still the same, but he had traded his signature overalls for sweatpants and his familiar flannel button up for a plain white T-shirt. The shaggier comb over hair style he once wore was now more buzz-cut in fashion, and I could see that his handlebar mustache I knew him by was gone; only a salt and pepper stubble remained.

"Hi, Thomas. It's Evan, Evan Clarke," I said it somewhat quietly as not to startle him. It was clear that he didn't hear me coming up from behind, either that, or he just didn't care. The feeling was a painful one to see the man I once knew as a kind and loving person who was loved by the world as a beaten and lonely man. He slowly turned his gaze to me from the view outside of the window. Staring at me with the same sad and forlorn look on his face for a moment, his eyes became wide and his jaw dropped.

"Y, y, y . . . You!" He stuttered and struggled to say his words. I couldn't tell if he meant that in such a way of saying that he recognized me, or if he was shocked to see a different person than usual.

"You! . . . N, n, n, n Not you! . . . B, b, b, Bad . . . Th . . . Things!" His mannerisms became frantic, and he began to rock back and forth in his chair. I was at a loss of what to do. I had no idea what was happening, or how to handle such an outburst. It seemed as though there was something about my presence that was troubling him. The motion over his back and forth rocking came to a grinding halt, and he slowly looked back up at me. That time something was different and very wrong. The same cold and brooding feeling from before began to envelope me. I was paralyzed as he looked me dead in the eyes.

"Evan, they come for you . . . come to take it from you . . . In the night, they sing . . . They sing . . . We're waiting for you . . ." His words came across in a deep voice, and there was no stuttering to be heard. He came across quite clear, and the look in his eyes was one of some understanding that was beyond me.

"What?" I could barely muster that, let alone to ask anything else. The statement made was one of frightening familiarity, and the cold feeling became all but overwhelming. I couldn't wrap my mind around what was said; I knew those words, but how did he? He told me that *they* were waiting for me. I shuddered and slowly stepped backward to the window sill, gripped in an unspeakable terror and unable to pull my eyes from staring into his; they were dilated to the point that they were almost black. I struggled to put it altogether in my head while fighting back the cold discomfort that was so prominent. Then there was a drastic change to his condition.

Thomas's eyes rolled back to reveal only the whites of them. At first, it seemed only that his jaw was trembling, but no sooner did that particular observation come to my attention, he began violently convulsing in his chair. Panic set in to horribly complement the already uneasy feelings; I had never dealt with anything like that before. There was only one thing that barely shot to the front of my mind:

"Nurse . . . nurse!" At first it came out as an escaped thought in vocal form, but a quick turnaround, and it was a yell for help. I had never been one for yelling; it just didn't ever seem to accomplish much but act as unnecessary noise; that case happened to be different. My view shot around the room to see if there was anything of aid that was at my disposal. I could feel my heart pounding harder and harder with each passing second as I glanced madly about the room for something, anything that could remedy the situation. The continued noises of him convulsing in the chair combined with the sound of my own heart now pounding loudly in my head made it very difficult to focus on anything that the room might have offered to stop his apparent suffering. Though it had seemed like an eternity, the time had only gone by for a few seconds, yet still no sign of help. It was then, through a moment of agonizing clarity, I saw the answer on the wall. There was a red emergency button on the wall, so conveniently placed that panic warranted my overlooking it. Propelled by an adrenaline induced dash, I made it across the room and smashed the button. It replied to my efforts by emitting a red light signaling that help was soon to come. Hardly a moment later, a doctor accompanied by a nurse rushed into the room to his aid.

"What happened?" the doctor shouted in my direction as he was trying to aid Thomas. The scene had left me almost speechless, not to mention the very unbelievable truth that sparked the fire for this trauma.

"I, I, I don't know! One second I was talking to him, and then this happened!" I suppose that my voice was heightened due to the situation, but it was all that I could bring myself to say. Besides, I got the point across without divulging information about the bizarre messages.

"Well, get out of here, we have to get him to the ER!" He was very stern in his projection, and it was clear that I was merely in the way of things there. The doctor grabbed the handles of the wheelchair and ran with Thomas out of the room. I was in the grips of despair as they scurried past me and out the door. The situation had become so intense that it left me distraught and disoriented. My function was one of basic operating procedures as I stood there trying to absorb it all. A short time passed, and I slowly regained some level of thought process; at least enough to find it fitting to respect the doctors wishes and flee the scene. Quickly, I exited the room and made my way down the hallway from whence I came. That same shared smell of all hospitals became poison to my senses with each passing step; I was being smothered in it, and I had to escape. The faster I walked, the louder my footsteps echoed in my head off the hard tile floor. I could think of nothing more than the event that had just transpired. I kept it on mental repeat as I drew closer to the doorway to my liberation from that terrible place.

The automatic sliding doors opened upon sensing my presence and met me with a rush of cool air. I was immersed in the much needed fall atmosphere as I stepped out my farewell to the bowels of the assisted living beast. Not too far out of the doors, I could do little more than fall to my knees and look up to the sad overcast sky. My mental status was falling; that much I knew for sure. I never quite believed that there was only so much a man could take before reaching some sort of breaking point, not so long as he persevered and fought through it. However, I felt as though that I could take no more of the insanity before I learned what a breaking point was. I had always prided myself for being an emotional and mental workhorse, a beast of burden when it came to matters of the heart and mind. But as a camel too is a beast of burden, the saying begs to mention the straw that broke its back. I was unsure about how many more straws could be piled on me before it became too much. Kneeling on the ground in the fresh air around me, my mind calmed enough to talk myself back to level ground. There was no need for panic. I was overreacting to a situation that happens all around the world most likely every day.

Be strong, I thought to myself as I let the breeze take me. After all, I was a journalist; my job was to find the grimy and gritty and put it on display for all other humans to view. The only difference then was that I wasn't digging into a story that I was third party in; the story was unfolding around me. Everything that was happening was a story to investigate, and I was the main character. There was still much work to be done as I had barely gotten past the tip of this iceberg. It was high time that I pulled myself together and focused on figuring out all those happenings, one way or another.

    I picked myself up from the ground and began to reorient myself. There were still things I needed to accomplish that day, and I always hated to disappoint. With a newfound sense of self-determination, I knew what had to be done. The question still remained about the man who jumped into the oncoming traffic. I needed to find out what the hell that was all about, and maybe find a clue about what was going on with all of the tragedies of late. Bending down, I brushed the traces of dead grass and leaf fragments from the knees of my jeans. I stood back up and headed for my jeep. Though Thomas's fate was a constant bother, I could not let it interfere with what I needed to find out. There was some twisted sense of justice in mind as my jeep once again welcomed the sight of me. The justice was not in Thomas's misfortune, nor that unknown man who I was seeking information on, but the simple fact that the story would prevail. It would prevail in the fact that all questions would be answered and all stories told, even if only to me. My loyal vehicle was patient and awaited my return to help me absolve myself of this mystery as I climbed in and turned the key inserted into the ignition. If there was, in fact, a story there, I was going to find it.

CHAPTER 5

The Rotting Man

Gray skies stretched across the horizon as I drove down the familiar streets of the town. There were a few guys I knew at the particular precinct of the police department I was about to visit; the roster of officers I knew was comprised of a cousin of mine, a man, and a woman I knew from high school. They would act as my informants to figure out a little bit of background of that nameless man that I had encountered. It all started seeming to me as some sort of puzzle; at least I supposed that was my way of rationalizing everything to put it into that perspective. With the way things were, it was all I could do to make sense of anything. The crossroads and stop signs along the way made ample time for me to think things out and try to make clarity of things, anything for that matter. It all was so confusing; though it all seemed linked, none of it came together in my mind to paint the picture. Snapping back to reality, I noticed that the next right would lead me to my next destination—the police department.

    I could tell that the wind had picked up since my leaving the nursing home; it was evident through my jeeps restlessness against it. Pulling into another vacant parking lot, a different strange feeling took me. It was not the same cold feeling from before, but more so one of loss and emptiness. As I parked my vehicle and hopped out of it, the lamenting feeling grew stronger as if that place was waiting for me to make my move. Despite those feelings, I knew that I had to deliver; like I said before, I hate to disappoint. I made way for the door, throwing all caution to the wind as I had to fulfill my goals. The concrete sidewalk guided me to my eventual point of intention with the clicking and clacking one normally hears from shoes on pavement. Silently, the door opened as I pulled the handle; I was almost worried about what I would be met with on the other side. I merged into the lobby cool and collected, despite what was going on in my head and the odd feelings that I couldn't explain. To perform the investigation properly, I had to appear unrattled and undisturbed—an act I pulled off well. The room was oval in shape, with five doors facing the center where there was a circular waiting bench. There was one door in front of me and two that had a large reception window between them on either side of me. On my left, the window there was concealed by a large roll-down metal shutter that met the protruding fake wood desktop; it was clear that it was not open for business. To my right however, the window was wide open with an officer sitting behind it. I casually walked over to the counter with a mind geared on confidence in my mission.

"Hi, I'm looking for Officer Brown. Is he in today?" My question was met by a blue-eyed glance. The man behind the counter looked like a cop in all respects. His dark brown hair was clean cut and combed to one side, and his almost comic book hero squared jaw was freshly shaven. If there was a poster boy for law enforcement, that guy would've been it.

"Yes, he's out on patrol at the moment. I can radio him if you'd like." Even his voice seemed as one of authority—deep and clear, much like something you'd hear from a radio DJ. I could hardly keep myself from laughing, not necessarily at him, but more because of the situation.

"Yeah, that would be great if you wouldn't mind," I said through grin. Normally, I wouldn't have found such a thing so amusing, but it was humorous to me for some reason or another. Perhaps it was the weirdness I was experiencing or that slowly my mind was beginning to crack, in any case, it felt good to smile.

"And who should I tell him is here for him?" It seemed as though he knew that I was smiling for some asinine reason as the bored expression of his face changed to one of a more puzzled nature.

"I'm his cousin, Evan." He looked at me for a moment and then turned around in his chair to some sort of radio console. I wasn't really paying mind to the indistinct radio chatter going on before me. My mind was more focused on piecing together what I could with the little to no information that I had. In all reality, I had nothing to go on, nothing really fit together in any way. Not that I had seen any uncommon places as of then.

The officer turned back around to me and told me that my cousin was on his way back to the station, and that I should meet him outside. Complying with the request, I thanked the officer and turned to the door. I had had enough of echoing, tiled, and droll environments as it was. Welcoming the thought of once again being outside in the wonderful fall setting, I grabbed the door handle and left the department without hesitation. Though my memories of the autumn up to that time had not been the most pleasant, the season was always my favorite of the four. Save for the times of my blissful adolescence, when the summer was my favorite time for the simple reason that I was out of school for three months. Much admiration was felt as I stood outside the station looking about at the seasons colored trees and gray sky above. In my older age, I found much beauty and poetry of that particular time of year; the vibrant colors and wonderful smells beautifully peaked just before succumbing to the death brought by winter. It was a simple concept and wonder that it was all the more lovely right before dying. All of the discomfort of the events prior released me as I surrendered to my view of the sky. I was so lost in all of my philosophical thoughts that I didn't notice my cousin pull up in his squad car.

"Looking at anything interesting up there?" The familiar voice brought my gaze from my surroundings to focus on where the voice originated from; it was my cousin, Patrick Brown. When I looked at him, I was almost taken back by our past. We were close to the same age and did a lot of growing up together. Though we grew apart over the years, we never had a problem picking up where we left off; it was always as if there were no gaps in time between us.

"Oh no, just admiring the view. How are you, Patrick?" I extended my hand, and my gesture was returned by a handshake.

"Yeah? You've always been a strange one. It's good to see you, man. What brings you to these parts?" he said jokingly. His thick figure and brown eyes were a great comfort to me as I was consumed by familiarity. Over the years, he hadn't changed; he still spiked his short, dirty blonde hair, and he was still built like a barrel.

"Well, my journalistic agenda has brought me here. There was a man hit by a car the other day, and I was right there. I saw it happen. I saw the guy once before, and it was a very strange encounter. My gut is telling me that there is a story somewhere here." It was the best I could do to put my situation into the short and skinny without sounding completely insane. Much like anyone else that I came in contact with, they didn't need to know the whole of the situation, telling those who could provide a piece to the puzzle could've been detrimental to my cause.

"I know the one you're talking about, and I saw your report. Let's get in the car. I'll take you to who you need to talk to." One can never deny the importance of those they know. Patrick was about to take me to exactly where I needed to go. Together, we walked toward the cruiser. I pulled the black handle that stood out from the all white and blue marked door and revealed what the front passenger side of a police car looked like. The seats too were blue, and there was a plethora of radio dials and other electronics that I'd never understand all geared toward the driver; I sank down in the seat as I got in. I looked over to the driver's side seat to find my cousin fill the emptiness of it. He adjusted himself into the seat, and I knew that we were ahead on our way.

"What the hell, man? You get all critically acclaimed and disappear for a few years. Then all of a sudden, you come back to life with a random visit. What's been going on?" His questioning of my current doings was not exactly what I wanted to hear. In fact, I found it more troublesome than anything.

"Well, I've been around, just busy I suppose." The uncomfortable topics of late were hard to think about with myself, let alone telling everyone else. I tried to keep the answers as simplistic and vague as possible.

"So, where are we going?" My change of subjects was functional as well as natural for me as I usually did steer conversations away from unsavory topics concerning myself. I felt no need to tell him of the current distresses of my life. I always found it to be unseemly to drag people into my personal issues.

"Well, I and the guy from the city morgue usually go to Griffon's for a beer every week. When we were there last night, he told me some crazy shit about that guy you were talking about. So I figured you might like to talk to him." His statement was intriguing to say the least. Perhaps the information I was soon to gain would be a link to make sense of some of the madness. The possibility that it could was almost relieving; I felt as though I was close to the end of all it and that I could resume my mundane existence in peace.

"What kind of crazy shit exactly?" It would have been a shame to let such curiosity fall by the wayside. I felt compelled to dive into the questioning; I'd always been pretty decent with interrogation.

"I'll just leave all that for him to explain. I don't think I could really tell you accurately myself." Though I understood what he meant, I hated just being left at that point. It would have to be a game of patience as he led the way through town to the morgue.

I can't say that the feeling was good as we made our approach on that cadaver hut. My stomach turned a bit, and I couldn't shake the notion that I had been there once today already, or at least been to the depot just before that near final stop that finally ended with one six feet under an epitaph. The building itself was very simple—a plain cinder block exterior painted a tan color, very few windows, and an average run-of-the-mill gray door. Just the image of the building was in no sense menacing; however, the purpose that it housed was quite troubling to me. In all aspects of the matter, I had no desire to be there. But I knew that if I wanted any kind of answers to any of my questions, I'd have to brave the dark and the unsettling.

"All right, we're here. Now the guy we're gonna be talking to is Ralph. He's a pretty mellow guy, so I think you two will get along." It was good to get a name to put to a face I had yet to see, just a shortcut around some unneeded pleasantries.

"Noted. Now let's get this over with. This place doesn't sit so easy with me." I had thought that if I expressed my distaste for such a trip, that I might get exactly what I wanted: all the information in as little amount of time in that place as possible.

"Damn you're squeamish." As he always did, he could not let an opportunity to poke fun at me slip away from him. It wasn't that I was that weak stomached, I just felt that I had been exposed to quite enough awful events over the last few days. Why willingly add to the heap of disturbing vibes all around me? He walked a few steps ahead of me to the door; as he did, I took one last look at the gray cloudy sky. It was just one last bit of comfort I needed before entering that mournful place.

All at once, the scene hit me as we walked through the door. There was a vacant reception window to my right, and before me was a long, gray, poorly lit hallway with light gray tiles on the floor. I couldn't help but think of how dull death really was.

"He's probably in room three. C'mon." Patrick led me down the chemical-scented hall a good thirty feet before we stopped in front of a windowless, flat gray metal door. The sign above it indicated that it was, in fact, exam room three. Patrick raised his fist and began pounding on the door.

"I said I'm running tests in here, damn it! If you can't figure it out yourself, then get the hell out of this profession!" A voice bellowed from behind the metal door.

Whoever it was in the room apart from ours seemed just slightly upset, and I say that in the utmost sarcasm.

"Open up, this is the police!" Patrick yelled at the lifeless door to the voice on the other side. I stood there silent for their banter, hands deeply inserted into my pockets. There was the sound of footsteps from the room adjacent that grew louder, indicating movement toward the door. A loud sound of a slide lock being moved to the open position was heard, followed shortly by the door latch releasing its keeper by the pull of a handle. Slowly, the door opened to reveal a brown eye behind glasses and a fragment of a face behind it. He peered out at us for a moment, and then the door swung open. Upon its opening, a man about my height was revealed behind it. He let us into the room, and I was better able to view him. He wore his black hair well-gelled and slicked back; it somehow complemented his thin pale face. Though he gave off the vibe that he would be a better-dressed man, he wore blue jeans and a green T-shirt under his lab coat that was draped over his thin build.

"Evan, this is Ralph." I extended my hand only to be met by a very weak handshake.

"Nice to meet you, Evan," he said, seeming to examine me as much as I did him. He seemed unsure of my presence there; much in the same way, I wasn't exactly sure what I was doing there either. I did know that I was there for answers, but it didn't go much further than that.

"See, this is my cousin Evan that I told you about before." I wasn't sure what Patrick was getting at with that statement, but I stood aside and let him say his piece.

"Really? This is Evan Clarke? I'm glad to have you in my office!" What he called an "office" was far from any conventional sense of the word; I was in an office of dissection of the human anatomy. Office to me meant paper clips, folders, and many other stationery supplies that I don't care to describe.

"I really liked your book *Find You, Find Me*. It really was a great dark romance, one of my favorites. I'm very happy to have you here." *What the hell? A fan of my work?* It was a situation that I had not encountered for quite some time. It was almost unbelievable that there were people out there who knew me through my works.

"Thank you, I'm glad you liked it." I couldn't help but keep my answer short and to the point. It was in a way embarrassing to once again hear such praise.

"Evan is also a journalist, and he witnessed the man's death that you mentioned the other night at the bar." Patrick's interjection acted as a catalyst to the conversation. I think that he somehow understood what I was feeling and was trying to get the ball rolling past the pleasantries.

"I see. So you're not just here for a visit, I take it." He seemed a little disappointed that we were there on a matter of business.

"Well, I'll tell you what was abnormal about the guy, but we don't know anything past that. No identification, no nothing. The guy's a ghost really." The look in his eyes became very serious as he told me that.

"We have nothing to go on at this point in time. The man's eyes were so cataract that I'd be amazed if he could've seen much at all. But it gets much weirder." Good, as if things that were going on around me needed to get any stranger than they had been.

"We tried to get fingerprints of him, but the surface of his hands and feet were smooth as glass, granted they were dry and cracking, but there were just not any contours resembling any kind of print." He had a look on his face as though he was still pondering the possibilities of that oddity.

"Wait, you mean to tell me that there were no fingerprints at all?" I found it so shocking that I had to express my confusion aloud. It, for some reason, seemed that no matter how deep I dove into all the mysteries, the less sense they made.

"Oh, but there's more. After trying to identify this guy for hours, we decided to move on to the autopsy. That was when we found something none of us had ever seen: his organs appeared to have been slowly decomposing long before he ever got here. It wasn't in any normal sense either. We tried to match it with all known viruses, diseases, cancers, everything. But there were gray and black marks on every single organ, brain included, that matched nothing. Even the tissue samples we took didn't show even traces of anything that was foreign in the body." His pondering look intensified more and more as he went on. I was struggling to take any of it in; my comprehension of everything was failing.

"You mean to tell me that there was no reason for any of his deterioration?" I said, once again not being able to contain my questioning. I wasn't sure why, but all the information was unusually unsettling. Had I been told something like that any other day, weird as I might've found it, it wouldn't really fazed me. I looked to my cousin in some hope of him telling me it was all a joke. I knew he liked to do such things, and I was hoping that it was one of those times, but my glance to him was answered by him shrugging his shoulders; no such luck on that theory.

"Basically, yes. From what we've been able to find, there was no explainable cause for this man's condition. Even right now, our senior medical examiner is in the room with the body, just as stumped as the rest of us." Ralph seemed to move from thinking about it to just pure frustration with it, and one sympathized.

The situations I was in were beginning to move from mystery to frustration with me as well. I had been trying to put it altogether, but anything close to a new lead that I encountered turned out to be another piece to an ever-growing puzzle that still didn't fit. We stayed for a few minutes after all information was set out. Just talking about your standard things between guys: beer, movies, and a little about my books. After the casual conversation had ended, Patrick and I found our way out of the exam room to the same gray hallway we came in to.

"So, do you think there's a story there?" Patrick crossed his arms and looked over to me. I wasn't sure what he was expecting me to say exactly. In my own thoughts, there really was a story—a story that would've been written by a madman and had no hopes of ever making sense.

"I'm sure there is, Pat, I just have to find it. Let's get the hell out of here." I had my fill of the prefuneral tutorial I witnessed that day. I was ready to go home and drink it all away.

"All right, man, let's go. I'll take you back to your car." Patrick seemed to understand my discontent with everything around me. Like I had mentioned, we grew up together. We had some form of wavelength shared between brothers. In situations like that, one tends to learn about how the other feels without saying a word. We walked side by side to the door that would release us from that terrible place; having him with me, it cushioned the full-on force of all the emotions crashing down on me. It was nice to be with someone familiar for the first time in a few months. For that moment, it was easier to cope.

His squad car had a look of impatience as we made our way to it. I grabbed the handle and pulled open the door. Just before I got in, I couldn't help but once again look to the late September sky. Its gray solemn look loomed over head, and it seemed to cry loneliness and solitude, a feeling I greatly understood.

"Are you gonna get in, or just stand there looking at the sky?" Patrick's talking snapped me out of the gaze I had with the clouds, and I set myself down in the car. He put it in drive, and we crept out of the parking lot. Some strange feeling of understanding filled the car as we made our way down the road. Not much after that feeling took me, Patrick looked over to me.

"So, I never asked, how is your wife doing?" So there it was. I knew that it was coming at sometime or other, and I couldn't bring myself to lie to him about that.

"We, uhhh . . . We are actually divorced now . . . ." That was it, someone knew. I knew myself that it couldn't be avoided forever. I just expected it to be put off a bit further.

"Well, I'm sorry, man. I've been there too." That was exactly what I was trying to avoid—sympathy. I always hated it when people felt sorry for me. Not to say that I was unappreciative, but I could never take the pity so well.

"I know. Thanks for the concern, but I'll be all right." Unsure as I was of the truth in that statement, it was the best I could do to be thankful for his sympathy.

"Well, you give me a call if you need anything. You know I'll be here." I could see it in his eyes, the care he extended was genuine.

"Thanks, Pat. I'll call you if I need anything." It was with that the conversation had ended; we had arrived at our destination. Then all of a sudden, another thought had occurred to me; the words that were written on that package I got: "Wrong Evan Clark!"

"Patrick, there might be something else you can help me with . . ." I said quietly staring out of the windshield.

"Yeah, sure. What is it?" He seemed confused about my sudden spur of thought.

"I think that there is another Evan Clark here in town, last name not spelled the same, without the 'E'," I explained. "Is there any way we can find him?"

He looked for a moment like he was deep in thought, and I could almost hear the gears turning.

"Wait here, I'll be right back." Patrick got out of the car and made a hurried stride to the front door of the police station.

I wasn't sure how long I had waited in the car, but it seemed like a quite a while before I saw him walking back out to the car with a few sheets of paper in his hand. The door clicked open, and he climbed in handing me the pieces of paper.

"What made you think to ask about him?" The way he asked seemed strange to me, and upon looking at the paperwork, I realized why. The information on the first page was a mug shot followed by information about his arrest for theft; his name was Evan Clark. I looked over to Patrick, but before I could say anything, he motioned for me to look at the next page. That page consisted of a missing persons report filed about four months earlier; the missing person was the same man from the first page.

"What does this mean?" I really had no idea of what else to say.

"I'm not sure. Do you know anything about this?" I couldn't tell if he was trying to sound accusing or inquisitive, but whatever the case was, there was no need for full disclosure of what had been going on. I would tell the truth or some semblance of it anyway.

"Well, I got a strange package in the mail, and written on it was 'Wrong Evan Clark', so I figured it had to be somewhere nearby for a mix up like that." It was the best I could come up with on the spot and at least keep the illusion that I wasn't psychotic. Patrick seemed to be put more at ease with my explanation.

"Hmm . . . What do you say we go do some poking around then?" The way he said it made me think that he was onto something; besides, it was nice to have some help on the mess at hand.

We were quiet on the ride over to the last known address of the other Evan. It was in what would be considered the not-so-great part of town, a few streets back from the main drag. The car pulled up quietly in front of a worn down and nearly condemned-looking house. It was almost too small to be called a house, more of a beaten up bungalow nestled tightly between the surrounding houses on a small plot of yard. The ever-growing familiarity with terrible feelings began again. Deep in the pit of my stomach was a pulling and unexplainable sourness.

"Well, let's take a look around," Patrick said turning off the car and stepping out onto the street. I got out just a moment after him and admittedly was hesitant to do so. The air surrounding the place was particularly fowl, and I held it close in similarities to the feelings I got when I received those nightmarish calls.

Patrick moved over to the dilapidated picket gate that was mostly in ruin and entered the yard. He walked cautiously about the brown grass and mostly dirt yard, looking for who knew what.

"I'm gonna check with the neighbors. See what they have to say about anything." My voice was quiet and low, and I couldn't help my guts from turning somersaults in me.

"Sure," Patrick said. "I'll keep looking around the house."

I nodded to him as I slowly walked to the front door of the adjacent house. It was bigger than the one we were there to investigate, but the condition seemed about the same: old and in need of some major TLC. I pressed hard on the doorbell, but there was no sound to go with it. I tried again to no avail, so turned my attention to the very faded red door and began to knock. There was no answer, so I tried again, and that time I heard something stirring in the house.

I waited there in front of the door as the slow and soft footsteps drew closer from behind it. I glanced over to Patrick who was at that point looking in the windows of the house with his flashlight. The door slowly opened just a crack as I was looking away and sort of startled me enough to stare back quickly. From what I could see, there was a little old woman peering from behind the scarcely opened door.

"Who are you? What do you want?" Her tone was harsh as her voice sort of squeaked out the words.

"I'm here with the police. I was wondering if it might be all right to ask you a couple of questions." I stood to the side so that she might see the squad car parked by the curb. She squinted at me hesitantly before opening the door just enough to show her face.

"What's your question?" she barked impatiently.

"It's about your missing neighbor. What can you tell me about him?" I got the feeling for a moment that it was going nowhere.

"He lived there only about five months. Seemed normal at first, but after awhile things started to get really creepy and weird." The old woman started to show some resemblance of fear in her expression.

"What do you mean exactly?" For some reason, the more I asked, although intrigued, I couldn't help but feel the same fear she was projecting.

"There was a lot of screaming and strange voices coming out of that house. He started looking really sickly over the next months: hair turned gray, got really pale, and started following people around, talking gibberish to them, drugs probably." I couldn't believe what he was saying: not to say that it wasn't true, but it was far beyond any measure of surreal to me. A quick glance over to Patrick, and I saw that he was talking to a person in the house next door to the one we were there for, and I couldn't help but wonder if they were telling him the same things.

"What else can you tell me about him?" My fists were clenching in anticipation, but I kept them in my jacket pockets as not to be seen.

"I called the cops and complained, but before they ever did anything, that man left one night all dressed in black and carrying some sort of box. I never saw him again. I think he was a satanist." The old woman's words flowed like ice in my veins; Could the other Evan have been one in the same as the dead man at the morgue? I couldn't even begin to think on those lines, not just then.

"That's all I need to know. Thanks." I started to walk down from the creaky wooden porch and back to the car, but the old woman had one last thing to say:

"You be careful . . . There's something strange in the air these days . . . ."

I looked back and gave her a nervous smile as I nodded. That wasn't the first time I had been told that.

I got back to the police car and got in. Sitting there in the quiet of the vehicle, I buried my face hard into my hands as I tried to formulate all of the recent information into some kind of reality, but it wasn't happening. I wasn't sure how long I had been sitting there like that before Patrick got back into the car.

"The old lady tell you anything?" I thought for a moment before answering, for the most part because I didn't know how to answer. On one hand, I could have told him exactly what she had told me and my theory as I saw it; on the other hand, it may very well have complicated things much worse than they were, and I still felt like there was far more to the happenings than I was even willing to admit.

"No, she wasn't any help and just said that she had made a noise complaint once." So I lied. However, as I mentioned before, I really did not want it to become more complicated than it had to be, especially with involving other people.

"Hell, the other neighbor wasn't much help either. He just told me some paranoid bullshit, nothing useful. I couldn't see anything in the house either. I think it's a dead end, Evan, sorry." I was glad that he thought so, because I didn't want to tell him that it wasn't a dead end to me.

"No, no, it's fine. Let's just call it a day," I said, slumping back into the seat.

We got back to the station and exchanged our good-byes as I exited the vehicle. I shut the car door, and he gave a wave to me as he drove off; I assumed that he was going back on patrol. There in the parking lot, I stood alone—a feeling I had been recently grown accustomed to. There again, above me, was the overcast sky; it had been with me since all the events had started. It was earlier that I had mentioned that the sky cried emotions, but that time it had really begun to cry. What started as just a few drops landing on my face quickly became a steady rain, prompting me to make way for my jeep.

My jeep had patiently waited for my return. Its cloth seats were welcoming to my presence as I climbed into the vessel of my return trip home. I needed to get back. I needed to stop those thoughts of the day from haunting me any further. There was too much thinking happening for my simplistic tastes. I wanted that to stop. The only way I knew how to keep myself from thinking along the way up was the same way it always was—crank the music. My tunes would help carry my jeep and me back home, free of all plaguing thoughts and ideas. I started my jeep and did exactly what I intended. With my music at the proper volume, I put it in gear and made my way for the highway. The town was as dead and quiet as it was when I first drove through—scarcely a car in sight. It was inconsequential to me at that time as my mind was preoccupied by the thoughts gathered that day. When the end of the town came and all of the stop lights were long passed, the highway opened up for me. I turned up the volume on my stereo too high, almost reaching capacity. The song that played was "Boulders," another song that helped me to cope with some terrible events in my life. I sang long and hard through it, and any other that came up, just to pass the time without thinking of anything other than the words of the song that was playing at that moment.

Chapter 6

Is It Coincidence or Is It Fate?

It seemed that the time I had with my music went by too fast as I pulled into my driveway. I had half considered driving the back roads until I fulfilled my musical needs, but upon coming up to the cabin, I renewed my will to drink. I was done with that day and all it had to offer. What I needed was a way to be rid of it. Shifting out of gear, I grabbed the emergency break and pulled it firmly up; I was ready to face another night. I turned the ignition off, and let the beast idle down before I exited. I opened the door and stepped out into the world around me. The surrounding pines and aspens could not have cared less about my presence as I stood there among them. I walked across the driveway and yard to the needy seeming front door. I pushed open the wanting door and revealed to myself the empty interior of the cabin and unwittingly welcomed the same forlorn feeling that I got when I first returned there. It was a lost and forgotten feeling that at that point, I was sure was more of a projection from myself. Upon my entry to the place, I knew exactly what I wanted—no, needed. As I shut and dead bolted the door behind me, I walked straight to the kitchen to fix myself a drink. The one hundred proof bourbon that I poured into the glass made for a satisfactory drink.

As I walked slowly back to the living room table, I was intercepted by that terrible electronic jingle of the phone that I then despised. I set my drink on the small counter below the phone and picked up the receiver.

"Hello?" The possibilities of what could be on the other end were endless, but I partially figured that it was going to be another eerie and awful voice commanding something. A strange amount of fear was present as I sat on the line. I could hear some rustling in the background, along with what sounded like arguing voices.

"Evan? Evan, are you there?" The familiar voice on the other end of the phone call was relieving.

"Yeah, I'm here." I was secure in the knowledge of the people who were calling me that time; they were my brothers.

"Oh good, you're there. We just got a new phone system put in all the damn studios, and we decided to do some test calls on this shit before we opened tomorrow. You're on speaker phone." The familiar voice belonged to my brother Michael, and being on speaker phone, I could well imagine that my other brother, Austin, was not far away. A few years back, they opened up their own sound and production studio that boomed in business and got them a few locations, much like my brother in Oklahoma and his body shops.

"Yeah, I am here. What the hell made you two think to call the cabin?" I knew that they had the number to the place, and the simple fact that they had just gotten new phones begged the question of the mystery phone calls. Did the calls spawn from the integration of their new system?

"Evan, you jackass! Why didn't you tell us what happened?" His question made me think deeper into the origin of the strange calls. What happened? What happened was too much to mention all in one statement, especially when I wasn't quite sure what he was talking about.

"What do you mean?" I didn't want to say too much in the off case that they didn't know what I was thinking about. I kept thinking that the fact that they changed phones might've been a root to the phone issues that were happening to me.

"What does he mean?" One said to the other. "You never told us you were getting a divorce! Does Mom even know?" It was Austin that time, and he somehow found out about my situation.

"Who the hell told you about that? I know I didn't, and no, Mom doesn't know. Is that how you guys knew to call me here?" There was some feeling of intrusion carried in my voice as I asked what I needed to, and somewhere in the back of my mind, I considered the fact that they might have gotten the information from Patrick.

"Well, we called your house, and Savannah told us. So we called where she told us you would be. I guess it doesn't matter much. Man, she was a stuck-up bitch. Did I ever tell you that?" That time, the voice came from Mikey. All thoughts that Patrick was somehow behind it were long gone.

"Yes, you did, at our reception. Remember when you got trashed, took the microphone, and announced to everyone that I made a bastard's mistake. Then she was pissed at me for a month because it offended her mother, who is also a bitch." I was laughing as I said it.

"Can't remember much about that night . . . Just that my face hurt the next day 'cause her brother punched me," Mikey said with a funny tone of voice.

"And then I found him outside and kicked his ass for it!" Austin chimed in. "So why did this happen?"

"Well, I guess because she was fucking someone else." It was a pretty harsh way of putting it, but it was the truth.

"That whore!" they said simultaneously.

"Yeah, that's basically it, but I have to go. I have some writing to do." Though I didn't, it made for a good excuse to end the awkward conversation.

"All right, if you say so. Don't get too drunk. Come by the studio some time, we're recording some fat-fuck rapper tomorrow. Later!" The phone call ended with what sounded like them fumbling around with the phone before eventually hanging it up.

    I couldn't keep the smile from my face as I headed over to my aid station, bottle in one hand, and glass in the other. If there ever was anyone who could make me laugh despite any situation, it was my two brothers. There was some degree of comfort reached in our conversation, however discomforting the topic of talk was and brief at that. Yet the news was prematurely learned about my marital fallout. I found it to be inconsequential at that point. It seemed to me that there were larger storms brewing in the horizon, though I wasn't exactly sure what type of weather to expect from them. The thoughts paced my mind as I sat at the table sipping away the whiskey. In all the passing thoughts, one surfaced to be coupled with the particularly troubling postcard that sat on the table in front of me. Who would have sent it? The even more disturbing question soon followed: How did the extra text get on there? Once again, my thought process jumped to full speed. I desperately needed something to fall into place; anything that could link any of those past events. I began to lay out the twisted timeline in my head; all of it started right after I left the courthouse where I signed my divorce papers. I had heard of life taking a downward spiral after a man goes through such an event, but a turn for the unexplained weirdness was just ridiculous. After the courthouse, I ran into that man in the parking lot. Shortly after my arrival to the cabin, heavy drinking, freakish phone calls, and angelic feeling dreams ensued. Next were the strange parcels and witnessing the death of that deranged man. Then, possibly finding that the very same deranged man could have been in possession of the package. Looking over all of the information I had, none of it really connected, no matter how much I dissected and spliced my thoughts. There were only a couple of commonalities in all the events, and it was more a gut feeling than fact: whatever they are that sing in the night. The phrase had been conveyed to me through multiple mediums at that point, yet the saying didn't even make sense all in itself. The other being that the package seemed to have something to do with it; anyone who had come into contact with it experienced something. Granted, that part of it was purely speculation on my part; I didn't know for a fact that the other Evan was that strange man and that the packages were one in the same, or even Thomas's side of the whole thing.

    All the toiling thoughts compounded with copious amounts of drinking led to far more abstract possibilities in my mind than I needed. I decided that it was time to stand up and take my weary soul to my bedroom. Upon standing, the spinning room and wobbling posture I held was a good indication of being too far-gone to think on those matters, let alone any other. In a slow, blurred glance, I turned to check the fluid level of the bottle: it was in a word, alarming. Damn near three-quarters of the bottle was progressively moved to my liver and bloodstream. It was a deciding factor in my need to move from my sitting area. A slow stagger to my bed made obvious that my brain was not properly communicating with my limbs. It was in that, that I had achieved one goal; at the point I had reached, I didn't give a shit about anything. Stumbling into the darkened room, I found my bed's location through hard contact between my shin and the bedrail—a pain that in the back of my mind, I knew would surface the next day. I slumped face down on the bed for the ensuing act of passing out.

A familiar feeling of opening my eyes came upon me; I was surrounded by black. There was another distinct feeling, but one not quite so familiar as opening my eyes. It was as if I was adrift in space or at least as close to what I could imagine it to be, complete weightlessness, surrounded by nothing. I drifted in the void for what seemed like forever. There were no thoughts to be had or emotions to be felt; I just simply existed. My thoughtless and feelingless drifting started to change as I felt some form of what I could best call gravity begin to take hold of me. A subtle downward coasting ever increased around me to a point that it felt like I was falling: to what I was falling toward, I didn't know. In my descent, the same spine-numbing cold took me; it felt as though whatever I was falling toward was not positive. The blackness began to formulate into clouds of gray as I fell into some unknown form of existence. Falling through what seemed like an entire planetary atmosphere, a deep winterscape and fog blanketed forest came into a distant view. I had never had a dream where I was falling, at least not before that one, but as I understood it, everyone does at some point. The cold feeling that I began to know so well grew within me the closer I came to the forest. Although the feeling wasn't good, in the back of my mind, I had no fear of death, even as I plummeted to the ground. The very rate of my falling began to slow as I entered the fog, almost as if the fog itself was acting as some sort of cushion for my landing. By the end of my downward journey, I hit a soft stop on the ground. I laid there for a moment, and all at once, my normal rational thoughts returned to me to replace the lethargic dream state ones. The lay of the land around me was enveloped in a deep fog; I could scarcely make out the trees outlines for fifteen feet at least. Though the scene around me depicted winter, I didn't feel cold, save for the ever increasing cold feeling that had started in my back and had spread to the rest of my body.

I looked around to see if there might be any kind of indication as to where I was. Yet there was nothing more than the fog, snow, and trees. It was at that time I decided that I needed to get up, but as I tried, I realized that something was amiss; every one of my limbs that I tried to move seemed as though they were heavily weighed down. Every appendage movement came as a struggle except for my head and neck, everything else did not want to move. I persevered; I fought my way up to a standing position to see what the hell I had gotten myself into that time. Totally surrounded by an unknown forest, I could hear the same strange pulsing energy sound I had heard before. It was not as prevalent this time, however; it was faint and lightly carried in the air. Though each step I took was a struggle, the invisible weights that troubled my stride seemed to loosen grip on me as I stepped heavily forward. The surrounding forest wasn't the only thing that was foggy; I couldn't think. It was much like having a bad headache, without the pain factor. An inability to focus was not what I needed at that moment. If ever there could be a smell of despair, it was carried in the light breeze that found its way through the fog and trees—a scent to the likes I had never encountered before. Yet the near indescribable smell was not the only thing carried over the eerie wind. All around me through the forest and mist, I could hear faint whispers of unknown origins. The sporadic dialog came from all directions, but I couldn't understand a single word uttered in the dull gray background. The shock of hearing all that around me at once cultivated my need to rapidly look around me. With each turn of my head, my vision blurred and the scenery trailed like a camera capturing too fast of a motion. My heart started to race and my breathing became heavy as the whispers increased in volume and frequency. The disembodied voices were clearer, but at that point, there were too many at once to fully understand anything. Through my panic, there were a few words that did surface to my understanding. As I processed the information, the grave discomfort I was feeling came to a point of high anxiety; they were saying "Norcrest."

"What the hell do you want from me?" I yelled out in some act of desperation for answers that I knew weren't going to come. All at once, the voices stopped, save for one.

"In the night, they sing . . ." The final whisper was a clear and simple statement. As little sense it made to me, at least I could understand it. No sooner than it completing what it said, I noticed a soft blue glow through the fog in front of me. Along with the glow, the humming sound that had been around me began to grow louder. Was it her? I began to make my way forward in some hopes of the soft blue illumination might be that girl from my dreams before. The closer I got to the light source, the pulsing energy sound intensified and sounded as if there was an electrical vibration with it. Walking was still difficult, but the weight I felt I was carrying increased the closer I got to the light. It became so damn heavy that I could no longer stand, and I fell to my hands and knees. I was determined though. I had to know what the hell that light was.

Keep moving . . . I thought to myself as I crawled ever closer to the intensifying blue glow. I finally came to a clearing, and in the center was the blue light, about ten feet out from me or so. It brilliantly lit the small area in which it hovered, and I was convinced that it was also the source of the pulsing sound. Upon closer examination, I could barely make out what looked like a metallic glistening around the light. Was that the medallion my father had sent me? I studied it for a moment, but I couldn't see clearly enough as the light being emitted was too bright to see passed. I had to get closer, but when I put my hand forward to crawl forth, the hovering light started to do something else. With a sound very similar to a wet finger rubbing the rim of a crystal glass, the light produced a ring of blue light from what I assumed to be the metal edge around it. The ring quickly expanded and faded into the forest surroundings. I watched with a kid's enthusiasm; even through my fear and the ever present cold feeling, I still managed to find beauty in the anomaly's spectacle. Then again, it shot another ring of light off into the surrounding fog with the same crystalline sound. Just after the second ring dispersed, the electrical vibrating sound and pulsing hum immensely grew louder and faster in frequency. The light began to intensify as it started producing the rings of light, one after another, each with its own high-pitched sound. All of it amplified to the point of sensory overload, I could hear nothing more than the sounds of the energy it clearly emitted, and all I could see was the bright blue light as it engulfed me. I laid myself flat on the ground and buried my head in my arms to avoid the severely intense light blasting over me. Everything around me began to tremble, the ground, me, and even the very air that was around me. I once again felt like I was falling. I opened my tightly closed eyes to once again find myself surrounded by pitch black. Gaining much momentum, I could see no end to what I was falling toward.

I was woken up from experiencing the very real feeling of literally being dropped onto my bed. My breathing was still heavy and my heart still pumping madly as I looked all around my room to make sure I awoke in the place I passed out in. It was, in fact, my bedroom; all was as I left it the night before. Lethargic and confused, I got up from the bed and made my way out to the living room. I squinted my eyes as I was met by the sun light pouring into the cabin windows. How long was I out? I glanced over to the clock on the wall; It was 1:30 p.m., much later than my usual over the last few unusual times of waking. Not that it mattered anyway, I had nowhere to be. I sat down at the table to go over the newest of terrible dreams in my mind, and that's when my attention was grabbed by the disk-like medallion across the table. I reached over the gun strewn, empty cigarette box littered, table top and picked up the metal object. I looked it over for a moment, but nothing seemed any different about it than before. Although I was sure that this piece was the focal point of my last night terror, I couldn't decipher whether or not the dream was caused by stress-induced madness, or if it was something else. At the point I had reached, I just didn't want to think about it for a while. I just needed to take a shower, something to wash away the anguish that I felt. The information I had gathered weighed too heavy on my mind. I desperately needed release. I set the medallion down on the table and got up to make way to the bedroom. I opened up the suitcase at the foot of the bed and pulled out the clothing I desired to wear. I went with the tried and true: a black sleeved and white-bodied baseball T-shirt, a gray and black pinstriped button-up shirt, jeans, and the rest of the essentials. It was once again a new day and a time for new agonizing reappraisal of some things. It would be a small step toward that anyway. After I gathered my clothing, I walked to the bathroom and started the water for the cleansing. The shower head chokingly spit up the water for a moment before achieving a steady stream. It took a good minute or two before there was any evidence of heated water. Then the rising steam signaled that it was safe to jump in. For a long while, I stood under the cascade of hot water; I thought about a lot of things. Mainly about what all those events were, and if there was even any meaning behind anything that had been happening. The constant beating of those questions wasn't helping though. It seemed that no matter how deep I drilled into the possibilities of answers, the less sense any of it made. The shower had started to run cold queuing my exit from the porcelain tub that had turned on me. Despite the unpleasant end, I was refreshed and ready to go.

Drying off and getting into some fresh clothes came with a good feeling—one of a few good feelings I had experienced of then. I stood in front of the bathroom mirror and studied my look as I buttoned up my shirt. My brown hair was kind of a wet mess, and the five o'clock shadow I was sporting could probably have used a shave. I leaned in for a closer look into my reflection's eyes; they were the same topaz blue as always, but there seemed to be almost a defeated look to them. I backed away and continued getting dressed. I didn't feel compelled to shave; it was fine how it was. Nor did I see any reason to do my hair. I'd just as soon wear my hat. After straightening my shirt, I looked at the mirror and gave myself a nod of approval and then left the bathroom. I walked over to the table and picked up the strange medallion that sat silently on the table. It, in all aspects, was a beautiful piece of craftsmanship. The unknown gem glistened and shimmered as the sunlight draped over it, and the fine silver metal that encompassed it was just as radiant. I couldn't help but wonder if the strange disk that I held in my hand was manifested by me in the latest of the nightmares I had been having. My admiration was suddenly disrupted by a series of terrible pounding sounds. At first, I had no idea in hell what it was, but I came to the quick realization that someone was knocking on the door. With that question having been answered, it surfaced an even more difficult question: Who was it at my door? The pounding annoyingly continued as I stared at the door. I reached for the pistol on the table in all hopes that I wouldn't have to use it. Cautiously, I reached for the knob, not sure of what might've been waiting on the other side. The sound of the hammer clicking back was simultaneous with the clicking of the latch releasing the door. I cracked the door open just enough to catch a glimpse outside. It was not anything I would have expected.

The man who was causing all the racket was the real estate agent that I had been neglecting to call. Behind him was a portly and elderly gentleman. His appearance seemed to be stereotypical tourist. He was clad in a Hawaiian-print button-up shirt along with khaki cargo shorts, sandals with socks, of course, and a white fishing cap on. I opened the door to better view the surroundings; behind the men in my driveway, there was the agent's car and another car with an older woman getting out of the passenger side. I looked back to the men standing before me, the door fully opened now, and the pistol set down on the entryway cabinet.

"Chase, hi. What are you doing here?" I was confused as to who the other man was and why they were at my door; I was too hung over, generally spooked, and definitely in no mood for any more shit.

"Evan, hello. What's going on? I didn't expect to find anyone here." I could see that the realtor was just as confused as I was, if not more. I had given him a set of keys so that he could show the cabin without the hassle of me driving all the way up to meet him. I'm sure that any showings that had gone prior to the last week had gone as planned. On the other hand, he had never told me that anyone had even looked at the place. Chase extended his hand in means of a handshake. I halfway didn't want to, but my manners overrode my aversion to the situation.

"Can I talk to you for just a second?" I met his gesture of a handshake. I led him into the cabin next to the doorway of the kitchen.

"I'm sorry. I meant to call you to let you know that I was here," I explained to him the short version of why I was there and told him that I had been there for the last week.

"I really am sorry to hear all of that, Evan, but these people are ready to make a real offer on the place if you're still interested in selling. They don't even need financing. They have the money." It took me a second to process all that he had just said. It was then that I remembered something that stood above all the odd events that had taken place—the postcard. Through the mental gears grinding, it all seemed to make sense to me somehow, and that same feeling, the need to flee, began to surface once more. Perhaps it was time—time enough in this state, in every sense of the word. I couldn't make clear judgment of my thoughts on the matter, and I didn't have to; it seemed that they had already made for me. The event, though random as hell, might not have been a bad thing—a godsend so to speak.

"All right, Chase, let's do it. If they want it, the cabin is theirs. I have to run back to town, and you show them around while I'm out. Stall them for a minute though. I have to clean some things up just really quick." I walked back toward the bedroom as Chase went outside. I didn't figure that anyone would want to walk in to find guns, booze, and empty packs of cigarettes strewn about, so I dashed around in a quick clean-up effort. By the time I was done, Chase was ready to bring the couple in and show them around. I walked out of the front door and stepped to the side so they could enter.

"All right, I'm off to town. Call me later," I told him as I started off to my jeep.

I really didn't have to go to town, but since I was more or less forced to go out and about, there was something I could look into while I was there.

Chapter 7

Leaving the Last Remnants

About halfway down the road to town, I couldn't help but ask myself if that was what I wanted: Did I really want to run? Did I really want to drop the little bit of my old life that I had left and flee for the unknown? There was a strange inclination that I did.

"This cabin is perfect! We love it! When would you like to sell?" In my mind, I knew that the potential deal brought before me was one of necessary action. If I were to solve any of the mystery, I was going to have to go where the mystery took me. If selling my house was a means to that, then I had to do as fate dictated. Besides, there was a bent appeal in packing up what little I had and running to where ever the clues led me.

It had started to rain more heavily as I got closer to town. My next destination was the house of that "other Evan." I had some strange feeling that something was left unanswered from the day before. However, there was something else that needed tending to prior to my stopping back at that house; I was starving, and I really needed to stop somewhere and eat. At the risk of horrid nostalgia and painful memories, I couldn't stop myself from taking notice of the French restaurant as I was coming into town. The last time I had been there was a couple of anniversaries ago, when things were still normal and made a hell of a lot more sense. Maybe that was why I had stopped to feel some resurgence of normalcy, to remember some time before all the bad events that had taken place. Generally, it's the type of place that takes reservations only, but I figured that they would make an exception for just one person.

To the extent of the before-mentioned exception, I was right, and I was right about the memories too. Upon entering, I felt a cool air of the past come over me, almost as if I had walked into a memory. There was an empty table for two in the corner that happened to be the very table I had once proposed to a girl, that being the table the hostess sat me down at. In the corner of the room, I watched the crowded restaurant and nervously twisted my ring around on my left hand. No matter how many people there were around me, no matter how nice the hostess or even the waiter was to me, I still couldn't shake the feeling of being totally alone.

It was the same feeling I had gotten the first night at the cabin, and the last thing I needed then. Almost in an instant, my appetite was gone, and my discomfort had gotten to the point where I could no longer stay. I took a quick, deep breath and stood up from the table. There were more important things at hand than stewing in the past, and they weren't at the restaurant. I quietly strode through the place as normally as I could possibly compose myself to be. I hated the idea of being an inconvenience, so I had dropped a ten dollar bill on the table for their trouble before I walked out the door.

By the time I got to the house of the other Evan Clark, I was thoroughly depressed; I couldn't quite explain my prior reasoning for going to that place, but getting back to my more abnormal circumstances took my mind off the more realistic. His house was dark and quiet; more so than it was the day before. I had parked down the street so my jeep wouldn't look so suspicious in close proximity, and I took the alleyway in hopes that none would notice a little bit of light "breaking and entering." I crept over the back fence and into the dead and abandoned yard. There wasn't much for a lock on the door; all that it took was the quick side of a Super-Shopper card that I had in my wallet and I was in.

I could hardly see a thing as I went into, as far as I could tell, the laundry room. I flipped on the light switch, but nothing happened. I figured his state had degraded to one passed upkeep on bills. The severely discomforting feeling deep in my stomach came on strong again as I continued further into the dark and vacant house. It wasn't until I got to the living room that I decided that the lighting of the opaque skies through the well-covered windows was not enough to see anything, so I pulled out my flip-top lighter to get a better look at my surroundings. Putting the palm of my hand toward the back of the flickering flame made a good enough makeshift flashlight for me to find a few candles on top of what seemed to be the entertainment center to light.

The lighting of those three candles led me to light five more scattered about the room; *candles were dangerously close to the walls*, I thought. When I lit them, the reason for their closeness to the walls was revealed: all the walls and even parts of the ceiling had been carved with various inscriptions and symbols. I drew a slow, deep breath in disbelief and stepped back; I had seen the markings before, but I couldn't quite remember exactly where. A strange and menacing presence loomed all around me and grew stronger every moment that passed with me standing there. I could feel my heartbeat starting to climb in rhythm, but more confusingly, I felt slight pulses of vibration in my back pocket. I reached in and pulled out the strange disk that had come for me in the package; I had forgotten that I put it in my pocket in my rush sprucing up of the cabin.

I held it in my hands only to find that it was, in fact, the source of the pulsing feeling, and it was that realization that brought on a whole new level of unease. I studied the piece carefully as it vibrated in a slow, metronome-like cadence, and it looked as if there was a subtle, almost unnoticeable glow emitted from the stone in the center. I disregarded the gleaming as having simply been reflections from the candles about the room, and beyond that, I found something much more curious; the engraved symbols that encircled the medallion matched many, if not all, of those carved into the walls. No sooner than my observation of the writings holding near exact resemblance, my attention was taken by a much more concerning observation; I could see my breath. The temperature around me seemed to drop in an instant, and a chill took my senses that wasn't just from the cold.

Unsure and seemingly petrified, save for my shivering, I tried like hell to formulate a rational answer to explain what was happening at that very moment, but nothing was coming. Then all at once, the silver disk stopped pulsating, and the gem in the center gave out a far more pronounced glow than what I had written off only seconds ago. Everything around me seemed quiet and still; though there wasn't anything moving before, an unexplainable void engulfed the room. My breathing became shallow and quick, and my shivering had grown to a tremble. Like the strange dream from before, I began to hear the disembodied whispers of indiscernible words emerging all around me. My once shallow breathing had stopped, and I felt as though my heart had done the same. I was no longer certain if I was actually in that house or in another fucked-up dreamscape like the nights prior. Regardless of what it was, it didn't take me long at all to find reasoning enough in myself to run.

I burst out of the backdoor and stumbled out into the backyard, falling over as I was trying to get my footing. The disk had stopped its pulsing and glowing, and as I laid there on my back, I was given a chance to catch my breath. I could hear no more whisperings, and I couldn't help but wonder if I was just going crazy . . . . That was, of course, if I hadn't reached that destination already. I stood up and brushed off the dirt and dead leaves from my jacket and pants; all the while my brain was struggling to figure out what the hell had just gone on in that house. It was very much the same in comparison to those strange dreams I'd been having, all except for some of the physical happenings that went along with it. The headache soon started to come about as I made my way to the decrepit fence. Just as I was about to slither back over into the alley, a voice called out from behind me that made me stop in my tracks.

"I told you, to be careful . . ." I slowly turned around to find that the voice came from the old woman that lived next door. She was standing behind the barely open back door of her house, peering out at me through the narrow opening. I didn't answer; instead I quickly looked away. As I did, I caught a glimpse of something out of the corner of my eye; there in the window of the house I just left, stood a figure in the shadows. I quickly looked back to where the old woman was as if to silently beg for some sort of confirmation that what I was seeing was actually there. I only caught the sight of the door closing behind her as she retreated to the confines of her house, and by the time, I looked back to the window, the figure had gone. A terrible feeling of nausea came on strong and, compounding with my headache, was cause enough for me to take my leave as fast as I could. I clambered over the fence and into the dirt drive behind the house; the same disorientation I had felt from those night terrors before clouded my head and choked my thoughts. Dizziness and blurred vision overtook me as I stumbled hopelessly down the alleyway, eventually collapsing against a fence.

A soft hand was placed on my cheek; it felt warm and cold all at once, and a calming sensation came over me as I sat there on the ground.

"Evan . . . Evan, wake up . . ." the soft feminine voice echoed in my ear as I slowly opened my eyes. I glanced about my surroundings to see that I had made it about halfway down the alley before I had passed out. I wasn't sure how long it was that I had been there; all I did know was that it had to have been quite awhile as it was well after dark by the time I came around. For a few minutes, I just sat there propped up with my back against the fence, just trying to reevaluate the events prior to my sitting in the alley. My head was splitting, and I feared that I had acquired the smell of the garbage cans next to me. I was pulling my aching body up from the gravel and dirt only to be taken by surprise by yet another strange vibration, that time in my jackets inside pocket. I had completely forgotten about my cell phone up to that point, and I was certainly caught off guard when it started to ring.

"Hello?" I answered groggily and annoyed.

"Evan? Where have you been? I've been trying to call you," Chase stated sounding just as annoyed as I was.

"Sorry . . . I was . . . I was at a movie." Cliché as the answer might have sounded; it was a much better alternative to answering what I had actually been doing.

"No, no, that's fine. I just wanted to let you know that they've decided to buy! I've been here at the office all night arranging the paperwork. So, is it good to go ahead?" I knew that his excitement stemmed from the fact that he'd been trying to sell the thing for months, not to mention the handsome commission he stood to make from it. I thought about it briefly but answered before I knew what I was going to say.

"Yes, let's do it." I heard the words as they came out of my mouth but wasn't entirely sure why I had said it.

"Great! I'll be there by tomorrow and we'll get all of this going! 'Goodnight, Evan'." He hung up before I could say anything else, and I was left standing there in the dark alleyway a bit confused and unsure of what the hell was happening . . . What was new, right?

The entirety of my drive back up to the cabin was filled with wonder and curiosity. I kept looking up to the postcard I had fastened to the sun visor in my jeep and couldn't help but think that there was something to all of it: something much more than happenstance or coincidence but more a culmination of events and dealings leading me in a particular direction. I knew that being rid of all the memories that plagued me might be met through the act of leaving the cabin far behind me and that the abrupt business of the real estate might've been the best thing for me. I couldn't shake the strong feeling that there was something big in the horizon for me. I just didn't know what. It all seemed to me to be some twisted form of fate; there was more to the events leading up to where I was that couldn't be explained in any other way. All those thoughts churning in my mind must have made for quick travel up the mountainside as I had made it to the driveway of the cabin almost without notice.

 I returned to the interior of my temporary castle. I closed the door behind me and took a good look around what was soon to be someone else's cabin. A steady thought began to form in my mind that would act as the answer to the deal I had made; the place was poison. It seemed to me that sitting there in the mountain retreat and drinking myself to death was not an option, at least not so long as the mysteries before me were beginning to unfold. However, I figured that one last "hurrah" in the cabin might make for an appropriate gesture as I fixed myself a good, stiff drink. I made my way over the creaky hardwood floor to my bedroom, sat my glass of scotch down on the end table, and picked up the suitcase at the end of the bed. I opened it up and set out a set of clothes to be worn the next day, and then I zipped up the opening and turned to the closet. Really, there were very few things to gather for the coming adventure, considering that most of the items I brought up with me were still in the back of my jeep. On the top shelf in the closet was a canvas duffel bag that had sat up there since I first moved into the cabin. I grabbed the bag off the shelf and knelt down in front of the gun safe. The door was still open from my last raid on the safe. All I needed that time was the rifle and its ammo. I grabbed the two boxes of bullets and shoved them into the bag. There wasn't much left to be done, all the contents from the bedroom had been collected. I walked out to the table in the living room and started shoveling everything into the canvas bag, guns, ammunition, and all. I had found a sense of release as I packed up my belongings as I believed that I was ridding myself of the last remnants of my former life—being free of all that halted my progress toward recovery and possibly discovery for that matter. After a quick hour, I had packed all that I needed into my jeep. I looked out to the horizon, jagged over the pine-strewn mountain tops, the moon shone down through the broken clouds in the autumn sky; both seemed to be bidding me farewell as I stood there next to the vessel of my next great escape.

 I woke early the next morning, slightly shocked that the night hadn't been teeming with despicable nightmares and disturbing phone calls. There was one phone call later on, from Chase, beckoning me to come to his office to sign some paperwork and some other amounts of formalities involved in what I would find to possibly be the fastest action of real estate I would ever encounter. It all came too quickly for me to second-guess any of it; in retrospect, it was probably for the best that way. The older couple got their summer cabin, Chase got his commission, and I got the freedom from memories and the severing of any ties that would have otherwise kept me from chasing whatever it was that I was hoping to find. After a short stop at the bank to deposit my newly acquired funding for my expedition,

I was ahead on my way. For a moment, I thought of everything over the last few months, especially up to then, and tried to decide exactly how I felt about any of it. There was a lonesome feeling tied to much of what came to mind, along with some strange sense of loss as I imagined my short yet very memorable time at the cabin. I pushed aside my feelings and got back into my jeep.

    Sitting down in the driver's seat and adjusting accordingly, I stared up to the sun visor just above and in front of me. I looked at the postcard fastened to it very carefully as I began to formulate some form of a plan. I had nowhere to go with having sold my home, at least nowhere I had ever been. I read the words written on it again; the words that somehow seemed to call to me, in fact, I knew that they did. If there was someone in Norcrest waiting for me, I'd hate to disappoint. As I took one last look at the fall blanketed town that I once called my home, a cold breeze through my open window brought on a longing feeling: Whatever was waiting for me, I would soon be there to meet it.

CHAPTER 8

Long Roads and Lacking Explanations

There was nothing left for me; all ties had been severed. The only thing left for me to do was to find my way to the open road and put all the shit from my most recent past behind me. Everything was set and geared for my final escape from anything that had confined me to that place. My jeep seemed as ready to get the hell out of dodge as I was as I turned the key in the ignition. It was about a 1900 mile drive from where I was to there, and all that was left to do was run a savage burn over the highway. Before my long journey would begin, I needed to fill up my beast with some gas and grab a refreshment for myself as well. I'd hit the station just at the edge of town and make way from there. I put the jeep in gear and drove toward the highway, east bound.

The road in town was littered with stoplights that impeded my timely leaving of that place—a feeling that usually surfaced just before any sort of trip came over me as I drove onward to the end of the city. Just ahead was the last stop I'd be making for a good long while, the gas station. I pulled in under the pump canopy and jumped out of my jeep. I slid my debit card into the appropriate slot on the gas pump and began to fill up. I clicked the handle into place for it to keep pumping without me, and I walked around to the other side of the jeep. From the concrete pad of the gas station, I looked out on the eastern Colorado plains. The fall had made the prairie more dreadfully dull than its usual lack of luster in the spring and summer months. I looked to the mountains in the west and followed them down to where they met the brown-gray high desert that was all that the eastern part that the state had to offer. I could hardly stave off the emotions of sentiment as I looked on the wild west that I knew so well. I was dancing on the edge once again, departing from my place of origin; much like the last time I left, I was unsure of how long it would be before I returned. The loud clicking of the gas nozzle shutting off broke me from my reminiscent trance over the plains. My jeep had its fill of fuel, and it was time for me to get mine; with any luck, the last I'd need before crossing the state line.

On my way to the convenience store entrance, I couldn't help but direct my attention to a beautiful classic car parked near the front of the store. The high-gloss black paint shined brilliantly with its chrome accents; yet the government service license plates made no sense to be put on a 1965 Rolls Royce.

My tax dollars at work, I thought to myself. I quickly dismissed the whole idea and proceeded on to what I was initially trying to accomplish. The door sounded an electronic chime as I passed through it, a mildly annoying gesture I always thought. I grabbed a soda from the rack and set it on the counter in front of me.

"Is that gonna be all for you today." The clerk seemed almost testy sounding as I brought my business to the counter, almost like he was offended that he actually had to do something other than stand there. He was definitely a younger guy and a bit on the heavy side. Judging by his sloppy uniform and his annoyed yet apathetic demeanor, one could speculate that it wasn't quite his dream job.

"Could I also get a pack of Marlboro Reds too?" I was sure that my additional request wouldn't have been met with much enthusiasm, and as he sighed and turned to grab my smokes, I was proven right.

"Total is $8.39." As not to be more of a burden than I apparently was, I paid and walked out the door to get my journey going.

Just outside the door, I stopped to open my pack of cigarettes. As I lit one, I caught sight of a man walking in my direction from the corner of my eye. The very presence that he carried brought an unsettling air as he came closer. I nonchalantly looked in his direction to better my view of him. He wore a black suit under a long black overcoat and a black tie around a white shirt to match. The man was quite tall, easily six feet if I had to guess, and his snow-white hair was mostly hidden under a black fedora. Though I couldn't see his eyes through the very dark sunglasses he was wearing, I did notice that complexion and posture wise, he looked too young to warrant such white hair. He stopped his rigid stride a short distance from where I was standing. He stood there staring at me even as I looked right at him.

"How's it going?" I said in hopes of breaking the awkward scene.

He said nothing and promptly turned to the door and went inside. As he did, I couldn't help but notice a heavy black embroidery on the sleeve of his coat. Though the symbol was familiar, I couldn't quite peg where I had seen it before. It depicted what looked like an architectural or drafting compass overlapping a thick V shape, and in the almost diamond formation in the void between the two was the letter "I." I knew that I had seen it before, or at least something like it, but it was hard to tell any details of it as it was black thread over the black fabric.

Walking by the Rolls Royce once again, I saw that the license plate brandished the same symbol of the strange man's sleeve. Putting two and two together, I speculated that it was his car, and it did strike me as odd that a government office would keep such a vehicle for a working purpose. The whole idea, however, was far from my spectrum of questioning, so I returned to my jeep and climbed in for the last ride out of the state. No sooner was it than me fastening my seatbelt, I saw that man hurriedly exit the store and enter what I presumed to be his car. He sat there for a good moment or two staring in the direction of my jeep. I returned his stare with my own in a strange curiosity as to what could've been so interesting to look at in my direction. We locked gazes for a short time before I had enough of the weirdness. I started up my vehicle and slowly drove my way to the station's exit. His eyes were no longer locked on me as I pulled out onto the highway hell bent on meeting the horizon.

I had long since upped the volume of my stereo to have my music help carry me over the long stretches of highway. The randomization of my mp3 player had seen fit to bring about one of my most cherished songs: "All On Black." The song filled me with a sense of righteousness about what I was doing, especially the line that simply stated: "I'll soon be sleeping sound, as soon as I leave town." The song, both poetic and dark, left me feeling hopeful that it would become a true statement on that quest of mine. At the point that I had reached, I wasn't sure if it was something I wanted, or if it really was much needed for my mental state. The road I traveled had taken me through most of Colorado and was soon to dump me out onto the seemingly endless stretch of road through Nebraska. I remembered having gone over that highway as a child; everything I saw seemed quite familiar as I crossed the state line. Although I could very well remember the act of traveling over that road, I couldn't pinpoint the context of which I had; it seemed that the memory was faded, I couldn't remember the purpose of the trip from those many years ago.

The late fall seemed to have been very unkind to the farmland territory as I passed by endless neglected fields and barren plains. The long since harvested stubs of corn stalks littered the open lands on either side of the highway, causing for a dreary and forlorn feeling over the terrain. That particular stretch of interstate would be one of the longest of the trip, and I knew it. So depressing was it to drive passed all the worn-out barns and forsaken farm equipment randomly set about either side of the road that I traveled. So much so, that it seemed to begin to weigh heavily on my psyche. I began to feel tired and hungry as I traversed the miles and miles of the seemingly deserted croplands. Hours out of my home state had crept by, and the darkness of night had fallen over the eerily vacant road before me.

It all looked as if to be on repeat; everything in the landscape surrounding the highway looked to be much of the same, only in different patterns. There was a forgotten tractor on the right, and then on the left; there was a rundown diner on the left, and then on the right. I could feel my eyes growing heavy as I continued along my path; I was certain of my road burned condition. A distant sign for a rest stop came steadily into view as I made progress up the road. The notion of pulling off and resting my burning eyes was one of necessity, just long enough for a power nap to recharge myself to be able to hit the road again. The thought that I was in some kind of hurry came to me as a surprise, considering I really had no time frame or schedule to follow. I suppose I just wanted to get there—reach my destination and put those troubling mysteries to rest. Or perhaps it was the only way I could justify to myself that it was something that I had to do to return my life to some degree of normalcy, provided that my life had ever known such a state.

I pulled into the vacant parking lot in the middle of the Nebraska nowhere. Besides ample parking, the rest area simply consisted of a small restroom opposite the lot from me and a dim streetlight looming above it. I put the emergency brake in place and stepped out of my jeep into the cold night air. A cigarette would help me relax and clear my head of the cloudy thoughts consuming my brain. Slowly I paced about the area surrounding my jeep just thinking of what I brought to my own attention just moments ago—normalcy, such a broad term. I walked along my same circle that I was making as old shattered thoughts and splintered memories unearthed themselves from long unvisited graves in my mind. Things from my childhood and memories from my days spent in college—they all seemed so vague and distant, in a sense, surreal. Much like a dream struggling to be remembered, all it can muster are distorted fragments and echoes of dialogue. The feeling brought on by the state of those thoughts was nearing one of depression. It seemed like I was losing myself in some way and had been for some time. Perhaps the strain that ended my marriage, the block on my writing, the ever-growing distance between family and friends, and even the odd things that were happening were all in some way or another my fault or doing, or perhaps I was just tired; I really hadn't done what I pulled over in that lot to do. The idea was to rest not plague myself with my own twisted thought process. I was letting myself get distracted, so much so, that I scarcely realized that I had lit another cigarette. Dismissing it all as merely being a victim of circumstance, I put out the smoke and climbed back into my jeep. Adjusting to some degree of comfort, I reclined the seat and used a rolled up jacket for a pillow. Sleep came with a shocking swiftness as I dozed off in the surrounding darkness.

I abruptly woke to the sound of tires on asphalt rolling by slowly. I glanced at the radio's clock to find that it was 3:42 a.m.; I had been asleep for hours. Reaching down beside the seat, I pulled the handle to adjust the back to where it once was and looked out into the parking lot. The dim streetlight from across the lot poorly reflected off a vehicle that wasn't there when I had fallen asleep. For a moment, the sight of the vehicle was not taken for more than it was, just another car sitting there. After a second look, however, the car seemed oddly familiar. I studied it for a moment through the window. I knew I had seen it before. It was a very distinct high-gloss black with what looked like chrome accents. Even from the distance and surrounding darkness, it would have been impossible to mistake the make and model of a '65 Rolls, and a deep creeping feeling from my gut led me to believe that it might've been the same Rolls Royce from hundreds of miles ago. Driven by the unpleasant feeling that was spreading over my body, I started my jeep and put it in reverse. After pulling back some, I threw it into first gear and crept toward the still car. The glow from the streetlight, though dull and faint, was just enough to see that the car was vacant. I needed no driver to confirm my initial thoughts; after looking at the car for a minute, I was certain that it was the one I had seen at the gas station back in Colorado. It had that same strange yet familiar symbol on the license plate, and one of the same that I didn't notice from before, in the space between the front and back doors with the same chrome look as the rest of the accents. Whether it was coincidence or something more devious, I wasn't sticking around to find out. I had gotten the rest I required and was more than willing to put it to good use on the highway.

After some more hours on the road, I completed my travels across Nebraska and into Iowa. Aside from the terrain becoming more like rolling hills, there was very little to stand out as evidence that I was making progress across the country. It all seemed like more of the same: farmlands and farm equipment in empty crop fields. I came to some small, spot-on-the-map town and decided that it was time to fill up the gas tank and grab something to eat. I drove through the seemingly desolate farming community until I came across a gas station next door to some Mom & Pop diner. It was right up my alley. I pulled up to the gas pump and got out in the sun drenched and windy landscape, and I took notice that it was one of the few times since any of those things had started that the sun was out and the sky was not overcast. After paying for my gas and picking up a pack of smokes, I stood there pumping the fuel into my hungry jeep. The surrounding quiet town, though far from my tastes of living, was radiant in its own humble charm. Across the street from me was a small Christian church and a few houses to either side of that. In a somewhat short distance, I could see the local Co-ops grain silos, looming quietly over the small town. It was without a doubt that those towering silos would be the tallest structures that the place would ever have. The loud click of the fuel handle signaled the completion of its task, and I set it back into its cradle.

I cruised my jeep over the short distance between gas pumps and gravel parking lot of the diner. Escaping the confines of my vehicle once again, I headed for the door of the very plain and simple-looking establishment. A bell chimed my entrance into the restaurant, and I was met by an interior that was to be expected: plain and simple. There was nothing special about the place, but the quaint environment brought some peace and comfort. I stood at the front for a moment before I was greeted by a short, thin, blonde girl in typical small-town waitress garb.

"Is it just you today?" she asked with a big smile. I couldn't say that I was prepared for such warm reception. I had been to those kind of places before, and admittedly, the employees of them always seemed a little on the burnt out side. Not to say that they weren't kind, just not so glowing as that particular waitress. She couldn't have been more than twenty or so, with her shorter hair worn up in a ponytail and her bangs to one side of her face. Her big blue eyes sparkled as she looked at me for a response.

"Yeah, just me thanks." She grabbed a menu from a slot in the cashier's podium that I was standing next to and said, "Right this way."

As the girl led me to some corner booth in the back, I looked around at the local color strewn about in random places in the diner. At one table, there was a group of old men in farmer's clothing and trucker hats carrying on over coffee;

at another table, a young couple that seemed to be sharing a milkshake and their hands clasped tightly over the table; and finally, a rugged-looking man in a green and black plaid flannel shirt drinking coffee alone up at the bar-like counter in front of the kitchen. Behind the counter, was a woman who looked to be in about her forties or fifties that more accurately fit my previously described diner waitress, and in the kitchen, there was a fairly heavy-set man in a white T-shirt and white apron. All of it formed a scene that could be expected in those types of places.

"Here we are." The girl directed me to the table, so I took off my jacket and sat down.

"Here's your menu. Can I start you off with something to drink?" I asked for a black coffee, and she promptly left assuring me that she'd be right back. I looked over the menu at what was to be expected. In my experience with diners, the menu rarely ever changes: breakfast all day, common sandwiches for lunch, and meatloaf, pot roasts, and various other large portion items for the dinner portion of the day. But, of course, how could I forget the hamburger listing of the menu. It was still early, and I felt no desire for something really heavy, so the eggs benedict would suffice.

The girl returned as promised with my drink in hand. I told her my selection, and she took the menu and headed for the kitchen. The lackluster environment that was charming and relaxing before quickly wore down to an almost still and boring setting. There was just some kindling feeling that I needed to get back on the road and out of that state. The amount of drive time left was somewhat daunting, and the multiple states still left to traverse could've been a factor. The waitress returned with my meal and asked if there was anything else I needed. Satisfied with what I had, I stated that all was well and began consuming my meal. It was exactly what I needed to continue my trek in the right direction. After a stop at the restroom and paying for the tip and bill, I was ready once again to blaze down the highway. I jumped into my jeep with a feeling close to excitement, started it up, and made for the road. There were still some hours left to be spent in Iowa, so I intended to waste no more time than I had already.

The clock seemed to spin rather quickly as I cruised the interstate blasting my music and singing along, occupying my mind from any troublesome thoughts that might have surfaced. Hours went on as I passed through Iowa into Illinois and from there into Indiana. Luckily for me, they were fairly narrow states, so they really seemed to go by quickly. Pennsylvania would be of some concern; it was quite a long state to be driving across. But it was getting late in the evening, and I had expired my tastes for anymore fast food and gas stations for the day. I wanted a hotel, preferably one with a bar. I judged by passing road signs that it looked like Columbus was the next city of any substantial size. I was sure that it would provide me the proper lodging.

The city of Columbus was nothing more than a large cluster of lights on the horizon as I made my approach. Coming into the town, everything seemed pretty lively; cars were bustling about the streets back and forth, and there were pedestrians walking around. It came as refreshing to see signs of life that seemed to be vacant from most other places I had driven through. Off the highway, I happened to catch sight of a hotel, with what looked like a conveniently placed establishment of drinking not a parking lot's distance from it. I took the next exit and drove over to the enticing view. Pulling up to the main office area, I could see that the hotel seemed to be well kept and pleasing to the eyes. More pleasing, however, was the wonderful sight of the bar next to it. I was in bad need of a drink; even with all of the miles I had put between myself and what I used to call home, the memories had no trouble catching up with me. I had to get checking in out of the way before I turned myself loose on the beverages. I climbed out of my jeep and walked toward the check in counter. Behind the desk was a tall, thin man who greeted me with a smile.

"Hello, sir. Welcome to the Columbus Inn. What can I do for you this evening?" His voice was surprisingly deep, but it carried an air of kindness with it.

"I'd like to check into a room please." I had to be to the point with that one. For some reason he struck me as the type that would talk forever if given a chance. I had no time for such pleasantries—not when there were drinks to be had. He hurriedly typed something into his computer and then looked back up to me.

"And will it just be you staying tonight?" His eyes were wide and staring as he waited for my response.

"Yeah, just me. Regular single bed is fine." I didn't need much more than that. Especially when I half expected that I'd just be passing out on it anyhow. The man returned his stare back to the computer and typed some other things that I was oblivious to. I handed him my card to swipe, and he handed me the key in return. A quick signing of my name, and I was set to stay in my room, number 222.

I rifled through the back of my jeep to uncover my suitcase that was buried beneath a pile of things I took from the cabin. There were a few keepsakes that I brought along, full knowing that I'd not be returning to that place I briefly called home. Under all that I had carried with me, I finally dug out my case of clothing and bathroom effects and promptly closed the hatch down. I stopped along the way to my room in the middle of the parking lot to look up at the starless black sky hanging over that Columbus night. The air around me was cool and crisp; a slight chill on the wind made it seem very bleak. Not seeing the stars on that particular occasion was a seemingly welcomed sight, almost as if escaping their illuminated gaze for even just a while was enough to feel a place in the world of the living. Strangely enough, however, their absence brought about a fond memory of a time when they were very much visible and being looked upon by two people in love. If memory served me correctly, it was about the same time of year—the fall, when we laid on the hood of my old car wrapped tightly in a blanket, watched the stars, and talked until dawn was about to break the twilight.

I wasn't sure how long I had stood there in the parking lot relishing in old memories, still feeling that they were some sort of lost and distant dream. I snapped my focus back to reality and the present, both of those being that it was all gone, it wasn't coming back; I was alone. As I realized such a perfect understanding of that concept, something new came to me; it was a thought that had occurred before, but I suppose it didn't really sink in: I was alone. For the first time since I started my quest, it actually came as a positive aspect. Maybe that's what it was there for, to accomplish it all on my own. No friends, no family, no significant other to help guide my way, just number one, me. I'll admit that the thought was very inspirational as I started to look at my situation as a personal trial of sorts. With that thought, I was reassured of what I was doing and that somehow I would reach something through all of it, and I proceeded to find my room in the hotel. After a few minutes of searching, I came to a door marked 222. The key fit as it should've, and I went inside.

The room was much nicer than I would have initially guessed. Not that I thought that it would be repulsive but more homely than its actual decadence. The nicely blue-and-cream-striped wallpaper was met halfway with a lightly stained wainscot trimming around the room. Instead of the usually expected wall-mounted lighting, there was a minichandelier mid-ceiling with a dimmer switch. The bed was the regular single-sized that I had asked for, but it was on a magnificent oak set with sheets and comforters fit for royalty. One couldn't ask for more for seventy-five dollars a night. As impressed with the room as I was, it did not negate the fact that I still had a mission to pursue—a good, strong drink. After some looking around at the very tasteful paintings of wilderness on the walls and the overall splendor of the room, I set down my suitcase at the foot of the bed and let room 222 for the time being. The bar next door to the hotel beckoned me.

I left my room basically untouched, save for the suitcase that had I left behind. I made my way across the parking lot over to the adjacent bar. From the outside, it seemed like a relatively respectable joint. The nice soft glow of purple and blue neon lights crawled calmly from under the outcropping of the roof. There were other signs of neon beer brands that hung in the windows, and it seemed from the outside that the interior might carry a comfortably dim ambiance. Even if it looked good on the outside and turned out to be some Ohio version of "Roadhouse," I didn't much care; I was just there for the drink. As I approached the door, I could tell that the very large and very bald Latino bouncer was eyeing me. I slowed my stride to make a sly entry but was foiled as I came to the door.

"ID" I would have written it as a question if it had come across that way. However, it came as a statement more than anything.

"Sure . . ." I pulled out my wallet and showed him my proof of age. If it had been any other situation, I probably would have given the bouncer a regiment of shit for asking before finally presenting it. But "tiny" there, was in the way of me and a nice glass of scotch, so I played ball.

"Okay, you're legit. Go on in . . ." he said it as stoic and solemn as before.

"Okay . . . I'm 'legit'." I muttered sarcastically to myself as I passed him to the door.

The interior was as calm and stress free as the outside had led me to believe. The music was low, but I could still hear it, and the crowd was quiet but loud enough to speak with a slightly raised voice. Really, it was picturesque of a proper bar environment. I sat at the bar for only a moment before service came my way, yet another great asset for me in a bar. I was greeted by a younger brunette girl as I sat down on the stool. I looked down the row of people sitting in front of the long wooden bar; it was crowded but not packed to the point of sardines in a can. The men and women along the row all seemed to have some degree of familiarity with each other, at least they were all in conversations anyway. The rest of the bar had people scattered about at the tables and standing in small groups. At one table, there was a group of guys, the frat boy-looking type, who kept eyeing a group of what I would've considered provocatively dressed young women. In fact, as I looked about the bar, most of its patrons did seem about college aged, save for a few of the older crowd in random placements around the room. It led me to think that there must've been some kind of higher learning establishment in the area to attract the crowd that it did.

"What can I getcha?" The bartender asked as she leaned over the bar to hear me. She was very pretty; her long dark brown hair fell over one shoulder, and her soft brown eyes somewhat shimmered in the dim track lighting above me. The girl looked as though she was probably in her late twenties, and she was in what looked like designer rural apparel. Her shirt was a pink and white plaid button up that she tied the two ends at the bottom into a knot around her stomach and just a plain white T-shirt under that. Her pants were just simple jeans one would see just about any other girl wear, and her shoes were just plain canvas converse.

"Give me a double Glenlivet on the rocks and keep 'em coming please." I was sure my order was one that screamed "full-blown booze fiend," but the truth of the matter was, that at the time, I wasn't far from it. I slid my debit card out of my wallet and handed it to her.

"Can I just keep it on a tab too please?" I asked as I gave her my plastic money.

"You got it. I'll be right back with your drink." She then turned and walked over to pour my golden beverage that I so eagerly awaited.

Time seemed to pass on slowly as I was taking care of my third glass and looking about the bar. The drinks weren't hitting me as hard at the lower elevation, causing the thought in my head that it could be a very expensive drinking experience. That was inconsequential though, I had plenty of money from selling the cabin, and it just didn't suit me to do anything financially responsible with it. Another wave of that lonely feeling came over me; it must've been from the thoughts dwelling on my newfound amount of money and nothing to do with it. My thoughts wondered to "what next"—what was next for me after I finished whatever mission I was on? Although I was unsure about what ends I would meet through all of it, I couldn't help but think that there had to be something for me when it was all said and done. Perhaps a new start was in order. Finding some place that I could call home, a place to plant roots and stay put to build a life again. I was brought back from the recesses of thoughts in my mind to notice something across the bar from me. There, sitting at the opposite side, was who I was sure to be that white-haired man I saw all the way back in Colorado—either him or his twin.

I studied him from where I sat for a moment, just to make certain that I wasn't just looking for something in nothing. That was not the case; I knew that I had seen that man before and possibly his car at that rest area all of those miles ago. It was starting to seem like running into this guy again was more than coincidence; there had to be some reason for it. The man just sat there alone, and not talking to anyone in the same fashion I was, sipping on some form of liquid over ice. He didn't stare at me, but as I sat there trying to watch him undetected, I could see that he would peer at me from the corner of his eye every now and again. Whether the guy was following me or not was of question, and I needed an answer to that particular query. I flagged down the bartender to come over in my direction; I had a plan. Though I hadn't drank myself to the point of complete inebriation, I had drank myself to the point of bold actions.

"Did you want another one, sweetie?" she asked leaning over the bar to me again.

"Yes, please. And . . . That white-haired gentleman across the bar, I think I know him. What's he drinking?" It was time to get some answers out of that guy.

"Well, he's drinkin' the same as you and a water, but I haven't seen him take one sip of his liquor since I gave it to him like an hour ago." I could tell that when I pointed him out to her, that it kind of set her uneasy.

"All right . . . Well, send him another one. I'll get my drink over there by him," I said standing up to go talk to him.

"Okay, it'll be right up," she said going off to fix the two double glens.

Making my way through the people standing around, I caught the man looking over in my direction. He saw me coming but made no effort to leave as I half expected him to. I made for the vacant stool next to him and sat down. I had enough to drink to be able to start up random conversation with random people, and I was going to use that state of drunkenness on him. The bartender sat down the drinks just as I was adjusting on the stool. I grabbed one of the glasses and set it down in front of him.

"There you go—a drink suited for men of good tastes. Drink up my friend, this one's on me." The man slowly turned his head to look at me, and then down at the drink. I noticed that the one he already had was a watered down mess that was untouched; there wasn't even a smear in the drops of condensation around the glass.

"Interesting measure of generosity extended from a stranger. Tell me, what's the purpose?" His voice was low and calm, very fitting of his rigid posture.

"Well, I'm glad you asked, because I don't think we're that estranged from each other, considering we've met before." I took a long drink of my scotch waiting for his response. It almost felt like verbal chess, strategically placing the proper words for a constructed conversation and the eventual checkmate.

"I would not be one to call seeing one another at a gas station for a brief moment 'meeting', unless you are that detached from people to use that as the definition." The way he said it was almost smug; however, it answered my question about him being the man at the station. Yet the question of him following me would have to be asked with near vocal "surgical precision."

"See, you know something about me, so there's something of a start—so interesting that we'd cross paths again after so many miles. If I didn't know any better, I'd say that we were heading in the same direction." The bait was placed. All I needed was for him to take it.

"Well, considering that we are in Columbus, Ohio, and you saw me in Colorado, I would say yes, we are headed in the same direction, East." As smooth and calm as his voice was, it was very easy to pick up on the light sarcasm he conveyed.

"You know, you drive a very distinctive car . . . One doesn't see many of those around, especially those in the employment of government services. Much like the one I saw in Nebraska. So what do you do for the government that they'll give you a Rolls Royce?" I was getting tired of the games, I just wanted answers.

"You are right. They aren't a more mainstream car. As far as my work is concerned, I simply drive what they tell me to. Now, if we are heading in the same direction, it must not be hard to fathom that we might just happen to be taking the same highway, is it? In any case, thank you for the conversation." He stood up and adjusted his heavy overcoat that brandished the same familiar emblem embroidered on the shoulder part of either sleeve. He began to walk away, leaving me to sit at the bar with the two drinks, but then he paused.

"By the way, I didn't mean to seem rude by not accepting the drink you ordered. I'm not one for heavy drinking. The one that I had in front of me was meant to be for you. Enjoy the rest of your evening, Mr. Clarke." It felt as though my heart stopped for a moment after he said that. I never did tell him my name, yet he knew it. I could've gotten up and went after him for more information, but there was something that told me that I would be crossing paths with him again.

I sat there pondering on the new collection of information. Though he didn't say much, he told me a lot. From all that was said, I could at least put together that he was some form of a government employee and also that he was heading for an eastern destination, at which point I assumed to be exactly where I was headed. The only question that I was left with was "Why?" Why was he either following me, or going to the same place as me? Perhaps the same things were happening to him. Or maybe whoever sent those things to me are of someone else's interest. Whatever the case, I wasn't going to find out anything at the bar. All would have to wait until I got there before I could achieve any real answers. I did the only thing I could do, given the situation and current setting, and that was to drink. I was there to have a good time, a relaxation away from the conundrum that surrounded me. All that plagued me would be put on hold, if only for a night. So I killed my drink, and I called over the bartender once again; the drinks were beginning to take the effect I had intended. It wouldn't take many more to get to where I wanted to be.

"Another one?" she asked as she dried a tall glass with a cloth.

"Yes, please. Another one would be great." It wasn't long at all before she came back with the wonderful liquid on ice. As she sat the drink down in front of me and leaned over the bar counter again.

"So did you know him?" For some reason or another, she seemed very eager for my response.

"No, he wasn't who I thought he was." There was reason behind my lie: if she thought that I did, in fact, know him, she wouldn't tell me what she really thought about him. It was that much I could tell that she had some comment about him; otherwise, she probably wouldn't have even mentioned it.

"There was something really strange about that guy. Something about him just didn't sit right with me." Although I wasn't sure why she was telling me all that, it was good to hear that I wasn't the only one off-set by his presence. It was a combination of things: From the way he spoke to the way he carried himself and just the general air about him brought on a nervous feeling.

"Yeah, there was something just a bit off about him. Oh, and I guess he's not going to drink this," I said as I raised my glass to my lips and pushing the drink he had left for me toward her. Not that *I* was making a rude gesture, but there was no way in hell that I was going to drink it: never take candy from strangers.

"Oh, well. Glad he's gone. He was just creepy." Before I could even get a chance to respond, she was gone and down the bar to get drinks for the other patrons.

Time passed, and as it did, many more drinks were consumed. It was just about closing time, and I was having my last call. The state I was in was quite a bit passed the one I was hoping for; I was trashed. By then, the bar had pretty much emptied out. The group of frat-boy-looking gents eventually made their move to talk to the group of girls, and they all left together. With them leaving, it started a domino effect of people filing out of the place. All that was left by closing was my drunk ass, and two other seemingly intoxicated individuals. That being queue enough for me, I began my swagger for the door. As I exited the building, I couldn't help but notice that clouds had rolled in and looked as though another onslaught of rain was on its way. When I was done staring up at the clouds like some lunatic in the middle of the parking lot, I fished around in my pocket for a moment and found the key to my room. It was far past my bed time, and I needed to sleep it off in the worst way. Much to my surprise, I didn't see a black Rolls Royce anywhere around. If that man was still around, he wasn't in the parking lot.

I awoke to the sound of the hotel room door opening, followed by a loud voice from a woman saying "housekeeping."

Oh shit! I thought out loud, *how long was I out?*

I looked over to the nightstand to view the cheap digital clock perched on top of it. It was already three thirty in the afternoon. I had beyond overslept and, needless to say, missed my 11:00 a.m. checkout time. The woman entered and seemed startled by my presence there. Luckily for the both of us, I had passed out fully clothed; otherwise, it would've been a needlessly awkward start of an already botched day.

"Oh, I'm sorry. I must've missed my alarm. Let me just grab my things, and I'll be out of here." My dismay in the situation caused for a rushed exit as I picked up my luggage and made for the door. I dropped my key off at the counter and hopped into my jeep as though I was running late for an actual schedule or deadline. The growing feeling of hunger was very evident, but I figured I'd just hit some form of fast food joint on the way out of town; I had wasted enough time as it was.

Chapter 9

All Roads and Nightmares to Meet

I followed the road for what seemed like days; ever since I hit Pennsylvania, the road couldn't keep a straight line. On top of that, I still felt like shit from the long night of drinking before. I had a lot of time to think on the trip, maybe even too much, although it was hard to focus through the hangover. So much of my past ran through my mind. A thirty-some-hour road trip alone can really make a man question some things in his life; at least, it did for me anyway. The biggest questions on my mind revolved around all the strange events from the time prior to my excursion, and I still was clinging to the notion that all questions would be answered by going to the place that didn't even show up on any road atlas that I picked up. Explaining the whole situation to myself in my head, it all seemed too crazy to make even remote sense. But I had gone that far, and I would be damned if I didn't see it through. All was constant for a while, but out of nowhere my music turned to a thought-disrupting static. Not seconds after it did, I frantically tried to find the source of the disturbance by turning radio dials and pushing buttons on my mp3 player. After a second of fumbling with the gadgets, it returned to normal. The odd part was that I never did find the problem in the first place.

The road kept winding on, and I followed, but I couldn't help but glance up at the postcard that I had fastened to my jeep's visor. For some reason, it seemed to call for my attention. I kept glancing up at it, and the more I did, the more a growing feeling of being watched came over me. The feeling began to grow heavy, and it felt as if my heart was dragged down into the depths of my chest. It was then that I made my periodic glance into the mirrors of my jeep. The side-view mirrors showed me that all was well behind me. Then I looked in the rearview mirror. As my eyes met the reflective glass, I saw that girl from my strange dreams sitting in the backseat. Terror took me, and I looked back only briefly to the road to make sure of my course, but in the split second it took me to look between the two, by the time I looked back to the mirror, she was gone. In a panic, I stepped on the brakes and pulled over to the side of the road. I looked back again, with my own eyes, to find that nothing was there. I sat back in the seat and rubbed my eyes for comfort. Clearly, there was still something going on; proof of that was just in my mirror leading me to think that my quest was not one in vain. The shape I was in was not conducive to good thought or state of mind. I needed more rest. New York would still be there tomorrow; that much I was sure of. What I needed was proper rest and a place to complete that in; I needed a hotel. In the confusion of what had happened, I must have missed the next turn I was supposed to take. I could tell by the signs that went passing by me in comparison to what the map was saying that I had no clue where I was, but I figured that it was something that could be figured out after a night's rest.

Not too far down whatever highway I was on, I found exactly what I was looking for—a room for the night. It was about ten miles down the road from the most recent episode of mine, which made it convenient. The general old and run-down look and feel of the place set me uneasy, but then again, what didn't as of then? The motel had clearly seen its better days, and so had the pub sitting across the street from it. Both were in dire need of a fresh coat of paint and regular maintenance, but it was a bed, and that was all I really needed, and possibly a shower too. I couldn't rightly say that my stay at the last hotel was very productive in any sense. By going for it a second time, I figured that it might work out better for me knowing the effects of the night before.

The gravel parking lot made a familiar crunching sound as I drove over it. Looking at the motel as I got out of my jeep, I could say that the feel of the place was anything but inviting. Its sickly and faded dark blue trim on pale blue walls stood out against the thickly forested backdrop behind it. I slowly walked to the main office as I still looked about and took in my surroundings. There really wasn't much to the place other than its "antiquated" mood. It definitely seemed as though time had moved on from this place and left it all in its wake. Oddly enough, I saw no surrounding houses or establishments to speak of other than the pub across the street, and it was in no better shape than the motel I stood in front of. It was as if someone at some time just decided that this would be a great location for a random place of drinks and lodging. Putting thoughts of the oddity aside, I grabbed the handle of the office door and went inside.

The office seemed uninhabited, and a stale smell lingered in the air. I looked around the room to see the pictures and old, outdated advertisements hanging about the walls. All the pictures looked as if they might've been family and friends; they had a very personal feel to them. Judging by the coloration of most of them, or lack of color at all in some of the cases, it looked to me as if the collection had been built up over decades.

"Can I help you?" A sharp and elderly voice came from behind me. I turned around to find a withered old man standing there with an expression on his face that borderlined a scowl. He was quite a bit shorter than me and was dressed in khaki polyester slacks and a light blue button-up shirt. His thinned-out white hair was fashioned into a comb over, and he peered at me through bottle-thick, wide-rimmed glasses. His posture as he stood there behind the counter was one anyone could expect a frail-looking old man to carry himself.

"Yes, I'd like to see about getting a room," I said my statement as nice and politely as I could without coming across as a complete weirdo, yet his expression never changed. The old man moved closer to the counter and made a sound that was somewhere between clearing his throat and scoffing.

"A room's forty-five bucks a night, no breakfast." Seeing his sharp and shitty attitude, it was no wonder to me why that place was such a dive.

"That's fine. How late is that pub across the street open?" Not that I really wanted to hear anymore out of the cranky old bastard than I had to, but I asked anyway.

"Midnight. So do you want the room or not?" He conveyed his impatience with the conversation well. Needless to say, my patience with the old man was also wearing thin. I wasn't used to such rude behavior, but I supposed that not everyone could be a beacon of human kindness.

I stared for a moment at the keys he had laid on the counter just a moment before and mulled over the decision to give the jerk my money. I knew what needed to be done, and after the transaction, my involvement with the old man would be minimal.

". . . Yeah, I'll take it." I reached in my wallet for some of the cash I carried and tossed it on the counter; he wasn't the only one who could be rude. He picked it up and counted out the twenty and three tens that I threw down. After a few grunts and sighs, he opened a cabinet below and handed me a five and a key.

"You're in thirteen. Checkout's at noon," he grumbled as he slowly made his way to the back room behind the counter. As I left the company of my bitter new acquaintance, I couldn't help but wonder about the story behind the place I was in. Thought's drove through my gray matter asking myself questions I hadn't had the slightest answers to. What was the motel like in its better days? What could've gone so wrong or badly in that old man's life to make him brimming with disdain? And, of course, who the hell thought it would be a sensible business endeavor to construct a pub and motel in the middle of the damn forest-covered nowhere? Sure they were pointless thoughts for not having any answers, but the entertaining of such things helped to keep a balance in my sanity. I came to the door of my room, number 13. As if I really needed to be put with such a superstitious relic, it set me uneasy. Again, at that point what didn't? I stuck the key into the lock on the heavy wooden door and prepared for entry.

I flicked on the light as I walked into the room, and it came as no surprise to me that it shared the same stale and old smell that the office did. I stood in the doorway for a minute to look around the room. The style and decoration was some form of cheap mid-seventies garbage; pukish green shag carpeting was sprawled on the floor, while it was horribly complemented by a dull-brown-and-orange-striped wallpaper pasted over the entirety of the room. Those two features alone filled the room with an almost dirty feeling. How many drug deals and serial killers had that place accommodated over the years? It was the kind of place that a high-profile businessman would take a prostitute after telling his wife he was working late and then killed the hooker shortly after. I will admit though, the room housed something I had never seen before, nor ever wanted to again; the comforter on the bed was one of a shit brown color and paisley print design. As sickened by the filthy, time-capsule ambience of the room as I was, I figured that there was no use in complaining; I had already paid, and I'm sure that the wonderful personality that ran the place wasn't one for refunds.

I had no desire to stew on the shitty conditions of that dump in the guise of a hotel room, so I decided that I would pay the pub a visit; after all, what better cure was there for a hangover and disturbing happenings than to drink some more. I tossed my suitcase and cell phone on the bed and made for the door. As I was about to leave, I looked back at the cell phone sitting silently on the disgusting bedspread with a passing thought to go back and pick it up. But I overrode my quick thought with another one that said that I didn't want to be bothered. And with that, I closed the door behind me and headed for the pub. I knew that I couldn't repeat the mistake of the night before with another visit to severe drinking, so before I crossed the street, I made a mental note to just pace myself and not get completely shit-canned on liquid misery suppressant. With my limit set in mind, I walked across the street in hopes of some sort of escape.

The sign on the front of the pub read "Lucky's Irish Pub," a place where I hoped to gain a little peace of mind and to drink one for my Irish ancestry. Though the worn and time-beaten exterior told a sad story, the interior told a completely different tale; it was very clean and neat, well kept with various beer and liquor advertisements hanging about the walls along with an abundance of Irish-themed decorating. The air inside was a refreshing turn from the hellish room I had rented for the night; the place was calming and almost therapeutic to a troubled mind. There were more people inside than the almost barren parking lot had initially led me to believe; there were people scattered about the place. I took off my jacket and wrapped it over the chair back and sat down at the bar. Almost immediately, the barkeep took notice and started down my way. He was a tall, burly man with short black hair and a thick black mustache. He wore a white dress shirt under a black apron and black jeans. Along with all the rest of his appearance, he wore a warm and inviting smile.

"Well, you're a new face! I'm Donald, and what might your name be?" His voice was deep and thunderous but not in an intolerable sense. The warm welcome set a good air over the dark cloud that had been haunting me. He gestured over the bar top for a handshake, and I promptly returned the gesture.

"Evan Clarke. Nice to meet you, Donald." It was nice to have some positive interaction to counteract the bullshit I had to deal with earlier from that decrepit old man.

"Evan Clarke, huh? Sounds familiar . . . Well, what can I get for you this evening?" Although I wasn't sure why my name would have been of familiarity to him, I gave my order anyway.

"Glenlivet on the rocks, please." I just had to remember to keep it in moderation.

"Right away, my friend." As he went off to go fix my drink, I peered about the pub at the people around. There was one man sitting at the other end of the bar from me. He was an older gent, maybe in his late fifties or early sixties. His interaction with Donald seemed as though they knew each other, probably a regular. Across from the bar in a corner booth was a group of girls giggling and sipping on their beers and other cleverly named mixed drinks. To the left of me sat who I figured to be a dating couple carrying away and laughing. Finally, at the table to the back left of me, there were two girls talking with one another, and there was a stack of books on the table. It seemed to me like a pretty average bar crowd from all the ones I had seen before.

"I've got it now!" The bartender's voice came as a startling surprise as he sat my drink in front of me.

"I'm sorry?" It was all I could muster from my broken concentration on the people around the bar. That, and I was unsure of what he meant by that statement. He then pulled out a familiar magazine and sat it in front of me.

"You did the article on 'Adultery in Modern Marriage' in this, didn't you?" His enthusiasm seemed to be a bit too much, but I humored him anyway.

"Yeah . . . I did that one . . ." My reply resembled disgust in some way. Perhaps it was the fact that I had to recently live through the topic of the article. It was one of the last pieces of my writing that had been published and not really too much of my pleasure; it was something "suggested" to me by my publisher as a way to get back to writing. So they set up something from a magazine and told me to write that piece of social commentary shit. As I mentioned, it wasn't much to my pleasure. In some way, it seemed that everything up to that time was just a mockery of my situation and recent fallout in life.

"It's so true. People just don't stay together anymore." His tone was more serious and nowhere near as loud as it was before. Just by his response to the conversation, I could tell that he too had seen the bitter end of love. I wasn't there to be anyone's shrink; as it came to mind, I thought that a bartender was the only mental therapist that prescribed booze, not former authors and journalists.

"Well, here's another one on the house," he said sliding a full glass of glen over in my direction.

"Let me know if you need anything else, bud." He turned and walked to the other side of the bar. I looked at the ring on my left hand just long enough to feel the burning of emotional hooks rip into my heart and pull it into the depths of my stomach.

"*I would* write that fucking article," I muttered under my breath as I took a drink.

I continued with my lovely beverage uninterrupted. That was until a girl walked up and stood next to me.

"Excuse me . . ." Her soft voice came as a surprise. I slowly turned around in the barstool to see who was talking to me. My eyes viewed a very pretty girl with shoulder-length, raven-black hair, thin glasses, and a fair complexion that was in some way fitting of her very petite and slender build; she struck me as an intellectual.

"Yes?" The way I said it came out a lot different than what I meant to sound. I came across as short and bothered, and I could see that she was a bit taken aback by that.

"Umm . . . Well, you see . . . I was just . . ." It was clear that she was shy, and I was sure that the way I responded didn't aid her nervous situation. She did seem very nervous too; she clenched a book tightly to her chest and was kind of swaying side to side. Her manner of dress told me that she was conservative, yet wanted to be pretty, and she accomplished it well. The girl wore a black sweater vest over a white dress shirt and a knee-length gray skirt. Seeing all that caused me to think that she was one for class. She stumbled over her words and was going back and forth between near laughter and seriousness.

"My friend and I have been arguing over whether or not you are someone we've seen before." The girl was acting more nervous than before.

"Who is it that you think I am?" I asked with a sort of laugh. I had no idea what she was going on about. In my mind, I didn't stand out from anyone else; my short and sort of messy brown hair was put to the side as it usually was, and I was still dressed in a simple button-up pinstriped shirt and jeans.

It was then that she handed me the book she held onto so tightly before. She acted as if she was trying to say something before she did, but I suppose action overtook her speech. I looked down at the book she had handed me, only to be met by a picture of myself on the back. Automatically, I knew what it was; it was the first book I had written and published. It was the publisher's idea to make me submit some crap-ass picture of myself on the back of it.

"Well, if you were arguing over whether or not I am the guy in the picture here, whoever said I was is right." I didn't want to sound haughty, but it was the truth.

"I knew it!" Her exclamation was not what I was used to seeing from fans, even when I had them.

"I told her it was you! I'm a really big fan of your work. This is my favorite book of yours." The book was titled *A Midwestern Boy*; it was somewhat of a modern-day *Catcher in the Rye* but much more optimistic. The oddest part to me was the sudden notoriety: my book signings were pretty much empty, my publicity was shit, and I only made two television appearances.

"Well, I'm glad you enjoyed it." My answer to her excitement was genuine; it was nice to feel valued again.

"Would you mind if I asked you to sign my book?" She exclaimed with the utmost energetic excitement.

"Of course, I'll sign it for you. What's your name?" It was always special to me when I signed any of my works for a person; it made me feel as though at least something I had done in my life was appreciated and worth a damn. A feeling I can honestly say had been very distant for some time. Up until then, I was admittedly down on myself for obvious reasons and, not to mention, the onslaught of weirdness that had taken over my life.

"My name's Elizabeth Mattox." Even in just simply stating her name, she expressed what I thought to be sort of funny display of nervousness.

She handed over the slightly worn soft cover book and a pen for me to sign it with. I scribbled my piece just inside the cover, addressing it to her name.

"Here you go. It's good to see that there is someone still reading my stuff." I handed it back to her with a smile. I couldn't help but be reminded of a memory I kept fondly in my mind—a time when I got to meet someone of admiration to me. He was the lead singer from my favorite band, and I met him after a show I went to when I was around seventeen years old. I recalled how he not only just signed some T-shirt or scrap of paper and send me on my way, but also took time and talked to me for a good hour and a half. I had always kept that memory not for more than just who I had met, but also for the impression his gesture made on me that he was just another person who happened to be widely recognized for their work.

"Thank you so much! This really means a lot to me!" She exclaimed in joy. As she started to ready herself to leave, a thought came to my mind.

"You know if you're not in any kind of hurry, we could sit here and talk for a while." In some way or another, I think I wanted to sit and talk to her just as much, if not more, than she would want to talk to me.

"Really? You mean you wouldn't mind?" She almost seemed in disbelief that I had asked.

"No, I don't mind at all. I'm not going anywhere until tomorrow, so it would be my pleasure." I suppose that I was also eager for real conversation; I had been pretty well alone for a while, and some actual dialogue with someone revealed quite a bit of appeal to me.

We spent a good long while talking. I found out that she was there visiting home from college and that there actually was a town, very near the seemingly deserted pub and motel; it was just down the road a bit. Conversation had gone from literary topics to life goals, and anywhere else in between. For once, I felt very comfortable with a stranger—not my normal withdrawn and vague self. Perhaps it was the alcohol that loosened the social tensions that I normally felt, or maybe it was simply that Elizabeth made for excellent company. She was very intelligent and wise to the ways of the world, especially for the younger age of twenty-three. She was very much a joy to converse with; it brought a calming peace to my mind. That was something that I really needed. Unfortunately, and it was more and more understood by me in the recent weeks, that all good things must come to an end, and that meant our time of friendly chatter. We stood from the barstools and exchanged our good-byes. I had even given her my e-mail address with a promise that she'd be the only one to know it apart from personal acquaintances. She gave me a hug at the door of the bar and thanked me for being so nice to her, and I thanked her for being nice enough to sit with me. We then parted ways as she went for her car on the other side of the lot, and I made mine across the street toward the motel.

It seemed much colder out than it had before I entered the pub. Of course, the night had progressed, and it wasn't going to get warmer. There was also a light fog over the area, and everything seemed more vacant than before. The setting was quite eerie and uncomfortable; even the clouded sky seemed too still for any normal weather. It struck me as odd too that the surroundings of comfort I had just left wore off in almost an instant as I was surrounded by the foggy night. A strange headache started manifesting as I got closer to my room across the gravel and dirt parking lot; something wasn't right. Deep in my gut shot a sharp feeling similar to acid indigestion, but there was something else to it; the feeling set off what I could only explain as a physical warning signal. I was overcome by the impulse, and I became dizzy and light-headed as the headache intensified. All the strange symptoms were something other than the drinks I had just consumed. I was barely buzzed; it was oddly reminiscent of what happened to me in the alleyway back in Colorado.

Coming up to the door to my room brought a very slight, minimal comfort but not enough to stave off the dreadful feeling that had befallen me. By that point, my vision had started to blur, and concentration became increasingly difficult. I pulled the room key from my pocket, but no sooner did it breach the top, it dropped to the ground. It was a struggle to bend down and get it, but once I crouched down, another dark feeling came to my alert. It was a piercing feeling—one that said I was being watched. I slowly picked up the key and halfway opened the room door, but the sense that something was observing me intensified. Turning around in the incompletely opened doorway, something across the street caught my eyes. In the distance, through the fog and under a flickering streetlight, something stood there staring right back at me. I couldn't see more than just a silhouette, but something inside me said that the simple image I was viewing was more than enough. Whatever it was held a very human resemblance, yet there were some things that were amiss. It seemed rather tall; just having guessed from the distance, I would've said somewhere between six and a half or seven feet. But the points of ill-fitting characteristics didn't end there. The arms and legs looked longer than any normal person, and not only were they longer, but they also looked as though they were disgustingly thin.

A contest of staring ensued as I looked at it, and it looked at me. The ever-growing familiarity with that same cold feeling from before reached a new level as I gazed across the street. Who or whatever it was cocked its head to the side in an almost animalistic manner and then straight up again with no visual motion in between. My heart rate significantly increased seeing that gesture; it wasn't normal. It then began to shake its head back, forth, up, and down in a very choppy but extremely fast motion. I could no longer stand the presence or the feeling that it brought; my heart was beating so hard that I could feel it in my teeth. I quickly turned for my room and slammed the door behind me. As I fastened the deadbolt and the lock on the handle, there was no idea in my mind about what had just happened; all I knew was that it wasn't good. I took a cigarette from out of its pack and brought my shaking hand grasping a lighter to ignite my nerve calming tactic. The headache and dizziness were still running strong, and I could think of nothing else other than what had just been seen.

"What the hell was that?" I asked myself. In the same case of everything else terrible that had gone on, I had no answers. I slowly moved to the window and peered behind the curtain, just enough to see to the streetlight. There was nothing. To a certain degree, I had to ask myself if I had gone mad. Even if I had, it wasn't like an insane man will ever admit to being crazy. I sat down on the bed and lay back, taking a deep drag of my cigarette. The headache and dizziness had subsided almost as quickly as it had began, and I wanted my gun more than anything, but there was no way in hell that I was going out to my jeep to get it. What was going on? Even the more positive experiences I had encountered were far from ordinary. In all my time writing books and articles, I never did gain a lot of notoriety, much less be recognized as anything else than just another guy. I sat up in puzzlement of everything, good and bad. None of it came together at all, and at the point I had reached, I knew that it wasn't just stress; something else was at work.

I lay in the bed in hopes of sleep that wasn't coming, and the plain and depressing view of the shitty hotel ceiling didn't help matters any. So many things danced wildly around my head as I tried to make sense of all of it. I stirred up my own thoughts so much that they became abstract and stopped making sense even to me. But all my racing thoughts were soon cut short as the phone sitting by the small table under the window began to ring. A terror took me; no one but that old man who ran the place knew I was staying there, and there was no reason in the world I could see for him calling me. The phone sat persistently ringing with a red light on it, flashing every time the noise came through. There was a large part of me that wanted to just let it ring, yet somehow I knew that even if I did, it wasn't going to give up so easily. I stood above the ringing and flashing phone for a moment just staring at it. My gut wrenched and my heart sank as I picked up the receiver to say hello.

Just as the receiver met my ear, I could hear something on the other line. It sounded once again of a labored and gasping breathing. Before I could even muster the word "hello," I was met by a horrific voice through gasping and wheezing.

"We're . . . waiting . . . for . . . you . . ." The voice was so distorted and surrounded by static that I could barely make out the disturbing message. Whatever was on the other line sounded horribly raspy and came across as electronically twisted and out of breath; it sounded evil. After a short time of more of the labored breathing, the call cut off and left me standing there nearly paralyzed with horror. In an instant, the headache and blurred vision returned coupled with my hands trembling and my focus far from reach. I dropped the receiver and left it to dangle off the table as I staggered over to the bed. All the traumas I was experiencing at that moment reached such a point that I could no longer bear. Slumping down on the bed, all around me faded to black, and a loud ringing consumed my hearing.

When I came to, I was no longer in my room. I looked around in a confused haze to know where I was and how I could've gotten there. It took a moment for my sight to regain proper focus and my mind to reach a point where I was able to process thoughts again. It was about then that I came to the very shocking realization that I was propped up sitting against a large tree. Again I looked at my surroundings; though it didn't make sense, I was able to understand that I was surrounded by a thick forest blanketed in a heavy fog. I looked up and could see that the ominous blue moon was trying to light the area, but the fog and as far as I could tell for cloud cover was thick enough to just bring about a soft blue-gray illumination over everything. The headache was gone, but there were still some groggy aftereffects from it. I curled my hand to the back of my head and rubbed it for comfort as I stood up from the ground. Then I noticed a sound in the distance. I was not sure about what I was hearing, but it sounded like a faint panting somewhere in the fog. For reasons beyond unclear to me, I was compelled to start walking in the direction the noise was coming from. It wasn't long walking before the faint panting sound became more audible; the sound I heard was of someone's crying.

The thought that someone might've needed help overcame any fear I was feeling at the time, and I quickened pace toward the source of the sound.

"Hello. Do you need help?" I began to yell across the vacant fog and forest, hoping for some kind of response. The crying grew ever louder as I forced my way through thick, dead brush and timber, trying to make haste. Just as I entered a small clearing, a vibrating and buzzing in my pocket startled me and caught my attention; it was my cell phone. As if the situation wasn't bizarre enough, the last recollection of my cell phone I had was it lying on the bed. I dismissed my recollection for the more important matter at hand and began wildly digging in my pocket to retrieve the incoming call.

"Hello!" I answered the phone in a near panic. There was something that came over me that brought my attention to high alert and to read the situation as dire.

"Evan! Evan! Where are you? Why aren't you at home? I need you! I miss you!" I knew the voice on the other line, but there was no way that it could have been. Through the sobbing and frantic manner of speech over the phone, I could recognize the familiar voice right away; it was my ex-wife.

"Savannah? Why are you calling, and what are you talking about? Are you okay?" It wasn't simply the fact that she had called that was off about the whole situation, but in all the time that I knew her, she rarely ever cried. Savannah was always very emotionally reserved; so one could imagine that if I had rarely seen her cry, I sure as hell never saw her in a hysterical state.

"Evan, I'm scared! I don't know where I am, and it's cold here, so cold . . . Evan, please help me!" Her tone became ever more excited and panicked as she spoke. So badly that it started to get difficult to understand her. Then I noticed something that stopped my heart and stole it from my chest; the crying over the phone mirrored the sound of the crying I heard in the distance.

I started a fast-paced jog to where the sound was coming from.

"Savannah, just stay there. I'm here, just don't go anywhere!" The sobbing grew louder over the air as I madly rushed through the forest. I came to the edge of the clearing and began to make my way through cutting and stabbing branches, twigs, and the like. The crying was getting louder, and the phone still played back exactly what I was hearing in the darkness around me. With the faint moonlight on my side, I could barely see that just up ahead was another clearing, and I was sure that had to have been where she was. I looked back at my cell phone to make sure that she was still on the other line, but the screen was black, and it seemed to have lost all its functions. I was in too much of a hurry to be bothered by the device though, I shoved it back into my pocket and pressed on.

I finally came to the clearing; the stinging from the protruding branches of the path before was fresh on my skin, and I was slightly winded. I looked around as I tried to catch my breath to see if I could find her, and then my eyes locked on what I was looking for. Against a tree, curled up and weeping, was Savannah. I came closer not knowing what to expect.

"Savannah?" I said softy and out of breath. She was in better view from the distance I stood at entering the clearing. The fog had made it hard to see her from longer range, but when I got closer, I could see more detail. She sat and cradled herself against a large, dead and rotting tree. Her face was hidden, buried behind her arms and knees as she cried rocking back and forth. She wasn't wearing socks or shoes, but what she did seem to be wearing added even more confusion to a situation that made for heightened curiosity. It was a dress, one that I recognized, but it was tattered, dirty, and torn; it was the dress she wore to our wedding. Aside from everything else that was going on, there was something very, very wrong. I could start to see as I got closer that her skin looked very pale and ill colored, and her hair looked jet black instead of her normal brown. Something was very wrong; I knew that it wasn't her, not the Savannah I knew.

"Evan . . . I am so glad that you came . . . Waiting . . ." She didn't lift her head to speak to me; she spoke in a whisper that seemed to echo around me, and it didn't sound like a voice that had been crying at all.

"Are you . . . okay?" I couldn't think of anything else to say as my nerves began to react in a fearful manner of the situation.

"We have been waiting for you." The voice had changed from the echoed whisper into something else. It had become what sounded like a conglomeration of high, low, and midrange voices that all came to sound in an echoed unison. Simply put, it sounded as something I would call nightmarish.

Just after saying that, she rose up off the ground like a marionette puppet being picked up by its strings. There was no motion or action that indicated her physically picking herself up from the ground. She rose up to a very limp posture but didn't stop until she was at a sight hover above the ground.

"What the fuck!" I said aloud just below my breath. I couldn't even begin to understand what I was seeing. The most I could do was taking a few steps back in disbelief and complete and utter terror.

"What's the matter, darling? Don't you love me anymore? You have something that we desire." It spoke with the same demonic tone as before, but the statement was followed by a hellish laughing that seemed to echo and resonate through the forest and all around me. She slowly lifted her head from her limp state to look at me, and that was when I noticed the most disturbing feature; its eyes, or the lack there of, to be more specific. As the creature looked at me, I could see that its eyes were a total black void. It didn't look like the eyes were missing but more that a void of the deepest black, almost cloud-like air seeped perpetually into the socket. A profound feeling of despair took me as I met the being's gaze. I felt as though my heart was about to explode and that my other internal organs were on fire, and it was the first time in my life I had ever had a definite fear for my very soul. The same ringing that had tormented my hearing before returned with a vengeance. Unable to bear the pain and intense throbbing sound waves coursing through my head, I fell to one knee and my vision began to blur.

"You belong to us, Evan dear . . ." Even though my head was throbbing with the severe ringing, its voice conveyed with just as much clarity as it had before. It began a slow and dragging float in my direction, and I wasn't sure what was about to happen to me. I looked next to me on the ground and happened to see a large fallen branch. In some last act of desperation, I reached over and picked it up.

"Get the fuck away from me!" I swung the branch as hard and wildly as I could at the levitating beast coming toward me.

The branch blasted in two upon what I thought was impact and sent a shock into my hands, arms, and shoulders, causing me to drop the half that I still had. The floating thing appeared untouched by my effort, and it let out a scream to the likes of something I had never heard or ever wanted to again. It writhed around in midair, screaming and retching with the most god-awful sounds I could have never imagined. As it belted out its blood curdling screeches, the ringing in my ears intensified so badly that I fell to the ground and rolled over onto my back, but I tried my damnedest to recover and crawl as far and fast as I could. My vision began to fade worse than before, but I was still able to see that the monstrosity still writhing above the ground not far from where I was. Hopelessness began to take me, and I felt as if that hell hole of a forest would soon be my grave . . . or maybe worse.

In an instant, all sound stopped; the intense ringing was no longer present, and I couldn't even hear the strong internal sound of my own rapidly pounding heart. A light that seemed to come out of nowhere began to shine in the forest clearing, and the creature began to flail and thrash wildly at speeds not comparable to human motion.

"Evan, close your eyes . . ." Her ever-more familiar voice echoed through the silence that consumed my sense of hearing, and instinctively, I did as I was told, closed my eyes as tightly as possibly could. As hard as it would come to explain, I felt the light around me grow to immeasurable strength; it was as if it were the only thing that surrounded me, and the only thing that followed was full body lightness that lifted me, embraced me, and carried me. An emotional overwhelming filled me, and I felt as though I was crying, laughing, and . . . divinity . . . I felt . . . divinity?

Consciousness came as a surprise hit as I sat up on the bed. My head was still feeling a dull and distant headache, but my body was revitalized and refreshed, more so than it had been in longer than I could remember. It took me a minute to come to my full senses as I looked about the room to see if my settings had at all changed. There was nothing more or less than before in that hellishly outdated motel room. The only real and obvious difference that I could see came from the daylight peeking out from behind the curtains. Whatever nightmare I had encountered had to have spanned the night, though it didn't seem like it did. I looked around for my cell phone to check the time, but it was nowhere to be found. With a deep breath and heavy sigh, I stood from the bed and turned to see if it had somehow moved elsewhere on the comforter from where I had left it last night. Careful examination of the bed yielded no results; my phone wasn't there. It wasn't until I stepped back from the bed that I felt a well-known feeling against my leg. I reached into the front pocket of my jeans to find that my phone was not where I had last left it. A heavy feeling developed in my chest as I pulled my phone out and flipped it open to examine its digital time capsule. Through the menu and to the recent calls list, I found that at some undetermined time, an unknown call was made to me; the date was blank too. For a moment, I stared at the phone's information that it gave me, and somehow I knew that it was the call I received that night. More confusingly, I wasn't even sure of the events that had happened. It was about then, that I knew I had to make a phone call to whatever ends it would meet.

Electronic chiming told me that the call was going through. The number I dialed was one burned into my memory from fondness and frequency of use. I couldn't explain to myself why, but I knew that I had to call her—if anything, for some peace of mind.

"Hello?" A familiar voice answered—a voice still as sweet as the first time I had heard it, the voice of my former wife.

"Hi . . . It's Evan." For lack of better things to say, all I could do was announce myself.

"Oh, hello. How are you?" She seemed just as confused as I was about the reason for the random call.

"I was wondering the same thing. Did you try to call me last night?" I saw no point in beating around the bush with pleasantries. I needed to know something, anything that could make me understand that night before.

"Yeah, I'm fine . . . Is something wrong, Evan?" I was unable to decipher her concern; she sounded as though she actually cared.

"No no . . . I just thought that you tried to call." My head was spinning with questions. Although I wasn't sure of why I even called her, I was even more uncertain of what information I had hoped to gain from the act.

"No, you sound different, Evan . . . Are you okay? Where are you?" I was still confused by her concern. I knew that she had said that she didn't want us to end on bad terms, but I couldn't see how she could show any degree of caring after what had happened.

"Yeah . . . I'm fine, I think. I'm somewhere in Pennsylvania. I should probably go. I'll talk to you some other time." Admittedly, I was somewhat annoyed with her attitude about the call, but it was clear that whatever had happened the night before didn't involve her.

"All right, if you say so. Why are you in Pennsylvania?" I could tell by her tone that she wasn't convinced, and to add to her confusion, I had to mention being clear across the country. I might have even told why I was there, if I knew the answer myself, so instead I was quiet for a moment.

"I'm . . . I'm not exactly sure. I should go." I didn't mean to come across so short and vague with her, but I felt that the conversation needed to end.

"Bye, Evan . . . Just . . . Please call me if you need anything." Her last words seemed to come as a struggle to her.

"All right. Good-bye." With that last bit, I closed up my phone and returned it to my pocket.

I somehow knew that she was in no way part of what was going on, and that last conversation was proof enough for me. I unpacked a fresh change of clothes from my suitcase and took them to the disturbingly clean bathroom. It wasn't that I minded cleanliness, but the question I had asked myself earlier about the number of serial killer visits the motel had accommodated came back to mind. Putting aside the powerful smell of bleach and cheap soap, I turned on a hot shower and climbed in anyway. The hot water felt so relaxing as I stood beneath its showering down, save for some stinging sensations on my face. I got out of the shower and dried off, the slight stinging sensations still felt on my face and even my forearms. I wiped the steam off the mirror to look at myself, and the sight I found was alarming to say the least; on my forehead was a small cut, and a couple of lighter scratches on my left cheek. I then looked down at my hands and forearms to find that the hot water had agitated previously unseen scrapes and scratches to a soft redness on my skin. All the same small injuries from running through thick timber; both to my shock and terror, the abrasions were real. With that having been realized, I couldn't help but ask myself if the rest of it could've been real as well. My mind toiled with questions over it but to no avail.

Standing naked in a foggy bathroom was not going to help my inquisition, so I tried to put it all aside long enough to get dressed, ready, and load my suitcase into my jeep. As for checkout, I walked into the office to find that nobody was there, and then a devious thought took control of my better judgment. I looked around to make sure that I wasn't being monitored. I pitched the keys hard over the unattended counter like I would a baseball and then ran out of the door. The jerk of an old man probably didn't have *that* coming, but he got it anyway, and I got to vent a little frustration.

"I don't know how much more of this I can take," I whispered to myself as I lit a much needed cigarette just beside my jeep. At that point, I was done with asking myself why all those things were happening to me. My head hurt from tormenting myself with asking; I was treading water with it anyway. There was no one to ask, and I sure as hell didn't have the answers; not then at least. I stomped out my smoke and jumped behind the steering wheel of my vehicle; I had spent too much time trying to get to Norcrest; it was high time that I made the journey complete.

The pub, motel, pleasant events, and everything from that last night were far behind me. I drove along the twisted roads of the New England setting and couldn't help myself from once again cracking the window to indulge in the smells of the autumn air. It struck me as odd too that though the vegetation was vastly different from the states I had previously gone through, the scent of the fall season remained the same. The immense power of the air around me overtook my blaring stereo, the nostalgia came soon after. My driving became almost second nature as I went down the road with memories passed. I couldn't help but find myself lost in thoughts and memories that were behind me: my father's funeral, my first dance, my first kiss, and my first love. I dwelled on all those things as I continued down the highway of rolling hills, completely engulfed in the glorious smells of the autumn.

There were a few times that I had to pull over to the side of the road and make point to my bearings and ask for directions. Norcrest was not an easy town to find; it wasn't on any map that I had or any that I purchased in hopes that it would be on them. I dug back into my journalistic past and asked around some of the small towns and villages along the way. There were very few people that knew what the hell I was talking about, and many of the people who did were very reluctant to talk to me about it. According to the one's that did know, and didn't act like I was a crazy person, the town was nestled deep in the Adirondack mountains, tucked away from everything. Making notes on my map of the road numbers and landmarks, I was confident that I could at least get to the town I was told that was closest to the Norcrest.

After about forty miles later, I came to Rosdam, the last stop before my destination. I lit a cigarette just before getting into town to calm the nerves that started to run stronger the closer I got to Norcrest. I was still relatively unclear about where exactly I was supposed to go, so I stopped at a gas station for a top off and hopefully some better directions. The ritual of pulling in, sliding my card, and filling the tank had become an automated nature at that point; the only real difference was the scenery. After my jeep had its fill, I walked to the doors of the store and went inside. Despite the small size of the town, the store was just as modern as anything I had come across in the bigger cities of my journey. I grabbed a water from the cooler and went to the counter for the rest of my purchases. The cashier ran the barcode on the bottle under the laser and looked back up at me. Before he could say anything, I asked for a pack of cigarettes, which he promptly slid under the scanner.

"Anything else for ya?" he asked in a surly tone.

"Yeah, directions to Norcrest." I was surprised at my own mannerism. It was beginning to seem that somehow, through everything that had happened and all that I had gone through, I had started to change; I was more assertive and less tactful in my actions and speech. Perhaps it was just nerves, or stress and lack of good rest.

"Norcrest?" He paused for a minute, and his round face took on a seriousness that replaced the apathetic expression that was previously shown.

"Why would you want to go there?" He seemed to grow more nervous as he asked the question.

"So you know how to get there?" My impatience was made clear; the trip and the unexplainable events had gone on long enough, I needed answers.

"Yeah . . . But why do you want to go there?" The clerk got more twitchy with my persistence.

"What the hell does it matter?" I started to turn from the counter, thinking I had hit another dead end with a person who wanted to play stupid with what I was asking them.

"Look, it's just that no one ever goes there or even asks about it." I could tell that he was getting very uncomfortable with the topic of talk, but why?

"Is there something I should know about that place? Everyone I've asked had about the same reaction, so what is it?" Facing the clerk again, I awaited his answer. I pulled the state map out of my back pocket and unfolded it on the counter before him to show what I had highlighted as the route I was given earlier. He studied it for a minute before slowly nodding and looking back up at me.

"Yeah, that's the way . . . I still don't know why you wanna go there. Some real weird shit happens in that place, and it looks like a ghost town. Everyone knows better than to go there. People are afraid of it." He was leaning over the counter and speaking in a much lower voice than before.

"So you've been there? Care to tell me what you mean by 'weird shit'?" The tubby little cashier behind the counter had my undivided attention.

"See, a few years back, me and a friend drove out there to see what all the talk was about. Anybody that grows up around here knows 'you don't go to Norcrest,' some urban legend shit like that. Anyways, we went out there one night, and it was creepy as all hell. There were only two places in the town with lights on, some church and a castle looking thing up the side of the mountain. Everything else looked dead." The more he got into his story, the quieter his voice was and the more he leaned over the counter.

"So it's creepy and weird because nobody had their lights on?" Even though he mentioned a castle looking thing that I could have taken for the same thing on the postcard, I was finding it hard to buy into what he was going on about.

"No no. The weirdest thing was when we parked and got out. We both could swear we heard whispering all around coming outta nowhere." After he said that I found myself to be the one reaching discomfort. My nerves began to fire off, and I shuddered a bit like I just stepped into a freezer. If anything he said was remotely true, I was on the right track.

I quietly thanked him as I folded up the map and grabbed my cigarettes off the counter. I had made it to halfway opening the door, before the clerk had one last tidbit to say.

"That friend of mine, he went back ya know. It was a few weeks after we both went, and he never came back. Nobody ever found him either." As concerning as that last bit was, I didn't show it as I simply thanked him again and went outside. Just to the side of the entrance, I discarded the wrapping of the cigarette box in the trash bin and pulled one out to smoke. As I put my hands up to light the smoke and shield the flame, my eyes happened upon a familiar and troubling sight—a very nice '65 glossy black Rolls Royce was slowly driving by the gas station.

"Motherfucker!" I said out loud and sprinted toward the slow moving car. Although I wasn't sure why, I knew that the man driving had answers or, at the very least, knew something that I didn't. My expended energy was in vein however as he sped off as soon as he saw me coming. I stopped just before the edge of the street and watched as his car turned right down the road. I myself would soon be going down. I moved my hand up to my face to take a drag from my cigarette, but somewhere in the commotion it was lost, so I pulled out another and walked back to my jeep. I was very close, just a few more lengths of road, and I would find Norcrest.

CHAPTER 10

Lovely Scenery and Devious Secrets

As I pulled my jeep into the one road leading into the town, I couldn't help but feel a slight relief knowing that I had made it. The village of Norcrest: I looked upon the valley setting of the town of the beautiful autumn colors that painted the mountainsides in almost amazement. I pulled my jeep over to the side of the road and got out to examine the sign that sat just before the city limits; it read:

"The Village of Norcrest Has Been Waiting For You"

The words were simplistic, yet haunting. They were very reminiscent of darker tomes that had been spoken to me in events prior. The sign was weathered and appeared to be very old as if the place were a long forgotten one. I looked up from the sign to once again view the sleepy little village down the hill from me. From where I stood, I could see that it wasn't very big at all. In fact, I was hardly able to imagine a population much over a few hundred people. It was all I could do to just speculate why anyone from a town of Norcrest's size and remote location would be sending me anything, let alone a postcard that begged my presence. For the first time, the thought of Steven Kings book *Misery* came to mind, but I quickly shook it off as not to scare myself with the notion that some depraved fan wanted to hobble my ass and keep me prisoner; I wasn't critically acclaimed enough for that anyway. But that was why I was there, the purpose behind the almost senseless trip—answers. I got back into my jeep and pulled away from the ancient sign and made my way down the road into the village of Norcrest.

The first building I came to at the edge of town was a small one-pump gas station. Conveniently, I could give the tank a top off anyway, so I pulled in next to the filling pump. I got out and looked around at the fall colors that surrounded every part of the valley. The scenery really was breathtaking, but the same couldn't have been said about the gas station. It was painted a dull gray and the architecture seemed finicky at best. Like many other buildings I had come across on my venture, time and ownership had seemed to be forsaken them. I turned back to the pump to find that it was an old lever-operated relic; prepaying for gas hadn't reached that corner of the world yet. I pulled on the trigger of the pump, but nothing was happening. I toggled the lever on and off a few times before giving up. Confused,

I walked around to the other side of the pump to where the door was to find the attendant who might be able to fix the thing. The sign in the window said open, but I could hardly see any evidence of it. I walked inside to find that there was no one behind the register or anywhere else in eyeshot for that matter. I decided to give the attendant a moment to come back before I started calling for them, so I began to walk around the store. It didn't seem like I could step anywhere on the hardwood flooring without hearing a squeak, and the walls were painted an atrocious brown color. As where most gas stations I had been to had large stand-up coolers in the back, this particular one did not. Instead, it had two waist-level coolers sitting next to each other in the back, and they didn't seem to be working either. A few shelves and racks seemed randomly placed about the floor, and all the items on them were long since expired and were brands that I had never seen before. I paced a few slow circles that took about five minutes to complete, and there was still no signs of life about the building. Impatience had taken its place in me, so I decided to find the clerk instead of the other way around.

"Hello?" I raised my voice to be heard throughout the seemingly deserted establishment.

"Hello!" I called again louder than before. If anyone was there, they sure as hell made no effort to bring me service.

I walked back over to the empty counter and waited for a moment. It was clear to me then that no one was coming, so I was set to leave it at that. Until just as I was turning for the door, I noticed something of interest; on a shelf behind the counter was a row of Lucky Strike cigarettes, an item that I was certain had been discontinued. It was far too tempting and not at all beneath me to go behind the counter and help myself to a couple of packs. I tossed a ten dollar bill on the counter and went through the door.

I got back to my jeep without making a single encounter with anyone on the way there. It did strike me as odd that no one would be there, but that wasn't of any real concern to me. What I needed was a place to set up shop so I could begin my search for the postcard's origin. I jumped back in to the driver's seat and started the beast up for our next task. As I drove down the main drag of the Adirondack valley hideaway, it became very clear to me how old the town was. All the architecture was very old colonial, the buildings stood thin and tall and shoved together for convenience of walking. Even the streets were so narrow that they could barely support proper two-lane traffic. However, the upkeep of the town in no way resembled the gas station I had just left; all the buildings, even though there was no space between them, all stood out from one another through colors, signs, and decor. One thing that could be said about the lonely mountain town is that it had a certain charm to it. If I could make any sense of it in words, I would say that it wasn't the right kind of charm; there was something in the air of the entire town that set me very uneasy. Everything past the filling station seemed very picturesque of a small village, but there were no inhabitants. I drove down the street without seeing a soul. It was either the lack of people roaming the streets going about their business or the fog bank rolling in down the mountainside that made for the rotten feeling I carried.

My driving took me to a crossroad where I saw an unmarked police car sitting parked on the road opposite of me. The officer sitting inside was the first person I had seen in the otherwise vacant seeming town; if there was anyone to give me information about the town, it would be him. I turned on the cross street he was waiting at, and I parked my jeep along the side of the road. I needlessly checked either way of the road to ensure clear traffic and walked over to the squad car. The car itself didn't look like it belonged; it was a gunmetal color and a newer model Chevy Impala. When I got to the vehicle, the officer didn't notice my presence, so it came as a surprise to him when I tapped on the window.

He jumped in his seat as if the devil himself had grabbed him. The officer looked over to me and then motioned for me to step back. As I did, he opened the door of his car and stepped out. He was taller than me but carried a bit thinner build. The uniform he wore was the typical navy blue police officer's uniform, and the color made his blue eyes quite noticeably stand out. He reached his hand up and ran it through his salt and pepper hair as if he had just woken up.

"Holy shit!" he said. "You damn near scared the life out of me!" He seemed to be shocked that someone came to disturb him.

"Sorry about that. I was just hoping that you might be able to help me," I said it in a most sincere manner, but I did find some humor in the whole thing.

"Sure . . . Help you with what?" He looked confused about my being there. Rightly so, Norcrest was the kind of place you could only find if you were actually looking for it.

"Well, I was hoping to find some lodging in this fine town, but I haven't seen anything on the way in . . . Or anyone else for that matter." I figured if I was able to explain my position a little, he'd be more apt to help me.

"Are you lost? Where are you looking to be?" He seemed even more confused when I told him I was looking for a place to stay there.

"No, I know where I am. I was just looking for a place to stay." I put it as frankly as I possibly could.

"Well then, you're not from around here, are you?" I could tell by the way he asked that he already knew the answer.

"No, I'm just visiting, kind of a random thing." There was no reason to tell him the true answer to my being there; he would have locked me up if I had told him the purpose of my presence.

"You're the first person I've ever seen coming through on just a visit. There's a bed-and-breakfast just up the hill. That's about the only lodging you're gonna find around here." He pointed up to a large stone building that sat upon the hillside overlooking the town.

"So, are you from around here? I mean, can you tell me a bit about the village?" I didn't mean for what I said to come out of the way it did, but to any end, I would find out my answers.

"Me? No, I'm not from around here. I just came up here from the city to check some things out. I don't know much about this place, save for some weird stories." Hearing that he wasn't from around those parts made for some comfort in knowing that I wasn't the only person foreign to the town.

"Well, that's good to know. I suppose I'll make my way up there." I could see the building up on the hillside looked familiar; it was the picture on the postcard. That sudden realization brought about that same sinking feeling that I had almost grown accustomed to.

"Now let me tell you just one thing," the Officer said. "Watch your back in this place. There is something strange going on. I can't explain it, but just trust me." He grabbed my arm and looked me straight in the eyes as he said that to me. Admittedly, that comment threw me off a bit. What could have been so abnormal going on to warrant such a statement? However, it did make some degree of sense with all the happenings in my recent times.

"I will. Thank you for the help." I left him with that. The night and the fog were rolling in, and I needed to get to that bed-and-breakfast.

I drove up the road quite a way through derelict neighborhoods and empty streets. Though there were parked cars along the way, there were no other signs of life to speak of, not to mention that none of the cars were post cold war era. Could that have been the weird something that the officer had told me about? Whatever the case, I wasn't sure. It seemed like I was driving in circles, at least that was until I came to a winding narrow road that led to the place of my interests—the bed-and-breakfast. The road was long enough up the hill to keep the building just outside of town and high up enough to where it seemed like it would have a pretty decent view over the whole area. But it wasn't the location of the inn that came as different to me; it was the building itself that just didn't seem right. In my experience, bed-and-breakfasts were usually housed in old Victorian homes for a cozy and exclusive feeling, but about that particular place of lodging I was wrong.

Driving up to the building, I could instantly tell that it was far from any other conventional bed-and-breakfast that I had seen before. Surrounding what I assumed to be the entirety of the property was a stone wall that easily stood a good seven feet tall. Fixed on top of that was wrought iron gothic pike fencing that added what I estimated to be another two feet to the walls overall height. Just where the road met a gap in the wall, the space was occupied by a large and heavy gate of the same style of fencing that topped the wall. Above the large open gate was a flat archway of black metal with the word "Norcrest" cut from the center. The fortified style of enclosure was enough cause for my curiosity about what the hell kind of bed-and-breakfast it was. I pulled up on my jeep's e-brake and exited my vehicle to take a look around and get a better feel of everything. I walked up to the gate and grabbed onto one of the black pikes that composed it. It was a cold and thick black wrought iron; it had definitely been around for quite some time. My gazing about led my eyes to notice something odd above me. The flat archway that spanned over the gate looked as if someone had taken a cutting torch or some kind of welding equipment to the bottom of it, but the scarring on the metal didn't span the whole sign. Before I could continue my wonderings about the place, my thoughts were interrupted by a bright flash and a loud crash. I looked back down the road I had just come up to see that a thunderstorm was encroaching on the valley town along with the fog I had noticed earlier. I figured I had spent enough time examining the gates; it was time to see the building that was kept behind such walls.

The building seemed almost too big to be a bed-and-breakfast; I had seen smaller hotels and motels. It was a large two-story stone structure, all except for the central portion of the building that stood a story taller and had some kind of turret or belfry fixed on top of that. The whole of the establishment was long and tall, but it was quite narrow. From a quick glimpse of one of the end sides, I could see that there were only four windows: two on the second level and two on the first, typical of seventeenth century New England architecture. The grounds keeping around the place was impressive to say the least. The grass was thick and bright green, radiant as it could be before the oncoming dead of winter, much like all the vegetation within the walls. Neatly trimmed hedges lined either side of the stairs up to the main door; they stretched all the way to the ends of the building and around to the other sides. The most impressive spectacle were the flower gardens. From each end corners of the building was the same style of wrought iron fence from the wall before, and they fenced in two immaculate rectangular flower gardens on either side of the road. Narrow cobblestone walkways that twisted and turned throughout the garden led to small gates covered by a thin archway. The place was very beautiful, and I was certain that it was the Norcrest Gardens from the picture on the postcard; they were identical.

As gorgeous as the setting was, I couldn't shake a bad feeling from deep in my chest. Perhaps it was that I had finally reached the place I sought after and nothing extremely crazy had happened yet; or maybe I was still somewhat shaken by what that cop had said. Whatever it was, the feeling wasn't leaving. I grabbed my suitcase and duffel bag from the back of my jeep, along with a bottle of the Glenlivet that I took from the cabin before I left. Opening the driver-side door once again, I set my suitcase on the seat and popped it open. I stowed the bottle discreetly inside of it, and I reached under the seat to pull out my trusty handgun. Putting it in the suitcase and latching it shut, I was ready to enter that place of deceiving hospitality.

I entered through the tall and heavy wooden front door, another relic of that place that seemed particularly old. The interior was a far cry from what the exterior might have suggested. A long regal-looking rug ran from the entryway to the decadent wooden staircase just in line with the front door and covering the smooth stone floor. I looked up to see the staircase come to a landing and a third smaller spiral staircase that took off to a smaller landing above the second floor. Hanging in the middle of all of it supported by four large chains that were heavily fastened to the stone wall interior was a grand silver, gold, and crystal chandelier softly illuminating the entirety of entryway. The windows about the room were all nicely fitted with thick red tapestries and sheer white curtains between them. Overall, it was far from what I had expected from simply viewing the outside.

"Is there something I can help you with?" Her voice came as a shock to me as I heard it come from the left of where I stood. I looked over in the direction the voice came from to find that in my distraction of viewing my surroundings, I failed to notice the wooden booth-like desk and the woman behind it.

"Yes. Sorry, I was just admiring the decorations. I was hoping that I might be able to get a room." I tried not to act so surprised by her presence, but I surely wore it on my sleeve. I walked closer to the almost bunker like structure she was sitting in; as I got closer, she moved a sliding glass portion of the window to better converse with me. The guard-shack-esque nature of where she sat did strike me as unfitting of what was supposed to be a more personal environment, but I set that aside to see about the room.

"We have rooms available. How long would you be looking to stay?" The woman came across to me as the no-nonsense stern type, and it wasn't in just her manner of speech. She was dressed like she was still caught in the Victorian times: very plain white and gray all wrapped up in a very conservative manner. Her white hair was worn tightly pulled back into a bun, and all she wore for jewelry was a gold chain with what looked like some kind of circle carved out of jade.

"Indefinite actually. I'm here to kind of escape to finish my book." Though that wasn't the case at all, it made for a good cover story.

"Oh, I see. We do have a more long-term room available if you are interested in that." She kept her tone stern and emotionless, a behavior that seemed strange to me, given the place of business.

"That would be perfect. I'd very much like to have it." The offer seemed pretty decent to me, plus it would give me a nice place of retreat as I did my research.

"Very well. You're in room 777, second floor of the east wing. Breakfast is served in the dining room through the door just behind you at seven in the morning. We can go through the details of billing after you've completed your stay." The way the woman spoke was almost mechanical—very cold and to the point. She passed a key over the table to me and gestured to a sign in book that lay open on the desk. I couldn't help but notice that I was the only one to be signing on the page.

"Thank you very much. I do appreciate it," I said as I picked up the key from the desk and my suitcase from the floor. I was about halfway up the stairs when she said something else, "Enjoy your stay here at Norcrest, Mr. Clarke."

The statement was creepy and unsettling to say the least. So much so that it was all I could do to give a half cocked smile and a nod, and then continue my way up the stairs.

The hallway before me was long and narrow and did not share in the same near-royal decor of the main entry to the building. Smooth and gray, the stone floor remained uncovered by long expensive looking rugs and reached far to meet the wall at the end. Simplistic wall sconces lined my dimly lit way as I searched the hallway for my room. I took notice to the European-styled community bathroom that was the first door on my right, and the rest of the rooms down the hall as I went seemed to be just that—guest rooms. My unmuffled and echoed clacking of footsteps filled the empty corridor until I came to the door marked 777. There was only one real feature that set this room as different from the others; at one point, I could tell that the wall between the door to the last room once had a door itself, but it was very visibly sealed over with what looked like brick and plaster. It was my guess that the room that was once there was conjoined with the last two for needs of the extended-stay guests. Whatever the reasoning behind it, I moved forward and put my key in the door and turned the lock.

I opened the door to find a much warmer and more inviting environment than the hallway had led me to believe. Though the room was small, it was filled with all the necessary amenities and creature comforts one could ask for in a bed-and-breakfast. In one corner of the room, just opposite the door, was a twin-sized bed. The pillowcases and comforter shared the same regal color scheme as the tapestries in the main entry. Though there was no carpeting, the stone floor remained mostly hidden beneath an assortment of rugs about the room. Against the opposing wall from the bed was a tall and skinny chest of drawers next to a narrow door that was left ajar leading into a darkened bathroom.

I proceeded into the room after a time of looking at it and set my suitcase on the bed. I had no real idea how long I was going to be staying there, or how long it would take to find what I was looking for in the town for that matter. I sat down next to my luggage and slumped back onto the bed. So many things were going through my mind as I lay there. One thought dwelled on what that police officer had said—another on how odd everything in town really did seem to me. The silence that surrounded me was steadily broken as the sound of soft and sparse raindrops turned to sound heavier and more frequent. Some light thunder followed the rain as it picked up, and it sounded to me as though the storm was one to stick around for a while. I wasn't sure if it was the sound of the rain or just weary from my travels, but the comfort of the bed and solace of the room put me to an ease that I hadn't felt for a long time, at least since the beginning of all my shitty happenings. I stared at the oddly tiled ceiling for a time as my eyes began to weigh heavy. My sight blurred as I fought to keep my eyes from closing, but the inevitable sleep soon followed. The last thoughts I had before my coming rest were aimed at that girl from the dreams before. Was it going to happen again? Was finally being in that place going to make a difference? The thoughts were then lost as I fell asleep and drifted off.

A loud crackling of thunder shook me from my sleep. I sat up quickly and looked about the room, almost having forgotten where I was. I stood up and stretched, unsure of how long I had been asleep. Reaching into my pocket, I pulled out my cell phone to see how much time had passed, and to my surprise, it was turned off. It made a quick vibration and sang its little tune as I powered it back up, and the first notice it gave me was that the battery was just about out of juice. Just before it shut itself off, however, I managed to get a couple of details from it; I found that it was two o'clock in the morning, and that there was no signal. I rooted through my suitcase and pulled out the charger and began searching for a power outlet. There was only one in the room, and it protruded from the wall connected to a conduit leading down through the floor. It seemed to me that the room, whatever it was originally, wasn't fitted with plug-ins. After getting my phone situated, I walked over to the window and pulled back the heavy curtains. A very curious sight came to my attention as I noticed that there were heavy iron bars fixed to the wall just outside of it. My eyes were then drawn to some lights that seemed to be coming from the middle of the town, some chapel-looking building that was hard to make out through the rain and the darkness. It was much like the clerk at the gas station had described to me—me being in one of the lit buildings and only one other in the town. I stared on for at least a minute before I was startled by the booming of thunder. I thought about where to go from there and even asked myself what the hell I was doing there in the first place; I felt like I was going crazy but decided that I wasn't going to get anything answered that night, so I climbed into the bed and went to sleep.

I'm not sure how long it was after that, but I was soon enveloped in the warmth of the light I had felt before. I fought my eyes to open and didn't even bother to try to move my limbs; I knew that if it was going to be anything like before, my efforts would be wasted. The room was filled with soft, white-blue light, and that strange euphoria settled over me. I turned my head to the left as much as I was able to, and there she stood next to my bed, standing over me with a soft smile. There were so many questions, too many questions without answers that burned through my mind. I could feel my mouth beginning to move as if to say something, but before the words could escape, the woman put her index finger over my lips as if say to "shhh." I obeyed her gesture as I lay and watched as she moved to the wall opposite of my bed. Her tracing movement was hard to keep focused as she slid her hand over a brick high up on the wall, and it looked as though it illuminated with her touch.

"You are close, Evan. Find it here. I've been waiting for you." Her mouth didn't move, but I could hear every word as if she were speaking right next to me. The woman's blurring motion as she walked back to the side of the bed was nearly too much for my eyes to keep track of. She stood above me for a moment, and though my mind was racing with things to say, not a word came out. Her hand, somehow cold and warm all at once, moved on to my cheek, and she leaned over, her face close to mine.

"You are close now. Be careful, in the night, they sing, and they have been waiting for you too." I had no idea in hell what she meant by that, and in that moment, I didn't care. There was a purity in her touch and a soft calm in her voice that made any anxious feelings surrender to inconsequence. She stood back up from me and reached into the collar of her soft blue gown, and from it, she brought out what looked like a silver chain with some sort of a pendant on it.

"It will help you," she said as she laid the necklace down on my chest, and though I could see that she put it there, I could feel no sensation from it. She stepped back, and as she did, the light had begun to intensify as it had before. Having a pretty good idea of what was to come next, I closed my eyes tightly as I felt the light become overwhelming, and the sonic ringing I had experienced before was present, but not nearly as intolerable as it had been with her leaving.

That next morning, I found myself waking up on the floor, tangled in sheets and blankets with a pillow over my head. I wearily sat up and looked about the room; nothing had changed, save for it being daytime. I crawled over to the stand on the other side of my room and grabbed my phone off it. It told me the time but still had no calling service. Seeing that it was eight thirty in the morning, I realized that I missed breakfast downstairs. Personally, it wasn't anything of particular bother to me, but the lady who ran the place seemed like the type that would be pissed off about something like that. I dismissed the thought as I sat there propped up against the wall, trying to think of matters I felt to be more important. Mostly, my thoughts belonged to that woman, whoever she was. I had finally reached the place she had told me to, but I felt no closer to discovery despite what her apparition-like presence had told me the night before. Apart from her, I still had no idea what I was looking for, or what to be careful of, although I had a sneaking suspicion that whatever else was supposedly waiting for me had something to do with the freak experience I had back in that hotel in Pennsylvania.

I stood up from the floor and opened up my suitcase to pull out the day's pick of clothing. I knew that sitting in the room all day wasn't going to get me any closer to whatever it was that I was looking for. After closing the lid of the suitcase at the foot of the bed, I saw something shimmering up toward the headboard; it was the necklace she had put on me the night before. Admittedly, I was not nearly as disturbed as I probably should have been; perhaps I was just growing accustomed to strange happenings. The piece itself was beautiful: it was a small, diamond-shaped pendant with a magnificently cut sapphire set in the middle, and the pendant hung from a thin silver chain. I dangled it in front of my face examining it, and I noticed that there was something etched into the back of the pendant. It simply said,

Dearest Dorothy,

My love, for now and forever,

Nathaniel

Although I wasn't completely sure, it occurred to me that I might have finally had a name that belonged to that woman; after all, it did appear to be her necklace. However, the newfound information started me begging new questions. Who was Nathaniel, and what was the connection with me, her, and the loving scribe on the back of the necklace?

Despite it clearly being a woman's piece of jewelry, I put it on for safekeeping while I changed into some fresh clothes. I got it in my head that I needed to get out and start looking around the town for clues about what was going on with me. I put my phone in my pocket and grabbed the other essential items, smokes, lighter, wallet, things like that, and a pen and notebook before leaving the room. I got out to the main entrance and looked around for the woman who owned the inn, but there was no sign of her behind the counter or anywhere else, for that matter. Just on the other side of the booth-like check-in desk, I saw a mostly empty rotating rack. More importantly, I saw a few postcards that were identical to the one sent to me, so I walked over and picked one up to examine. It was, in fact, the same print of card, except the writing that was on the one I had, and after a few seconds, I returned it to the rack. There were very few items on the rack itself; really, all that there was were a few varieties of postcards, different pictures, and the like, and all in very few quantity, I might add.

"Did you find something of interest, Mr. Clarke?" The old woman's stern voice echoed through the lobby from behind me. Startled, I turned around quickly to find her standing just a bit behind me in the middle of the room.

"Uh no. I mean, yes, I was just admiring the postcards," I said nervously.

"I see. You missed breakfast this morning. Was everything all right?" she said as she walked slowly toward me. I'm not sure what it was about her exactly, but everything about her was absolutely unsettling.

"Yeah, everything is fine. I just slept in a little longer than I meant to. Say, I think I've seen a postcard like this one recently. Has anyone bought one lately?" I took the mirror-image card off the rack and handed it to her. Her already unpleasant expression turned to more of a glare as she looked at the postcard and handed it back to me.

"No. You are the first guest here in quite some time. Now, if you will excuse me, I have things to tend to. Good day, Mr. Clarke." Her voice was cold and was only followed by the sound of her rigid footsteps walking out across the room and away from me.

"Well, that wasn't weird," I sarcastically said to myself as I walked to the front doors.

The sky was a bright gray with the morning overcast, and everything around me had that wonderful smell of fresh rain and fallen leaves. The lonely ambience of the scenery wasn't nearly as menacing as it appeared the night before; however, I could still feel some subtle oddness in the air around me. There were definitely pieces of something stacking up with all of it, but that's all that they were—pieces. Nothing was fitting together, and it seemed that with each new thing that came about, the farther I was from putting it all in place. All of it compiled on my brain as I climbed into my jeep, and as I closed the door, I sat there for a moment just thinking. I really didn't have a set destination or any real idea to start looking for whatever the hell I was there to look for.

She told me I was close . . . The thought came so quickly and prevalent above all others that I couldn't help but say it aloud. Grabbing the necklace and staring up at the postcard fixed to my sun visor, I figured on going to check out one of the more obvious points of interest to me—the chapel. It was, just like the clerk had told me, the only other light on in town—peculiar too at such an hour for when I had seen it.

There wasn't much for a drive over to where the church-like structure was. I think the longest part of the distance was the road coming down from the bed-and-breakfast. A light and misty rain had begun to fall as I pulled up to a park just across the street from the chapel, and I reached into the backseat to fetch my heavier coat. I slid it on as I stepped out onto the street and looked around in all directions. The wet, glistening streets were barren, and it looked as if the few houses that were around were vacant and had been for some time. It was an eerie and unsettling sight to see such emptiness all around me, and not just because of the houses but because it seemed like the parked cars and motionless bicycles were also without any present owners. I turned around and looked at the park behind me, and it too looked to be long ago abandoned. Although I had no idea what, I could tell that something had gone very wrong at some point to cause such desertion.

I started my way over to the church entrance and took notice that the steeple was easily the tallest piece of construction in the town; it wasn't far from the thought that it could easily be seen from anywhere in the village. I got to the large, heavy-wood, arch-topped doors, and despite having been in service the night before, the day told a very different story. The church doors were locked up tightly, along with all the shutters on the windows, and even the tower's belfry had shutters closed up over the openings. I took a slow stroll around the side of the chapel to see if there was anything I could get or see into. The other side showed much of the same, locked up and no way in. Behind the church, starting against the back wall, was a huge stone wall about nine feet tall and surrounded the entire property behind the building. I walked the entirety of the stone mass, and to no avail, there wasn't an opening for the whole length that damn stone wall. There was only one thing that I did notice as I made my way around it, and that was the unmistakable stench in the air of something rotting. Faint though, as it was, it was still enough to turn my stomach and add for a displeasing feeling over the whole place.

As I got to the other side, I saw a couple of weathered crates lying next to the wall, and I considered stacking them to maybe get enough height to see over the wall. It was a short debate, as curiosity got the better of me, and I lifted one of the crates on top of the other and started to climb up. After getting both of my knees on top of the boxes, I greatly started to question their structural integrity with each creak and twist of the old wood.

"Do you go trespassing around new towns often?" The man's voice came as a surprise, so much so that I fell off the boxes and onto the ground. I heard him laughing as he walked over to me. I picked my head up enough to see who it was talking to me; the voice was from the police officer that I had met the day before.

"Hell of a fall you took," he said it as he held out his hand to help me up. I took the gesture, and he got me to my feet, though I couldn't help but wonder why he just "happened" to be there at the same time I was.

"Thanks," I said brushing off the dead leaves and other debris from the ground that had collected on my clothes.

"I'm sure you hear this a lot, but it's not what it looks like *officer*." It was in a sarcastically jocular manner in which I made that statement.

"Sure, sure . . ." he said, "But what are you doing here?" I could hear a seriousness in his voice.

"Well, honestly, I'm not sure. Like you said before, there's something wrong with this town. I'm a journalist by trade, and some leads on a story brought me here." So I lied, but I felt that full disclosure would not have been exactly believable.

"Here's an idea." He paused and looked slowly around as if expecting to see something.

"How's about we go somewhere to compare notes?" The way he asked the question was strange to me, but I picked up on what he was getting at right away.

"What were you thinking?" I asked full knowing that he had some destination in mind.

"There's a little Italian restaurant in the town just north of here. Care to come along?" Though it sounded like a question, I could tell that he was pleading with me to take the drive with him.

"Sure thing." After my speaking, he simply nodded and started walking to his car that was parked just off the street by my jeep.

"By the way, I'm Scott Redding." His making his name known reminded me that though we had met before, we never did really make introductions.

"Evan, Evan Clarke," I said as we walked to his car.

The road was long, and I spent most of the time looking out of the window at all the fall colors. There was something that the collage of brightened leaves meant to me, and the inclination that there was grew stronger as the days went on. We really didn't speak a word or at least any of consequence as the drive went on. It wasn't until finally, we reached the parking lot of the restaurant, that we really began to talk.

"So you're after something, and so am I." His simple statement brought a heavyweight to what I really was doing there, in Norcrest.

"Yes . . ." I said as I got out of the car and closed the door. It was clear that he knew something that could either help or hinder my quest for solving the mystery.

We got into the Italian eatery and sat down before we began talking again. It was a corner booth far from the windows and tucked back in the corner.

"All right, you tell me yours, and I'll tell you mine," he said simply after the hostess had gone.

"No, you tell me," I said in a calm and cool way. I sat back in the booth and draped my left arm over the back of the seat, and my surroundings began to make sense. The room was dimly lit and done up in old Sicilian decor, and there was a soft sound of opera music playing in the background. The whole thing seemed like an old New York Mafioso movie given the "hush, hush" meeting and Italian setting.

I could see that he contemplated for a while before answering.

"Okay . . . My partner was friends with some antiques dealer, and this dealer started to think that someone was after some ancient thing he got a hold of. So, as a courtesy, my partner started checking in with this friend of his, and then things started to get weird. He started talking about how that friend of his was getting more and more paranoid and talking about the antique as some kind of key. Then, about six months later, his friend goes missing, and my partner takes time off work to search for him." He stopped talking as if to drift away in thought.

"And you are looking for him?" I said to try to bring him back from his distance.

"Yeah . . ." he said still somehow far away from the conversation, and then he looked down at the table.

"I think something bad has happened to him . . . So I'm here to find out what." He looked back up to me, and there was a deep, serious look in his eyes.

"Now, why are you here?" It was the very question that I had been avoiding.

We sat there eating, drinking, and talking as I tried my best to tell to him my end of the story so far without sounding completely out of my mind. The officer seemed to understand most of what I was telling him, at least as much as I understood. Scott was quiet for a while, and I could see that he was mulling over everything that I had just told him—everything that had happened up to that point.

"Shit . . . That's a hell of a lot to happen after a divorce." He chuckled as he said it.

"Yeah, tell me about it . . . Everything that's happened lately makes me think that I've gone insane." I stated laughing with him.

After the laughter calmed, we were quiet again; I could only assume that we both were thinking of all that was going around us, whatever it was. I paid the tab, and we got up from table and made our way out of the restaurant. When we got outside, a black Rolls Royce quickly pulled out of the parking lot.

"Friend of yours?" Scott asked quizzically. I had told him about the car in my more recent happenings, and in a way, I was glad; it showed as some proof of the story I had told him only minutes before.

"I'm not sure yet . . ." I stared at the car driving away with a serious and convicting expression.

"He showed up in that town just before you did, and by what you said, I don't know either." We both stood there and watched as the car drove down the road, presumably to the same town that we all seemed to have business in. Another long and mostly silent drive later, Scott dropped me off back where I had parked my jeep. We exchanged our farewells, and I got inside of my vehicle with an ever-increasing amount of questions. I looked up to the sky, and I could see that there was another storm coming down over the mountains—another night of rain and thunder. I started up the vehicle and drove my way back to the bed-and-breakfast.

Walking into the building, it seemed more open and vacant than it had the previous day.

"Finding your stay here to be a pleasant one?" The old woman's voice echoed throughout the empty halls.

"Yes, I think so." The abrupt noise had caught me off guard; clearly, she was good at that.

"Good, good," she said slowly. "I am very glad. Is there anything that you need before I turn in?"

"No, I'm fine, thank you." Her presence was more off-setting to me than it had been before.

"Then good night, I will see you in the morning, Mr. Clarke." She walked away stiffly down the main level hall and disappeared behind a door. I shrugged the whole scene off and made my way upstairs.

I walked down the echoing halls until I got to my room. As I got to my destination, the door to my room opened by itself slowly, beckoning me to come in, and I did. I slowly walked in, put my coat down on the desk, and made my way for the bed as if summoned there. Before any of the more recent events had happened, I would have been greatly disturbed by such a thing as doors opening by themselves and the like, but at the point I had reached it somehow just made sense to me. The thought of such things were very heavy on my mind as I took my place on the bed. As my eyes began to weigh down and all my thoughts began to delude in the passing from consciousness, I could feel the sensation of petit fingers run through my hair and a slender hand touching my cheek. She was trying harder to get to me, and it was my hope to soon find out why.

CHAPTER 11

In the Darkest Places the True Histories Hide

The same white light haze filled the room as it had done so many times before, and the woman who seemed to be growing desperate to reach me, from where, I did not know, stood by the wall of the room as she had done in my last vision of her. For the moment, my thoughts came to me much clearer than they ever had in that state, and I seemed to be better able to control my movement. Perhaps I was getting more and more accustomed to the experiences, or maybe it was some form of adaptation on my end of things; in either case, I was able to get up from my bed with only a little resistance.

As I made it to my feet in what felt to me like an extremely sluggish motion, I could see a smile come to the woman's face as if to express happiness or being proud of what I had just done. She didn't speak but simply raised up her hand and motioned for me to come to her. My feet were heavy as I made each step, and I swaggered as if I were drunk; granted, it was a much greater improvement to times before in which I was seemingly confined to lying in the bed with very little capability of motion at all. Staggering over to where she stood, I couldn't shake the words she spoke from her last appearance from encircling my brain; the words telling me that I was close. I took notice as well that the pendant hiding behind my shirt felt like it was pulsating and vibrating, and the sensation was ever growing the closer I moved toward her.

After what felt like a great distance of swaying and sloppy walking, I made it to her side. With my final step to the apparition, she greeted me with a smile evermore inviting and warm. I looked her deep in the eyes and muttered the first thing that came to mind:

"Dorothy?"

The woman's eyes seemed to light up more than I had ever seen before, and their emerald-green color became almost too much to look at directly. She nodded excitedly, still with her near-paralyzing smile; then she took my hand and placed it on the wall in front of me. I didn't understand, and I must have conveyed my confusion with the expression that I wore on my face.

"I know you do not understand, but you are very close, Evan." Her words seemed to come from thin air; her mouth did not move, and it sounded closer than a whisper in my ear.

She still had a hold of my hand, and she led it up the wall just a brick's distance down from the top and then began to move my finger tips around the brick, tracing the mortar lines. It was then that I began to understand what she was trying to show me as the lines in the mortar stood out from the rest of the bricks.

"What's . . . what's in. there?" My words were beginning to come as a struggle again, and I had the distinct feeling that the dream was about to end.

"If you go there, you will find me." The voice started to echo in my head as everything around me started to blur. I could feel myself swaying much more than I had before, so much so that I fell backward, the last thing I saw being little more than white light.

The feeling of being thrown onto the very bed I was laying in brought me out of my slumber. I looked around the room very confused but still very calm. As I sat up, I couldn't help but wonder what kind of side effects would come of all the strange happenings.

"God's sake," I said aloud. "This shit's going to give me a tumor."

Pushing that thought out of my head, I began my morning rituals of setting out my clothes and toiletries for my venture to the bathroom. Everything was going as routine until I noticed something out of the window—a black Rolls Royce pulling out of the bed-and-breakfast's driveway.

"Son of a bitch!" I said as I dropped the shirt I was unfolding and ran out of my room down the hall and down the staircase to the ornate front doors. I only made it in time enough to catch sight of the car's ass end going down the hill.

"I see you finally decided to come down for breakfast, Mr. Clarke." The sharp voice of the old woman didn't come as a shock that time. I turned around to see her standing there with her arms crossed in front of her, one hand clasping the other. To me, it seemed like she wore the same thing every day, or at least I couldn't recall seeing her wearing anything else since the first time I had seen her.

"Oh . . . Yes, breakfast, that's why I came down." I didn't mean to come off as nervous, but there were too many things going on for me to compose myself in any other manner, and besides, the old innkeeper just gave me the creeps.

She slowly walked over to the tall, narrow window next to the door and peered out of it.

"Were you expecting someone?" she said slowly without turning her head to look at me. I didn't say anything for a minute as I really wasn't sure what she was getting at or even if maybe she knew something that I didn't.

"No . . . No I wasn't. I just thought that I was the only one staying here." I could feel my eyes narrow in suspicion of her odd question, even though I didn't mean to show it. The old woman turned to me again with the same stern and humorless expression that she usually carried.

"Come now, Mr. Clarke, your breakfast is ready." No sooner than that statement, she rigidly turned and walked down the hall to a door toward the back of the room, so I followed.

The heavy wooden door loudly creaked as I swung it open. Behind the door, was revealed to be what looked to me like a very old and small cafeteria type of setting, and to be honest, it threw me off quite a bit. Walking slowly into the room, I took my seat at the end of a long, oak-looking table where there was silverware and a glass set out. I assumed that the place was set for me, and as I sat there, I couldn't help but wonder what the hell function that building used to serve; given many things that I had noticed about the architecture and just the general feel of the place, I knew that there was more than a history as a bed-and-breakfast for the building. My train of thought was derailed as the woman came over and placed a plate down in front of me.

"I do hope that you enjoy my cooking, Mr. Clarke," she said to me through the same stoic expression she always wore.

"Thank you. I'm sure that I will. Oh, and you can just call me Evan." I told her with a half-smile on my face.

"Forgive my formal ways, but I prefer to call to you properly, Mr. Clarke." She had a very strange and unsettling look in her eyes as she said it, like I had insulted her or something.

"Fair enough then." The smile that I had just a second before dissipated, and I began to dig into the meal sitting in front of me. It was a very typical New England breakfast: eggs benedict, fried chunks of potatoes, and wheat toast. Though it tasted rather good, I couldn't say that I was particularly able to enjoy it as the old innkeeper just stood in the corner of the room staring at me.

"Breakfast is very good, thank you again." I told her in all hopes that she would leave me the hell alone or at least stop staring at me. No such luck on my end of things.

"What is your book about?" Her manner of speech was so cold and direct that I really didn't think that she cared at all. As I'm sure that I had mentioned before, I didn't really have a new book, or even a well-formulated story idea for that matter, so I winged it.

"It's about ghost towns." It was the first thing I could think to say, and given the general look and feel of Norcrest, I thought it fitting.

"Ghosts, you say?" she said quietly walking toward me.

"There are no ghosts here, Mr. Clarke. I assure you." She bent down and took the plate that I was only part of the way finished with. For a brief moment, I thought about protesting, but I figured that it was just as well so I could escape that freak scene.

"Thank you," I said as coarsely as I could muster. "I didn't say ghosts though, I said ghost towns."

"What makes you believe that Norcrest is a 'ghost town', Mr. Clarke?" She was halfway to the kitchen and had her back to me as she said it.

"Well, I had spent some time in New York a few years back, and everyone I asked about ghost towns said that this was the place. Besides, you are the only other person I have seen here." I made it a harsh point to be as blunt as I possibly could. The lady was setting me very uneasy with her questions and actions and becoming pretty damned annoying I might add.

"Norcrest is no ghost town, Mr. Clarke. I'm afraid that you are misinformed." She stopped dead in her tracks as she said it but never once turned around to look at me.

"All right . . . Then where is everyone? Why haven't I seen anybody else?" I felt a strange anxiety brooding deep in my chest, and some heavy chill brushed over my skin.

"Many in our town have gone off to a better place. Those who are left are simply waiting. Good day, Mr. Clarke." She started walking off to the kitchen again but stopped just before the door and turned around just enough to look at me with that same unsettling look in her eyes.

"That man, who drove up earlier seemed to find particular interest in your vehicle. I just thought that I should let you know." She stiffly walked back into the kitchen and didn't come back out, which was fine by me. I had just about my fill of her special brand of weirdness. It took a minute for the brew of strange feelings in me to subside enough for me to fully realize what the last thing she said was, and when it hit me, I bolted from the table and to the front door.

Opening the large and ancient door, I was embraced by the cold autumn air; I left my coat up in my room, and I wished that I hadn't. Besides the noticeably brisk march to my jeep, there were other cold things to be felt. The sinking feeling gained in the kitchen wrapped its frigid grasp harder around me as I made it to my vehicle, and much to my horrified surprise, someone had in fact been there. The back hatch was left just slightly open, something that I was sure that I had shut and locked, and looking into the back, I could see that the other duffel bag that I had left in there was noticeably disheveled.

"Dirty bastard, motherfucker . . ." I muttered aloud under my breath.

There were no signs of any kind of forced entry; he had to have used a key. With that thought, I checked under the hood where I always kept a spare hidden in a small magnetic box, and sure enough, it was missing. I stepped back after putting the hood down and latching it shut and thought for a moment in near disbelief; there was something very specific that he had to have been looking for, and I knew damn good and well that it wasn't the guns or my booze. I reached into my pocket and pulled out my pack of smokes, took out a cigarette, lit it, and enjoyed. Taking the first deep drag, the thought of that odd metal disk came to mind; whatever the hell that thing was, I could guarantee that's what he was after.

"But why?" Another internal thought escaped through my mouth. Apart from the bizarre occurrences that I'd had with the thing, I really had no idea what it was for, if anything. However, despite not knowing really anything about the silver object, I knew enough to say that it had to be what that "agent" was after. On top of that, the cop's partner seemed to know that the one that he had was something of consequence. I closed up everything in my jeep that had been violated, but before I made my way back inside of the building, I grabbed a hammer and a flathead screwdriver from the back; there was something that called for my attention. Peering in through the scarcely open front door, I made sure that the disturbing old woman was nowhere in sight as I really didn't feel compelled to explain the hardware that I was bringing in. A full minute passed as I waited to make sure that the way was clear, and when I was confident that it was, I shot into the door and up the stairs before anyone could notice.

Slamming the door behind me, I leaned up against it to catch the breath that I ran out of; consequently, it was one of those moments that I didn't like the fact that I smoked. A cough and a shake off later, I made my way over to the wall opposite of the bed. I studied the bricks for a moment until I was sure of the one I remembered her gesturing to. Reaching into my shirt, I pulled out the pendant that I was wearing.

"Okay, Dorothy... Here goes whatever this is." I spoke as though she would hear me, and hell, maybe even answer. The screwdriver was in position, and the hammer was in hand. I brought it down with a hard-hit on the screwdriver's handle.

"Oh shit!" I exclaimed; the noise was far louder than I had anticipated, and it was quite shocking to me. I dropped the tools, ran over to the door, and stuck my head out into the hallway to see if my demolition act had gone without notice. After a few seconds of looking down the hall like a scared child, calmness found me once more and I returned to what I was doing. When I got back to the wall, I noticed that the screwdriver had gone all the way through the mortar line, and looking closer, I could tell that the mortar itself was unusually thin; though I was no mason by trade, it was at least that much that I could tell. After taking the time to study that little observation, I rethought my chiseling efforts and started chipping away lightly and slowly at the mortar line around the brick. After what seemed like hours had passed just quietly chipping away, I had finally made it all the way around the brick and it was loose.

The brick slid out with little more than a light pry with the screwdriver and fell right out into my hand. I examined the brick, and it seemed to me that it was merely the front portion, so I looked back up to the wall, only to see a dark hole where the piece in my hand once was. I swallowed hard and felt a hesitation to put my hand in such a place, so I closed my eyes and took a deep breath; something very odd happened as I did. As my eyes were closed tight, I could have sworn that I heard her voice.

"It is safe, go on . . ." It came as little more than a light, breathy whisper, but it was more than enough to cause my eyelids to snap back open. I looked around the room in rapid confusion before I settled enough to reach my hand into the hole in the wall. I could feel something about three inches tall, about six inches wide, and made of what felt like leather. Grabbing the object firmly, I pulled it out of the wall to find that it was some sort book. It looked and felt very old, like it had been there since the building had been established. I brought it down in front of my chest, peeled back the weathered leather bindings, and opened up the front cover. Some of the ancient leather split and cracked as it opened fully, and on the front page there was antiquated writing:

"The Journal and Diary of Nathaniel McClaren"

"Nathaniel McClaren?" I whispered to myself as I read the words written on the brittle first page. I slowly turned the page, completely transfixed on what secrets the journal could hold.

May 12, 1687

To begin properly in this account of the happenings in my life, I must first introduce myself. My name is Nathaniel Edward McClaren. My profession is that of masonry, and this journal was given to me as a gift from my beloved. She found infatuation in my writing so fitting was it that I have an avenue for my personal literature. I am twenty-three years of age, was born in Ireland, however reside in England. At this given moment, I am not terribly sure of what more to write about myself, so I shall leave this as my first entry in this diary.

Signed,
Nathaniel McClaren

Though the entry was short in both text and information, I found it to be unexplainably riveting, and I turned the page.

May 28, 1687

I have come to a time of truth in my life, and I am frightened by the present circumstances. My love, my beloved, is to be married. Not by her choosing, but rather her father the Duke has promised her hand to another. He would never have his daughter wed to a lowly mason, but we are deeply in love, and our secret tryst grows dangerous. I cannot keep myself from her, I long for her night and day. We meet under the cover of night in the carriage house for our short times of each other's company. What am I to do?

Signed,
Nathaniel McClaren

I could not quite explain my interest in the self-portrait of Nathaniel McClaren. However, I knew that the peak in my fascination couldn't simply be of my own curiosity; it was what Dorothy had been trying to get me to find, and it was somehow one step closer to figuring out what all was going on in that place. So there it was, another turn of an ancient and antiquated page of the journal, and I read on.

June 7, 1687

It would seem that events have led my beloved and I to a proverbial fork in the road. She is to be married in less than one month, yet our secret love can no longer be so easily hidden. With that in the forefront of my mind, I have formulated a plan for us to elope. I have yet to tell her of such a matter, yet in my heart I know that she will agree. For the sake of me, she must agree. Though I could not yet afford the cost of a proper ring as I have put forth all my funding to our prospective plans, I could little more than afford a strange and beautiful necklace made of silver for her. I bought it from a foreign trader who told me that it had special power and that it kept the very essence of love. I know it to be rubbish, but it is very pretty, and for a little extra cost, the man etched words into the back of it for me. It is my greatest hope that this will work.

Signed,
Nathaniel McClaren

I was starting to get the feeling that I knew what was going on, but I couldn't be certain. There was little more that I could do than to read on.

June 18, 1687

My plan has found a catalyst, and it was much to both my beloved's and my own surprise. She is with child, my child, and her father is demanding blood for who the one responsible is. It is now known that the father is not her husband to be, and punishment will be swift to the man who is to blame. They know not that it is I who in a moment of passion brought life into the one that I love, as they do not know of the love that we share. I gave her the necklace and the promise of a new life together, and she has accepted openly and lovingly my proposition. A small religious group had commissioned a ship to take them to the colonies in the Americas to seek their own freedoms of worship. For a fee, they have agreed to let us stow away with them to the new world. They seemed particularly touched and enticed by our predicament, and I expect that they will be a lovely asset to have with us on such a voyage. We leave this place tonight, under little more than the light of the moon. Tomorrow, we set sail for the new world, a new life for us, and it will be in a place called Salem.

Signed,
Nathaniel McClaren

Before I could turn to the next page and read on about the story of Nathaniel and his dearest love, I heard a faint noise coming from outside of my window; it was the sound of a car rolling up the driveway. I carefully closed the book and set it down on the nightstand to go see who on earth might be coming there—either that or to ready myself to go down and knock around some snooping agent. By the time I got over to the window and a clear enough view to see, my mind was put at ease when I saw the police car pulled up next to my jeep. Without a second thought, I grabbed my coat, the book, my room key, and made for the door. Before going down the long hallway, I made damn sure that I locked the door to my room. Just as I got to the bottom of the grand staircase, I was met by the innkeeper.

"Not much writing can be done so far from pen and paper, Mr. Clarke." Her voice was low and stern, and it was quite a presumptuous thing to say I thought.

"Half the writing is in the research, ma'am. Any good writer knows that." I made it a point to be sarcastic and short.

"But, of course, you would know best, Mr. Clarke." She sounded more resigned than before, but it didn't make it any less offensive.

"Tell me, what was this building before it became a bed-and-breakfast?" It was a question that I meant to ask her earlier, but because of the strange breakfast episode, I had abstained.

"We have always accommodated guests in this building, Mr. Clarke." Her speech was right back to the stern and cold one that I had come to expect from her.

"Right . . . Well, good day." I didn't believe her, though I really didn't know why. There was just something that kept getting more and more peculiar about her. Regardless of that, I shrugged it off and walked out the door.

As I walked out into the all-too-familiar fall-scented air, I could see Scott standing next to his squad car expectantly. He wasn't in uniform that time and, oddly enough, was dressed a bit like I usually did: jeans, long-sleeved button-up shirt, and some plain undershirt.

"Good morning, Officer. What brings you to this kind of place?" I said jokingly. He didn't smile, didn't even give a response, and just started quickly walking toward me. Admittedly, it made me very nervous, and I couldn't help but feel like something bad had happened. As he got near enough to me, he grabbed my arm and pulled me close to him.

"There is something very, *very* wrong about this place, Evan. Come with me." I couldn't quite say for sure, but there seemed to be a slight air of fear carried in his voice.

"What happened? Is something wrong?" I couldn't keep myself from asking.

"Get in the car. I'll explain." That time, I could definitely tell that he was shaken, so I did as he asked and walked around to the passenger side of his car. I hardly had time enough to get the door closed before the car shot backward and just as quickly down the driveway.

The colors of all the trees and other foliage blurred by the window as the car sped down the road.

"What the hell is going on? You're driving like I do when your fellow boys in blue aren't around! What happened, Scott?" There was something in his eyes that I somehow identified with, and I knew the look well; he had seen something unexplainable.

"Have you gone out around this town at night?" he asked sharply.

"No, not really. I really haven't done much of anything around here. Why?" He was making less sense, the more he talked. Finally, he slowed the car down to a stop, and I finally got a chance to comprehend our surroundings. By the best I could tell, we were parked up on a ridge overlooking the town, opposite of the bed-and-breakfast. He reached up, turned off the ignition, and sat back in his seat.

"Last night, I went out for some surveillance, and I think something bad is going on around here." His voice was quiet and the tone seemed grave.

"What do you mean? I don't understand what you're talking about." I didn't mean to sound cross with him, but the conversation was getting frustrating.

"I was walking around, and there wasn't a soul in sight. Then at two thirty in the morning, people started showing up all around the streets and sidewalks. I hid behind a fence and watched them all file into the church, the one I found you at. Something smelled horrible. It was all over the air. Smelled like something rotting." He went quiet and stared out of the front window of the car.

"And? . . . What happened after that." He snapped a look at me as if I startled him from a trance by speaking.

"After about half an hour, I could hear all this weird chanting. I never heard anything like it . . . I never want to again . . . Then . . . Then I heard something else . . ." He grew silent and still again.

"Damn it, Scott! What the fuck happened? What has you so rattled?" I had no idea why I lost my cool like that. It was far beyond uncharacteristic of me. He looked back at me with an expression that could only be taken as terror.

"I could hear screams coming out over the chanting . . . Screaming 'No! No! I don't want to go back! Don't do it! Please!' . . . I think it was Sam . . . I think it was my partner, but there were too many of them. I couldn't go busting in there. Then, something started glowing up in the tower of that place you're staying at. Then I ran . . ." His hands were trembling as he buried his face in them. No sooner he put his face in his shaking hands than he looked straight up and turned his head to look at me, and all tremors subsided. He stared blankly at me with a dead expression on his face and hollow eyes.

"In the night, they sing . . ." Though he only said it as a whisper, the words penetrated my very being, and I felt a dread that I hadn't felt for a while.

"What . . . What did you just say?" I whispered, more questioning what I had just heard than him directly. My eyes widened. I even felt my pupils dilating, and my heart pounded out of my chest. I could somehow hear the whispers of those words repeating and echoing in my ears as an instant headache came over me to complement the horror I was feeling. I could do little more than stare back at him as I panicked and rapidly searched for the door handle behind me. His cold stare quickly turned to a look of utter confusion, but it didn't break my stare or stop me from popping the door open behind me.

I must not have realized that I was pushing my back so hard against the door because when it came open, I had a hard fall backward out of the car onto the ground. Scrambling to my feet, the only thought on my mind was one of escape, to run—run fast, run far. Whatever the hell it was that made him say that to me was inconsequential at that moment. All that I knew was that I had heard those haunted words before and from too many sources to write it off as any kind of coincidence; no matter the mystery behind it, it seemed to be gunning for me. I sprinted as fast as I could through the trees and the thicket with no other destination than the hell away from there, but it didn't seem long at all before I realized that I had no clue where I was. I looked around madly to see if I could get any kind of bearing on my position, but to no avail; I was lost in the woods. A thought of simplicity crossed my mind as I told myself just to go back the way that I had came, but that was the problem. I didn't know what direction that was.

I wandered around for hours, still completely unsure of where I was or what I had gotten myself into. For reasons I couldn't explain, the surrounding forest in its dying solstice state brought me back to strange memories, much like my drives back in Colorado did. I almost instinctively sat down on a nearby rock and surrendered to my lost memories. It was once again myself as a young boy—that same scene on a derelict hillside . . . dressed in black? Why was I in a suit? The memory bank opened up in full with that small detail, and everything then on played like a movie. I was at my father's funeral. I remembered that he passed away, but I never could remember how. Then it hit me; he hung himself. I was beside myself with not only the memory but also the fact that I couldn't remember before. And like a brick shot from a cannon into my brain, it hit me. He had possession of that disk at some point, and he killed himself.

The shocking realization brought me some new understanding of the artifact that I was then in possession of; it all made some sick sort of sense—my grandfather committed suicide, my father, suicide, and as far as I could recall, my great-grandfather as well. I felt sick; I wanted to scream, cry, punch something, and anything to release the newfound feelings of pain and understanding that I harbored. Sliding off the rock and onto my knees, I chose to exhale, releasing all the air in my lungs and look up to the sky. So many things flew around in my head, and not one of those things could stand still. I only wished that none of it had ever happened and that any of it made the least bit of rational sense. Although I didn't recall, I had to have fallen asleep or passed out at some point because the next thing that I remembered was waking up. Darkness surrounded me as I stood up and looked around. I couldn't see anything through the pitch black forest, and that same terrible feeling of doom and dread crept over and enveloped me. Blindly, I started walking forward; to where, I didn't know.

I tripped over tree roots and ran into everything in my path; I couldn't see a damn thing. There was an ever so faint light overhead from the moon, but the cloud cover didn't allow enough illumination to find my way. I could feel my heart rate increasing, or so I thought; I reached into my inside coat pocket to feel that the disk was beginning to pulsate.

"In the night, they sing . . ." I whispered to myself as I felt it vibrating and sending out its humming sound. At least that much began to make sense to me, as it seemed to sing with its pulsating song of energy, and that it only occurs at night, or so I guessed. Pulling it out of my pocket, it was very clear that the gem in the center of it was emitting a strong glow, much greater than the faint light from times before. I held it out in front of me to use it to light my way; though it wasn't a flashlight, it revealed more than I was able to see before.

I continued on through the woods still unsure of where I was going, but I figured that it was better than waiting around where I was.

As I came to a clearing, a stillness took the air that previously didn't exist around me, and feeling that could be best described as stagnant filled me. The forest around me erupted in whispers from every angle, and it was then I knew that I wasn't where I thought I was. I quickly returned the artifact to the inside pocket of my coat, and as I looked around, I could tell that the environment had changed. The trees around me were dead instead of the autumn covering that they had when I entered the forest, and there seemed to be a foggy haze starting to blanket everything, though it was still too dark to see much of anything. I took a deep breath and carefully walked forward a few steps, and out of all the indecipherable whispers I could hear all around, I could make out that some of them were talking about me; they knew that I was there. There were mixed feelings in me of being trapped and needing to run, and neither of which I could decide what to do about. The whispering got louder, and the many breathy voices seemed to call out to me, some going as far to say that they knew what I possessed and that they wanted it from me.

A sharp and piercing cold came out from all over and triggered me to make a decision; all I could think to do was run. I took the disk back out of my pocket to light my way, and as I did, the whispers became snarling screams and vicious taunts. I sprinted from where I was off into the woods, but it still wasn't fast enough to escape the ominous and hate-filled cries that came from everywhere. As I ran, I could hear the brush and thicket moving behind me as if something was coming after me, but I didn't dare to look back. I was running out of breath, and all at once I regretted smoking, but no sooner than that thought came to me, the terrible voices stopped. Stumbling and coughing, I took a knee next to large dead tree. I leaned back against it and was breathing heavily to catch my breath. The same headache associated with the strange phenomenon began to take a hold of me, along with that, the slight dizziness that usually did as well. I looked out around the tree to behold a nightmarish sight; that thing, the woman-looking creature from before, was coming toward me, and it wasn't alone. There were at least a dozen of revolting entities emerging from the forest, each resembling some human appearance but some far less than the others. The more human-looking ones floated about looking in all directions, while the things that were much less person-looking trudged around looking for something as well, and I knew that it was me that they were looking for. I held my breath and sat back tight against the tree, and the thought that I was completely screwed jumped to the forefront of my mind.

I peered out again from around the tree, and the beasts were drawing closer. I couldn't help but observe one of the hulking creatures that were lumbering around near my location. It was tall, maybe six and a half or seven feet tall, with elongated and twisted limbs, some of which looked as if there were bones protruding in various places. Though the lighting was poor, it looked to have grayish skin, and its face was lacking in features, save for large eyes that were the same heart-wrenching black voids that I had seen before. And a twisted mouth that bore a grimace was the end of the thing's features. A great discomfort grew in my chest as I felt a cough trying to fight out of my lungs, and to my displeasure, I knew I had to hold it or else. There were very few options that were coming to mind that I could execute, and time was running out as the fiends drew closer. As I heard them gasping and wheezing and encroaching on my failed position, my mind was made up for me. I got to my feet as quietly as I possibly could, and then inhaled slowly and silently to fuel my lungs for another sprint. One last moment of mental preparation passed, and I could wait no longer. I dashed out from behind the tree and ran as fast as I could in the opposite direction of the hellish beings. Inhuman screams, and demonic shrieks and shrills rang out from behind me, and I damn sure was not going to look back.

Never in my life had I run as fast as I was running then, yet the demons behind me were still in hot pursuit. The unholy noises that they released were a strange combination of frightening and infuriating as I fled. The deeper into the forest I ran, more creatures emerged trying to intercept me on my course, and with each one I passed, more howling and screaming followed. In the midst of everything that was going on, I caught my foot on something as I ran. I stumbled and fought to try and keep my footing, but to no avail as I fell and hit the ground rolling as I did. The impact knocked the air out of me, and there was little more that I could do than lay there and try to move. I knew that the longer I took to get back to functional, the chances of survival diminished. The demon creatures began to appear all around me, and the only thing I could think was "I'm fucked." The beasts did not speak or make any significant noises past snarling and growling as they came up on me. The one that I mistook for Savannah came closer than the rest.

"I found you, Evan," she said with that sound of multiple vocals. I looked at it with a disdain that I couldn't even harbor for my worst enemy. I briefly thought about saying something clever for my last words, but I figured that since they were inhuman and wretched monsters, that nothing I could say would matter. It was then that I felt some warmth on my chest that was growing in heat. I reached into my shirt and pulled out Dorothy's necklace that she gave me, and it was glowing. Instantly, I noticed the fiends backing off from the glowing item as if it were something that they feared. I stood up to face them, then fearless with what I was holding at them. The pendant's glow intensified, furthering their distance from me. Slowly, I walked toward the abominations, fending them off with the bright blue glow; they twisted and moaned with each step I took to them. I could feel the disk inside my pocket vibrating violently and erratically as if it too was repulsed by the light. It was at that moment I knew that there was a distinct difference between the light from the necklace and that of the disk—a clear line between a positive and a negative. I held the pendant high as its light grew and enveloped everything around it. The creatures fled, and then I could see nothing more than the intense white-blue light.

I woke up on the ground unsure of how much time had passed and unsure of where I had ended up for that matter; my surroundings were different than what I had last recalled. Just in the middle of my confusion, I saw headlights through the trees. I made my way toward the source of light to find that the ground changed from earthen forest underbrush to worn and crumbling asphalt. The lights from the car drew closer, and part of me wanted to hide, but I didn't. I waited there on the side of the road until what was soon a familiar sight pulled up; it was Scott. He pulled up next to where I was standing and rolled down the window.

"Where the hell did you go? One minute, I was talking to you, and you were gone the next." He was talking like I was used to hearing him, and there was no detection of fear or trauma about him at all. As confusing as that was, I was still relieved to see him.

"I'm not entirely sure what happened . . . Like you said, 'There's something very wrong with this place'." I told him before making my way around to the other side of the car.

As I was getting settled in, Scott alarmed me by pulling out a pistol, cocking it, and setting the hammer back down.

"What are you going to do with that, Scott?" I asked nervously.

"Nothing," he said slowly and turning the grip of the gun toward me. "This is for you. Ya know, just in case." I didn't feel the need to tell him that I had a small armory of my own. Besides, I didn't mind having another gun, especially if it was a cop who was the one giving it to me.

"Thanks," I said taking it from him. "Hopefully we won't need to use them." I meant what I said too; the last thing I wanted was for events to turn to such an extreme.

"So since you already got lost in the woods all day, what's your plan for tonight?" Scott asked in a quirky manner. Even though I knew that he was joking, I couldn't shake the thought of what caused me to take off the way I did, and more disturbingly, that he did not seem to remember.

"I really didn't have anything planned, but there were a few things that I was hoping to look into." I wasn't yet sure if I wanted him to come along on my investigations. Not to say that I didn't like Scott, or that I didn't trust him, but after that episode in his car earlier that day I wasn't sure what to think anymore.

"Well, I have a few ideas if you're up for it," he said putting the car into gear.

"Sure . . . Does this town have a library?"

It was close to midnight by the time we got to what we thought to be downtown. The scenery was as I had come to expect from the forsaken town; there wasn't a soul to be seen. We stayed in the car for a while just watching the surroundings for anything unusual or at least anything more unusual than that place had to offer. Scott reached under the driver's seat and pulled out a familiar-looking bottle.

"You drink?" he said holding up a beautiful bottle of Jack Daniels.

"I'm a recently divorced, out of work writer, of course, I drink," I said with a defeated smile, taking the bottle from his hand. The burning sensation of the Tennessee sour mash delight was a welcomed comfort for my troubled mind. I pulled out my pack of cigarettes, picked out one for me, and gestured the pack toward Scott. He looked at it for a moment and then hesitantly took one.

"Ya know, I quit these about three years ago. But hell, why not?" He took out a very nice-looking Zippo lighter with "Love & Faith" engraved on the side.

"Not to pry, but why do you still carry a lighter if you don't smoke?" A fairly good question I thought.

"It was a gift from my daughter and ex-wife. I hang onto it because it was from my little girl. She's my world. Well, at least every other weekend." After his admission, he took a stout swig of the whiskey and a long drag of the cigarette. We were quiet for a minute as he passed the bottle back over to me. I thought for a moment as I took a drink of Jack's lovely serum.

"Savannah and I never had kids . . . Well, we tried like hell to anyway . . ." I was in the midst of some horrible recollections of the many disappointments we faced when we were married.

"So what happened? I mean, was there some kind of problem?" I could tell by the way that he asked that he was hesitant to do so.

It all came rushing back to me in some disgusting and disruptive form of nostalgia and horrifying memories.

"We . . . Well, the doctor . . ." I paused for a minute before I continued. "We found out that I couldn't have children." It was the first time that I had ever said the words out loud, and they painted a clearer picture than I had ever really wanted to see; the truth was that it was something that I didn't want to accept.

"That's when it started to go south . . . She became distanced from me, and I could tell that she felt robbed of something . . . Something that I took from her." Trying to come to terms with something that was right in front of me all along, I took a long, slow swig of the burning, charcoal-filtered medicine. I could feel something falling apart inside of me as everything that had transpired before, slowly and painfully transformed into a revelation. At that moment, nothing else came to mind: not Dorothy, the mysterious things that had been going on, and not even the terrors that I had faced.

"It wasn't more than a couple of years later that she found herself in the arms of someone else, and probably someone who could give her what she wanted . . . Savannah always wanted kids . . . more than anything . . ." Another stiff drink and damn near half of a cigarettes worth of a drag, and I resided to surrender to the truth; it was my fault, and I blamed her for everything.

Both of us were quiet for some time—smoking cigarettes and passing the bottle back and forth. A different sort of sinking feeling had come over me then, as I allowed myself to realize what I should have so long ago. My refusal to talk about kids and my unwillingness to listen to her about adoption, all of it was a bullet train to the ultimate end, and it was my fault. There was a large part of me that wanted to call her, just to talk to her and hear her soft voice again, and to tell her that I was so incredibly sorry for everything that I fell short on. But it was too late for all that, even I could recognize that simple fact. All there was left to do was for me to suck it up and deal with the matter at hand.

"If you feel up for a bit of breaking and entering, there's something that I want to check on in that library." My change of subject was worn on my sleeve, but I didn't care; there were bigger things at hand than my pathetic past.

"Yeah sure, but what's in the library?" he asked sounding unsure of what I was getting at.

"I'm not exactly sure, but I just have a feeling that there is something in there." I couldn't explain it myself, but there was a feeling that I needed to chase.

The vacant streets combined with the heavily overcast sky made for an eerie setting for our nighttime dealings. We got to the front door of the ancient-looking library and to not much of a surprise to us, the front door was heavily chained and the windows barred with thick wrought-iron grates.

"Well, looks like we got some work cut out for us," Scott said clearly disgusted with the situation.

"Maybe not," I said noticing a flaw in the bars over the window to my left. By the look of it, time and weather had not been very kind to the metal work, and it was badly rusted.

"Do you have a baton or something?" He reached for a button latched pouch on his belt no sooner than I had asked. The item he handed me was a metal collapsible baton, and I immediately put it to good use. Wedging the baton under the grate, I pulled with everything that I could, and finally managed to pull the old iron bolts from the aging brick wall. It came down with a crash, startling both Scott and me, but it made a clear entryway for us into the building. After taking one last look around to make sure that nobody was around to see our illegal activities, I busted out a corner portion of the window and let the two of us in. The timing couldn't have been better on our part as the black sky opened up and released the cold lamenting rain just as we went inside.

Two sounds of hard clicks from turning on the flashlights echoed softly through the hollow room. The beams of light were very visible through the dust we kicked up when we jumped in through the window, and with that observation, I could tell that it had been a long damn time since anyone had been in there. Neither of us said anything as we crept through the rows of empty, dust-covered bookshelves, and spiderweb-draped tables and chairs. It was quite evident that the place had been abandoned some time ago, why it was, I couldn't have guessed.

"What the hell is it you think you're going to find in here?" he asked me just above a whisper. I wasn't sure what to tell him mostly because I had no idea in hell myself.

"I don't know . . ." Just as I spoke, I noticed something in the back of the room that stood out from the rest of the otherwise uniform setting. The wall was made up of different bricks than the rest of the building; it seemed much older, and there was what looked like a date etched in stone on a large center brick: 1694. And just below it were inscribed the words: Praise Be to Our Fallen Family, May They Find the Other World in Peace.

Just below that, was an ornate doorway with narrow stained glass windows the full length of it on either side, and at the top was a semicircle stained glass window depicting what looked like someone being burned at the stake. As I studied the bizarre architecture, a sharp ringing started low in my ears, and nausea with a terrible headache set in on me.

"Oh, god . . ." The words slipped out of my mouth as I felt the dizziness take me. I dropped the flashlight and grabbed my head in pain.

"Evan? Man, are you okay? You're pale as hell." Though I could hear his concern, it didn't help as I fell to my knees, in anguish, and the ringing became deafening.

"Evan? Evan!" I could hear him, but it was like he was yelling at me through water.

With my trembling hand, I managed to reach into my shirt and grab the pendant that Dorothy gave me. As I clutched tight the metal piece, it was an almost instantaneous release from the plaguing effects that I was suffering. I shook my head as the symptoms subsided, picked up the flashlight, and got to my feet.

"What the hell was that?" Scott asked both concerned and uneasy.

"I'm not sure, but it's been happening since the beginning of all this shit," I explained as I rubbed the back of my head.

"Is it just me, or does it look like the whole front of this building was an add-on?" A convenient derailment of topic but still functioned as a valid point.

"Yeah, but what of it? Are you sure you're okay?" I could tell that he was concerned, but we really didn't have time for such things.

"Yes, I'm fine. Let's move on. I want to see what's back there."

"All right, if you say so," he said it slowly as if in disbelief as he followed me through the arcane and disturbing corridor.

On the other side of the wall, there was much of the same as far as dust and spiderwebs, but the architecture told a completely different story. The room that we entered was much older, in far worse repair than the front half, and there was a menacing air over everything. I shined the light over the walls to reveal very strange and troubling paintings hanged about the room. What came to me as the most traumatizing was recognizing some of the things that were depicted in them. One was of a person completely obscured in dark robes holding a familiar-looking silver disk. I walked over to examine the picture closely and read the title: Those Who Hold the Keys Will Find the Way. I slowly moved on to the next one which was equally, if not more, disturbing than the first. It looked like what was a snow-covered forest drenched in moonlight. In the center of the clearing, there was a hazily painted woman in a tattered white dress. The sight alone was nauseating, and it brought with it flashbacks of that horrendously fucked-up night back at the hotel. It was all I could do to read the title, it read: She Sees the Truth in the Black of Night. I could no longer look at it without the feeling of a strong despise. My concentration was quickly broken, however, as both Scott and I heard noises coming from the other side of the room.

Looking at each other, we understood simultaneously without saying a word and drew our guns. We pointed our flashlights and weapons in the direction of the sound's origin and slowly began walking toward a staircase leading down to what I could only imagine to be the basement. Creeping down the steep stone stairs, we both could see the subtle traces of a flashlight moving around between the long forgotten bookcases, and we clicked our lights off. Scott looked over and gestured for me to go around to the left, and he would go around to the right. As I walked my designated course through the towering bookshelves and debris on the floor, my heart started to pound and my hands began to shake and sweat. The adrenaline was running strong, and for the first time in a long time, my focus was sharp. As I cautiously peered around the corner, I could only hope that Scott was at the same point with me. The sight that I caught from around the bookcase took my breath away; it was the agent that had been following me from the beginning, and as luck would have it, he was ours.

I quickly rounded the corner, gun drawn, and ready for whatever came next.

"Don't you fucking move!" I yelled through the shadows. Though sight was difficult at that very moment, I could still make out the distinct silhouette rapidly turn to look at me. No faster than catching sight of me, he turned to run away. What came next could only be explained as pure impulse; as the shadowy figure of the agent tried to make his escape, I threw the flashlight as hard as I could, hitting the agent directly in the back of his head. As quickly as the contact was made between skull and lighting tool, he dropped to the floor, and Scott knelt down on top of him. He turned on his light and pointed both it and his gun at the agent's head.

"You damn well better start talking. I know that you are involved in this shit somehow, and I want to know." Scott showed a ferocity that I had yet to see him display; clearly, the cop in him had come out.

"You . . . you idiots . . . le. let me . . . go," he said between gasps. Given that Scott had his knee pressing down on the agent's throat, I could imagine that it would be hard to talk. I walked over, gun still pointed at the man lying on the floor, and picked up my flashlight and pointed it down onto him.

"You've been following me since I left Colorado, went through my jeep, and God knows what else, you bastard! I want answers!" I tried my best to sound convincing, but there was some strange feeling that I got from the man—something that I couldn't put my finger on; there wasn't just something "different" about him. There was something very off. I could see that Scott rocked back enough to let some pressure off his neck, but his pistol's aim did not waiver.

"You have no idea what you have gotten yourself into, both of you. Do you honestly think that the things that have been happening to you are simply freak accidents? You are fools. I know what you have in your possession, Evan Clarke. It would be in your best interests to just give it to me." The man's speech never lost its mellow or cool, and he talked in a way that made my skin crawl.

"That doesn't answer a goddamn thing! Why are you following me, why do you want that disk, and most importantly, how the hell did you find me in the first place?" As off-putting as the man was in just his general demeanor, it was to a point of pissing me off.

"Stop wasting time, as there is precious little of it left. Give me the seventh piece or face the consequences." His voice was piercing, and for no reason that I could fathom. Scott pulled back the hammer on his .45 and pressed it firmly under his chin.

"You really should answer his questions." I could see the look in Scott's eyes, and even I was more than taken aback by it. The agent stared at me with a gaze that could petrify, and to be honest, it kind of did.

"In the night, they sing . . ." You have heard those words before, haven't you? They have a much more grave and sinister meaning than you could possibly imagine. As for you, Evan, we know everything about you. My organization sent me for containment purposes, and you are impeding my objective. Nothing takes precedence over my orders, and I will kill you if it means completion of my assignment." Both Scott and I had no idea what to say to what the agent just was talking about. It seemed that the stakes were rising, and I still had not a clue in hell what the stakes were in the first place. It was then that I noticed the man on the floor slide something out of his coat's pocket. Before I could even speak a word, the room was instantly filled with a blinding green light; it was all that I could do, just to shield my eyes from the unexplained blast.

I wasn't sure how long it was before I could see again, but when I was finally able to, I soon discovered that Scott was just regaining his sight as well. As we both shook off what had just happened, the agent was gone.

"What the fuck was that?" Scott asked, picking himself up off the ground.

"I have no idea . . . I've never seen anything like it . . . What the hell was he doing down here in the first place?" I picked up my flashlight and pointed it toward where we found him standing in the first place. There in the glow of the beam was an open book sitting on an old decaying desk. Getting closer to the book, I could see that it was written in some strange language that I didn't understand, but I had seen before. Whatever the language was, it was one in the same with what was etched into the disk, and all the bizarre writing on the walls of the other Evan's house back in Colorado. Next to the book was a small notepad and pencil, and to the best I could tell, there were translations written down on the first page.

"What is it?" Scott asked as he dusted himself off.

"I'm not exactly sure, but I think he was translating whatever is written in this book." As I examined the text further, I found that my observation about it being written was more accurate than had initially thought; the words and symbols looked handwritten and about as old as the journal I found in the wall of the bed-and-breakfast. As I was gathering up the book and translations, I set down my flashlight; when I looked back up to grab it, I noticed that the light was shining on yet another peculiar picture hanging up on the wall. After studying it for a good long moment, I couldn't stop from thinking that it looked like an old drawn out schematic for the bed-and-breakfast that I was staying in, but the label said otherwise. I shined the light closer on the words to make sure I didn't read it in error, but I was unsettlingly correct; it was once called the Norcrest Sanitarium.

There was little more than silence for a while as both Scott and I looked at the small plaque attached to the picture.

"So . . . You've been staying in a crazy home?" he said it jokingly, but I could tell that it made him as about nervous and uneasy as it did me.

"I guess so, and it does explain some things. But there are way too many things left without answers. Can you take me back there?" In my mind, there was quite enough literature to go over and keep me occupied for the rest of the night.

"Sure, if you don't mind staying there after seeing this," he said pointing up at the sanitarium drawing.

"I don't have much of a choice. Besides, I need to figure out what is going on in this book and see what the hell is so important that the guy that just got away would kill me over." As the sound of my voice stopped its light echoes through the basement, another faint and distant sound took its place; it sounded like chanting. I broke the glass of the frame surrounding the picture with the butt of the gun and then pulled the schematic out and rolled it up. I looked at Scott, who was clearly shaken by the noises from outside, and I motioned for us to go back up the stairs. He slowly nodded, and we made our way up the stone corridor. When we got to the main level, the sounds of low chanting voices was louder than before. Guns still drawn, we quietly walked up to and crouched down by the front window to see what was happening outside.

The view for us to see was just like the one Scott had described before; there were a lot of people, and all of them cloaked and in black robes, slowly staggering and chanting all in the same direction down the street. I looked at my watch to see if it was the same time he had told me that it happened before, but my watch had stopped, and the glass over the face had broken.

"What time is it?" I whispered to him. He raised his arm to look, but his watch was in the same state as mine.

"My watch is broken. Must've happened in the mix-up downstairs . . ." I didn't say anything but just looked at him. I reached into my pocket and grabbed my cell phone, but it wasn't much help either; its screen was cracked, and the digital images on it were little more than a multicolored pixilated mess. Before I had time to question what had happened to my watch and phone, that sharp ringing in my ears began again, and my head felt as though it was about to explode. A faint and familiar sound began to emit from my coat; it was that same crystal glass, pulsating sound. Scott quickly looked over at me as the sound started, but before he could ask me what it was, he looked back out of the window just as fast as he had looked to me. Whatever image he saw, must have taken him by surprise as he fell backward and scooted back across the floor.

"Evan . . . They know we're here." His voice was quiet and low.

Through the ringing and the pounding in my head, I managed to pull myself up to the window sill to see what it was that he was talking about. In the middle of the street outside of the library, all the people who were out there had stopped and were then staring directly at the building in which we were. None of them moved, and the chanting had stopped, and every one of them solidly transfixed on our location. As the crystalline pulsating sound continued, I noticed that there was a vibration in cadence with it coming from the inside pocked of my coat; it was the silver disk.

I fished it out to see what it was doing, and as I did, the people standing outside of the library started to move closer. The round object was vibrating more than it ever had before, and the blue gem in the center emitted a distinct blue light, not like the faint gleaming that I had seen before.

"What the fuck are you doing? Let's get out of here!" Scott yelled as he picked me up from the floor. We ran to the back of the library, and I returned the disk to the pocket inside of my coat. There were few options for an exit, just two windows at the stairwell that led down to the basement, and I could hear whoever those people were pulling at the front doors. In an urgent manner, Scott picked up one of the old chairs strewn about the place and threw with all the force he had at the back window. With a loud crash and the sounds of metal and glass hitting all over the place, the window was gone and the wrought iron grate was partially pushed from the wall. The help I could offer to his effort was minimal as the ringing and pain in my head increased with each passing moment. I could do little more than stand there as he wildly kicked at the grate that covered the window. I looked back to the front of the building and was terrified when I saw that the robed figures were starting to climb in through the window we had first entered. Whatever was going to happen, I knew that it needed to happen then.

CHAPTER 12

Vicious Traditions and the Hell That They Bring

Scott had finally managed to bust out the grate in time for our escape before the cloaked figures could reach us. Me, in some horrible stupor, could barely function enough to run when he had prompted me to do so. Jumping out of the back window and landing on the dead grass and leaves, I lay there and couldn't help but wonder why all of it was happening and why the air was thick with the smell of rotting meat. What on earth could be going on to cause such a menacing scene and terrible events to transpire? I felt as though I was right in the middle of a horror story and that I was the main character; it was the only way that I could make sense of it to myself.

"Get up damn it! They're coming! We have to get out of here!" My thoughts were beyond collection because of the headache and the high-pitched ringing, but I could at least gather a bit of what he was telling me. I stumbled to my feet. Scott grabbed my arm and started running, causing me to do the same. I could only trust that he knew where he was leading us; I was too far out of it to ask, let alone lead myself to any semblance of safety and reason.

The pulsating vibration and the harmonic sound coming from the disk in my coat pocket faded the farther we got from the library, and with the fading of those two things, so faded the physical and mental abnormalities that came with its presence. Granted, I still had no idea where we were or even how far we had gone, but I was at least happy that the rotten smell had faded with distance we traveled. We finally stopped under a large tree far from the road and sat down to catch our breath. We were soaked from the rain that seemed to be falling without end, and the cold air of our fall surroundings made an already cold early morning simply miserable.

"We have to get out of this town, Evan," he said between breaths. I knew that he was probably right, but on the other hand, I knew that there had to be some reason for my presence there. It was something that I could not explain and something that

I was far from understanding, and even though the face of danger had shown, I still believed that there was more to all of it.

"She told me I was close . . ." I really didn't mean to say it, and it came as hardly a whisper.

"Who said you were close to what?" Scott asked sounding confused.

"Oh nothing. You're right, we shouldn't stay here. But . . ." I noticed something not far from where we were as I was talking to Scott. There on the mountain side, I could see the faint lights of the bed-and-breakfast, and I knew at least enough to want to go back.

"But what?" he asked still with a puzzled look on his face.

"I'm going to go back to the inn to get my stuff. If you go get your car and meet me there, we can get the hell out of here." He seemed to agree with what I was saying as he slowly nodded on almost every word.

"Okay. It might take me a bit. I'm going to try to sneak to it . . . That, and I really don't know where we are. Are you going to be all right?" I answered his question with a quick nod, not even sure myself of whether or not I would be all right from there. With that, Scott disappeared into the trees, and I was left to try and figure out what to do.

The cold, wet, dark autumn night was the only company that I had as I made my way through the bushes and trees. There was an odd comfort in the smell of the damp and dead leaves as I tried to piece together again all what had led me to the point I was at. In all honesty, I would never in a million years have guessed that anything could have led me to where I was. At least, there was a small fortune in being under the cover of the forest; though the rain was falling fairly hard, the trees covered me from getting anymore soaked than I already was. It was just then that a strange thought occurred to me as I walked alone in the darkened woods; the threat of danger had become grossly unavoidable and very real, and there was something that had to be done in the worst case. I carefully reached into my pocket and pulled out my cell phone. As I flipped it open, I noticed that even though the screen was still cracked, the background picture was back to its normal state, and I had one bar of service. I let out a long exhale as I slowly dialed the number, and I was riddled with uncertainty about why exactly I felt compelled to call her. The line rang, and rang, but to no answer, only the answering machine picked up, and I figured that it would have to do; I didn't know when I would get another chance or if I would get one at all.

"Savannah, hi. It's Evan . . . Look, I had a chance to really think about some things, and I just wanted to tell you that I am sorry . . . Sorry for everything. I never talked or listened, and this is exactly what I get for that. I don't blame you for a single thing, and I understand why you did what you did. I'm about out of time now, and at this point, I don't know what's going to happen to me. If I make it out alive, maybe I can tell you what has happened here. I'm sorry, and I love you . . . Bye."

I closed my phone, and my eyes looked down and took a deep breath. I couldn't figure out why I had such a compulsion, but I got it out of my system and was ready to move on. There was only a short distance between me and the inn, and it was there that I hoped to find some answers.

The closer I got to the former sanitarium, something strange began to happen; the disk in my pocket started up with its vibrations and high-pitched sound, something it hadn't done around that location before. The ringing and headache that usually accompanied the disk's odd doings came over me just as I got to the tall stone wall that surrounded the inn. I ignored the symptoms as best as I could and pressed on to the front gates of the property. The crystalline harmonics got louder and the vibrations more intense, but there was something else radiating energy in my possession; the necklace that Dorothy had given me felt as though it was pulsating in rhythm with my own heartbeat and the ringing in my ears and the headache did not get worse with the disk's cries growing louder. The words that had been told to me so many times before made a clear and perfect sense or, at least, were starting to formulate some sort of meaning.

"In the night, they sing . . ." I whispered to myself as I clutched the part of my coat that concealed the strange disk. Whatever the cause or the reason for the piece's reaction was unknown, but what I did know was that its bizarre harmonics could easily be called it "singing," something that had only occurred at night. On top of that, with that agent's admission, the particular antique in my pocket was told to be the seventh: In the night, *they* sing. Scott's partner had one, and who knew how many others there were.

All those strange realizations swarmed through my head as I reached the front door. The thought that any of the heinous events that had taken place and led me to where I was could be chalked up as stress-induced psychosis was far behind me; there, in fact, had to be something very real and very other worldly going on with all the nightmares, the disk, and even Dorothy herself. I looked up to the belfry to see that Scott was not exaggerating when he spoke of a light that came from up there. I could see that there was a pale blue light that was emanating from above me. It was quite unclear to me of what exactly was going on in the town of Norcrest, but there were some things that fell into place that hadn't before; the disks had some sort of power or energy. That bastard agent knew that it was something bad and that the feeling that something big was about to happen couldn't be shaken. I entered the hollow and vacant building with an unsettling feeling brought by the recently gained knowledge of what it once was. The castle-like architecture made more sense in knowing that it once served the purpose of housing the undesirables and misunderstood cases of the era in which it was built. Not to mention such practices performed in the earlier days of psychological understanding that would be considered torture and murder in the eyes of modern times and sciences. I couldn't be sure of how long Scott was going to be with getting his car, so I wasted no time in getting up to my room to see what I could sort out in the time that I had.

No sooner than opening the door to the room, I threw the Nathaniel's journal, the other book, and the agent's notes onto the bed. I ran my hand quickly through my hair, lit up a cigarette, took a healthy drink of the Glenlivet, and dived right in. The agent's notes were well organized with translations and what seemed to be his personal observations. What he had translated from the book so far read as some kind of incantation or ancient ritual—a prayer of sorts. It described some very ambiguous things having to do with ascension and another world—a place where only through righteous means may one enter, and the seven pieces must be placed in such an order. Further reading led to more things that I could only presume to understand. It spoke of things such as only pure hearts and the sacrifice of women can open the door, and only a partial translation about the grace of the moonlight being essential to the opening of the gate. There was so much of it that made absolutely no sense to me and really something that I felt that had nothing to do with me. What I was most interested in was Dorothy and her connection to both me and that journal. I could only assume that it was her Nathaniel was talking about being his beloved, all the pieces fit as far as that was concerned: the necklace, showing me the journal, and even in the confirmation that her name was Dorothy as the necklace was inscribed. The only real question was why her ghost would appear to me, and what happened so long ago that would cause her to bring me to that place then.

I tossed the notes of the agent back down onto the bed and flipped them off as I did; admittedly, I was still a bit spiteful of his death threat earlier that night. I picked up Nathaniel's journal and read on from where I had left off. Much of it was inconsequential to anything that was going on; there were many entries about the hardships over their ocean voyage, a great deal of their life with their young son, and the difficulties while establishing their life in Salem. There was one very interesting detail however, and that was at the first point that they had come over to the colonies. Nathaniel took on the last name of Clarke as not to be found by anyone who could possibly be looking for him. The journal didn't yield too terribly much information until May 1692, and then everything got incredibly interesting.

May 1, 1692

It is a strange day indeed. Today, the members of the church with whom we had come over were in great delight to see that the rest of their following had come over from our homeland. I found it as odd that a great many of them were Irish, and furthermore, only a few of them spoke the king's language. I recall from my early years as a child hearing the Gaelic language spoken, and though very similar, their dialect was different. The words sounded both ancient and arcane, unrefined as it were. They all seemed to be in rejoice at seeing one another, saying things such as "it is finally time" and other oddities. They even went so far as to invite my family and me to dinner at their church just outside of town. I cannot explain why, but I have some apprehensions at the very thought of going.

Signed,
Nathaniel Clarke

I was entirely captivated by the man's entries in the journal. I could only imagine that it was close to how an archeologist might have felt while unearthing ancient history for the first time in centuries. The slices of past tense happenings were gripping with every turn of the page; even the seemingly trivial matters were interesting to me. It was then that I noticed about a month long gap in his entries, and it was also the point of great speculation on my part.

June, 1692

A great deal of strange and troubling happenings as of late. The townspeople are afraid to go out at night, and the air is foul over everything. Whispers of witchcraft and black magic are heard about the streets, and secretive town meetings have been held to discuss such matters. The religious group with whom we made our voyage have withdrawn from all social circles, and they spend most of their days locked away in their church outside of town. The very few times of my seeing any of the members, they try to entice me to bring myself and my wife to one of their services, something I have not and will not do. My good friend Jacob Clarke, the man who is told to be my brother, has been telling me that there is something amiss with those in that church, and I believe him. The most disturbing of the events is that young brides to be have been vanishing, to where not a soul knows.

Signed,
Nathaniel Clarke

Some memory surfaced in my brain of an all but forgotten lesson in my school days, more specifically, history class. I couldn't put my finger on the event, but I could recall some importance to the year of 1692 in early America, and I read on.

July, 1692

The town has been in utter dismay as the count of young betrothed women who have disappeared grows. Trials have been set forth for those being prosecuted for witchcraft and dealings with the devil himself. Many are to be burned at the stake, and of those many, most are from the church outside of town, if it could even be considered as a house of proper worship at all. A large number of the members now

> hold strong resemblance to the walking dead. They smell of rot, have very little color, and seem devoid of their very souls. Fears of vampirism and necromancy plague the town and all who live in it, me included. I fear that we would have been better off to have eloped to Virginia as I had originally planned. Another ship with more of their followers arrived, and they seem to be making ready to take their leave of this place. Good riddance, I say. I do not care where they go as long as they leave in peace, nothing I will lament in losing, and no fare thee wells will be heard from me.
>
> Signed,
Nathaniel Clarke

It was what came next that I found to be the most disturbing in the scribes and the most disturbing event to happen to me for that matter. The vibrations coming from the disk were growing more intense with every page, and if the necklace's harmonic vibrations were keeping the disk's in check, they weren't strong enough to fight back the malicious physical tolls that the disk caused. The symptoms were getting very hard to ignore as I tried to bear it and read on, somehow holding on to concentration as if it were the only thing left that I could cling to.

> *August 1692,*
>
> On this day, the darkest of days in my life so far, they have taken my beloved. They have taken my Dorothy. In the dead of night they came, these followers of the church with no crucifix nor crest. They beat me unconscious, took my wife, yet in some bit of luck, my son managed to escape to Jacob's house. A note was left for me to find when I had finally awakened. The words taunt me and beckon me to follow them into the wilderness in which they disappeared. On this night, I will heed their words, I will follow them into the darkness, and may God help them when I arrive. I will come upon them with all the fury of Michael, the archangel, and God willing he be at my side through this endeavor. I have left my son, Alexander, with Jacob, and I have bargained with some of the more savage natives to help me track down and kill those responsible for this atrocity. I make my leave this night. I am coming for you Dorothy, my love.
>
> Signed,
Nathaniel Clarke

I could read no more, and not because I didn't want to, but because the sharp ringing had come to the point of drowning out all other sound, and the headache was so severe that I felt like throwing up at any given moment. I dropped the journal to the floor and grabbed the sides of my head tightly. I could not think or function, and I could feel a tear roll down my cheek as I simply wished for the pain to stop.

My footing suffered, and I stumbled about the room helplessly as the torment continued. Vision became blurry to the point that I could not distinguish anything specific, and the dizziness peaked so badly that I fell backward onto the floor. I felt like I was dying, and in my mind, if that was what it took to stop such an agony, I was content to do so.

I awoke on the floor, the headache and ringing subsided to a low key but still noticeable. My vision was slowly coming back into focus, and I was in what looked like the same room, but the size and shape was where the resemblance stopped. There were no rugs on the floor, no furniture to speak of, nor were there any other amenities. Then I saw him. Chained high up against the wall was an emaciated-looking man; he was hardly more than skin and bones. His flesh was a pale blue color, and he had deep lacerations all about his naked body. He had very little hair, save for random patches of long lengths on his head, and he looked as dry as leather; even the deep gouges in his skin looked like dried-up wounds that never healed or turned into scars. At first, I thought he was nothing more than a dead body; that was until he spoke, "Why have you come to this house of pain?" He didn't look up at me, and his voice was gravelly, raspy, and low. And it echoed terribly about the cold, gray stone walls of the empty room. I could never come close to describing the terror I felt at that very moment, sitting there on the floor of the poorly lit chamber.

"I . . . I, uhhh . . . I don't know." My voice was jittery and soft as those were the only words I could seem to muster.

"Leave now . . . Leave before they do this to you . . . Death is a far greater fate than if they find you, traveler." The sound and tone he spoke in sounded antiquated and rough, and though I didn't know what he was talking about, the warning he offered seemed very real and very clear.

"How . . . Who did this to you? How . . . did you get here?" The man's condition and situation begged many questions as did my own.

"I am held prisoner in my own creation . . . I built this for them, and this was my reward . . . Torment and anguish my only solace . . . My lament my only friend . . . Why have you come here to this hell, stranger? Did they send you to this woeful realm as they did to me and my beloved?" In a strained, shaking motion, he raised his head to look at me, his bones and skin making a ghastly cracking sound as he did. As disgusted, shocked, and utterly horrified as I was, my brain managed to formulate something, that though impossible, somehow made sense.

"Are you . . . Are you Nathaniel McClaren?"

The tortured man stared at me and cocked his head to the side as if in some sort of consideration.

"Nathaniel . . . Yes, that was my name . . . How long has it been? Every moment is an eternity in this domain of anguish . . . Impossible to know the span of time . . ." I couldn't believe what I was hearing. To me, there was no possible way for it to even make the vaguest sort of sense.

"They have kept me this way . . . They thrive on suffering, feed on torment and sorrow . . . Those fools believe it to be ascension . . . They deserve what will come to them for such misplaced beliefs . . ." His words were haunting and brought little more than despair to my mind. What hellish place could I have somehow found?

"Your beloved . . . Was her name Dorothy?" Although I didn't know what, something was clicking in my head and becoming ever clearer. The tortured man fastened to the wall began to tremble, and it almost seemed as though he would fall apart at any given moment. He let out a strained and sorrowful moan that echoed throughout the hollow and forsaken stone-walled room, and then began sobbing uncontrollably.

"My Dorothy! My love and companion! What fate has become of her I could never guess, nor ever would I try to imagine. A fate such as my own should never have been brought to an angel such as her! A saint among us, she was, and *they took her from me!*" He screamed out loudly and clearly in unimaginable pain. How long? How many years had he been forced to live with such pain?

I was at a loss for words; I knew that there was nothing that I could say or do to stop the travesty that had taken place centuries ago and carried on into the present time. I couldn't stop the tear from my eyes as I sat there on the floor in the pale moonlight shining through the heavily barred window. We were both silent as he continued to weep there in the ill-lit room. Then, something started to happen in me. I felt something deep in my chest. It was like the deepest feeling of inspiration, like looking the love of your life deeply in the eyes; it felt like falling in love. The necklace that I wore started to sing its own song, and it sounded like a much clearer and more harmonic sound than that of the disk. I pulled it from my shirt to find that the gem was glowing and the very silver of which it was made seemed as if it radiated a glow of its very own. Immediately, Nathaniel looked at the necklace with his blackened and dried-out eyes; though he had been crying, there was no evidence of the moisture of tears. Both of us looked on in wild amazement as to what the piece of jewelry was doing. It filled the room with a warmth that was absent before, and the sound that it emitted gave a radiance that lifted my very soul. An unexplainable compulsion came over me and brought me to my feet, almost as if the necklace that I was wearing had picked me up. Then all at once I felt like I was standing next to a heater while an air conditioner blew cold air on me, and Dorothy stepped out from me as if she had been inside of me the whole time.

I was beyond confused and in a way felt sort of violated; I wasn't sure what was happening, but I was pretty damn sure that hitchhiking in my body was never anything that I agreed to. Apart from being upset with the idea, and though I felt physically taxed immediately after, I was far more than eager to see what would happen next.

"Dorothy? My Dorothy? How . . . How are you here, my love?" Nathaniel asked her through his crying and his pain. She said nothing as she moved closer to him with exactly the grace that he had earlier described—like that of an angel. Dorothy put her hand on his face, turned around, and pointed to me, who at that moment was kneeling on the floor. Her face was taken by the most pleasant smile, and she looked back to Nathaniel.

"He brought me to you, dearest Nathaniel . . . You are safe now. Come home, my love." Just as the sound of her last word began to echo, a light started emitting from the hand that she had on his cheek, and the light steadily grew to consume the entirety of his body and then the room as a whole. I surrendered to the brilliance and beauty of the warm divine light that engulfed me, and I felt a peace that I had never felt before. I could barely make out the words from what I could only have assumed to be the voice of Nathaniel whispering.

"Thank you . . . Thank you my love, and blessed be the stranger who brought you back to me." His voice had lost the roughness from before and was then a soft Irish-accented sound.

When the light had finally faded, Nathaniel was gone, and all that remained was Dorothy and me.

"So . . . you *are* the woman from the journal. You are his beloved. You found me to find him. Where . . . where did he go?" I was beside myself as I could only sit there on the floor in utter awe of the pristine wonder.

"He is home now, in truly a better place where he will find everlasting peace and happiness. Thank you, Evan. You have done a great and wonderful deed. Dear, you have saved your kin from this realm of suffering." Her voice was soft but powerful somehow and couldn't explain the way that I could feel her words as she spoke them.

"Kin? Do you mean to say that . . ." I stopped what I was saying midsentence as I tried to dismiss such a crazy notion.

"Yes, Nathaniel is your ancestor, and so am I. Read the journal, and all will find sense with you, dearest Evan. For now you must go. You have done what you have come so far to do. Now you must escape this loathsome place . . . Find peace in life, Evan. I will be with you always." The light radiated from her as she spoke, and I felt like little more than a wretch in front of God as her spirit filled the room. There was at least something that finally came to some conclusion, and I felt at peace. As I sat there still kneeling, succumbing to the white and blue of her light, I felt a profound sense that I had done something good for once and that everything would find a way to be all right for me.

I felt that I had woken up from the best dream I had ever had as I came to on the floor of my room. I sat up, lit a cigarette, and took a nice long drag. I thought for a moment, as I was picking myself up off the floor, about all that had transpired up to that point. All the weirdness that I had gone through and all the bizarre uncertainty—all boiled down to what had just happened to me only moments before. And that was something that I was okay with. Also, I suppose I learned a bit of family history. I picked up and uncorked the bottle of scotch that was lying on the bed, and before I could swallow down a congratulatory and celebratory drink,

I heard a loud crash from outside of the window. The sound snapped me from my thoughts of self-satisfaction, and I ran over to the window to see what the hell was going on out there; my celebration was apparently to be short-lived. There in the parking lot of the bed-and-breakfast was what I could only call a horde of the cloak-wearing people, and that smashing sound was the sound of them breaking the windows of my jeep and lighting it on fire.

"Oh my god! No fucking way!" I yelled out at no one in particular.

The mass of them were moving up the driveway and to the best that I could tell the front doors of the inn; they were after me. I had almost forgotten that I was still in possession of the disk, and from what I had gathered from the information at hand, it was a pinnacle piece to their religion, whatever the hell that was. My mind was racing, and I had no idea what to do as the group made its way closer to my location.

"Oh shit, oh shit, oh shit!" I exclaimed as I stood there at the window. It was then as if by some divine providence that I saw a much welcomed sight—a police car tearing up the driveway, lights blazing and hitting anything that stood in its way. I had no way of knowing how long I was out for, and at that moment with the given situation, I really didn't care. I grabbed the gun that Scott had given me and put my own gun snugly in the back of my pants. Luckily, I smuggled the shotgun and a box of shells up to my room in the duffel bag, but unfortunately my rifle was lost with my jeep; even then I could hear what 30-06 rounds I had for the rifle firing off in the inferno. Having collected the three guns and all the texts that I had gathered over the days, I left the room and headed downstairs to meet Scott and in all hopes of make a daring escape.

By the time I got downstairs, Scott had driven the car through the front doors and into the main chamber, a move that I didn't quite understand. He jumped out of the car and fired his gun out of where the front doors were once hinged, as opposed to where they were then laying clear across the room.

"I don't know what you did, but they are pissed, and there's a whole hell of a lot of them coming this way!" he yelled at me as I came the rest of the way down the stairs. From behind us, I heard a second source of gunshots, and I looked back to see where they were coming from. It was the agent, and he was quickly walking backward and firing out of the backdoor that he just came through.

"What the hell are you doing here?" I hollered at him as he came closer to our position.

"Clearly, the same thing you both are doing. This is why I tried to warn you!" He had stopped firing and had a very shocked expression on his face.

"You mean to tell me you knew that this would happen?" It seemed to me that telling us a little more than he did might have made for a better understanding of what we were getting into, or at least some idea of how to prevent it.

"Not exactly . . . I had no way of knowing that this would happen." He was clearly distressed, despite trying to hide it behind his calm demeanor. It was something that no matter how weird or troubling things got for us, we could never have seen coming.

"There has to be a way out!" Scott yelled between changing magazines.

"We are surrounded! They came out of nowhere and closed on this position!" The agent said with a slight air of arrogance. I thought as hard as I could and searched the recesses of my mind to think of something, anything that we could do to get out of that mess, then it hit me; I remembered seeing something on the schematic that I took from the library. I took it out of the small satchel that I had and quickly began to study it. There wasn't much for things we could use. Then I saw that there might be a saving grace; in the wine cellar, there was an old tunnel that led out to the carriage house further out on the property. It was something that I figured would put us out at least far enough away to get ahead of the mob and maybe escape. It was definitely worth a shot as it was about the only choice that we really had.

"I got it! Our way out! Grab a flashlight and follow me!" I told them both as I ran to a door that was just behind the main staircase. As I had instructed, they followed me to the door. Scott kicked it in, and we made our way down the stairs as fast as we could.

The beam of Scott's flashlight shined onto the door to the tunnel, and it was in my utmost hope that it was still intact after so many years. As he kicked down that other door and let the light lead the way, things began to look up as the tunnel appeared to go all the way back. There was no need for words as we all nodded at one another and sprinted down the empty hallway. Though there was an abundance of spiderwebs and small puddles of water, the way was quite clear as we came to a square room with nothing more than a thick iron ladder leading straight up to an old wooden hatch in the ceiling. I climbed up first, followed by the agent, while Scott stood at the bottom lighting our way up, and then followed suit as I opened the hatch. The room I came into was about as equally unused as the tunnel—full of spiderwebs and a musty scent lingering about. Thankfully, there was nothing amiss with the carriage house, save for the thought that it was quite large for what it was. It must've been the equivalent of a three car garage in comparison to present standards, but it was quite vacant.

After a minute of surveying the scene, I climbed the rest of the way up and into the room. "I think it's clear," I said to the other two, and they climbed up the ladder to meet me in the room. When they reached topside and finished dusting themselves off, I felt that it was a proper time for an evaluation of our inventory.

"All right. So how much ammo do we have? I have a full clip and a box of shells," I said wishing that I had carried an arsenal.

"I have three clips plus four rounds in my gun," Scott said with a tone that I imagined to mirror thoughts of an armory. We both then turned our attention to the agent, and I at least hoped that he could add some good news to our poor supply of ammunition.

"I have two full magazines, a full one loaded, and this." He reached into his coat and pulled out a very peculiar-looking device. It was about the size of a hand grenade, but the resemblance ended there. The device was chrome cylindrical object with a small clear window showing a dark blue liquid. There were also a series of smaller clear cylinders filled with a deep purple liquid surrounding the main cylinder, and at what I could only guess to be the top of the device was what looked like a red button under a piece of glass about the same size.

"What the hell is that?" Scott exclaimed. He seemed to be some strange combination of excited and confused as he asked.

"A last ditch effort," The agent said calmly and simply.

"What 'organization' are you with anyway?" He never did say, and that conversation had been the most he had said to either Scott or me, and to beat all, without being cryptic or threatening. It was my best guess that given our predicament, he realized that it was best that we all worked together because if we didn't, we could only speculate what horrors we would be subjected to.

"I cannot say. But rest assured that even if I did, you would not believe me. Simply put, those who found more light," the agent said it so matter-of-factly that it almost seemed as if he didn't expect either Scott or myself to further question him. But before I could make a smart-ass comment on it, trouble had found its way to us once again.

"Son of a bitch! They're coming this way!" Scott yelled as he stood in front of the window. I ran over and looked to see what he was talking about, and sure enough, the horde had wised up to where we had gone.

"Damn, they're relentless . . . What are we going to do?" I tried my best to not sound panicked, but it was not an easy expression to mask at a time like that.

"We can use my car. It is hidden back just over the wall behind here. There is a small gate that I came through to get to the back of the building. I will get you out of town to safety, but you are on your own from there," the agent said with the first sign of human expression that I had seen from him.

"Fair enough, but it looks like we're gonna have to fight our way out! They're here!" Scott yelled as he broke out the window with the butt of his gun and started firing wildly at the crowd. The agent and I followed his example as we broke out windows and opened fire into the mass outside of the carriage house.

Despite our efforts and flying bullets, there seemed to be no end to the black-robed individuals who clearly wanted inside.

"Brace the doors!" the agent yelled as he dropped the empty and loaded another magazine. Scott ran to the first large door and pulled down the old wooden door bar across it. I was reloading the shotgun as he made his way to the second door, and our agent friend was keeping the mass of people at bay. By the time Scott finished with the third door, I was blasting buckshot into the crowd; at long last, they seemed to be thinning out.

"We can't keep this up! I'm about out!" I screamed out as I tossed the shotgun aside and cocked the pistol Scott had given me.

"Last ditch effort then! Whatever you do, do *not* look at the blast! Tightly close your eyes and cover your ears! *now*!" The agent's orders were very clear, but I could not keep my curiosity at bay enough to stop from watching how he would engage the thing at least. He turned the odd cylinder button-side down and smashed it hard upon the stone ledge of the window sill and threw it out into the mass of beings outside. It was then that I figured it to be a good time to acknowledge his instructions, and I covered my ears, closed my eyes, and crouched down for good measure.

The blast that followed was like nothing I had ever in my life experienced before. It pulled me back and onto the ground like it had imploded, but no sooner than that happening was an outward concussion that rolled me to the back of the carriage house. Not to mention the state of the three main doors afterward; they were all three rounded inward and quite concave in contrast to how they were prior. I was amazed that they didn't blow into the building in which we were. I picked myself up from the ground utterly shocked and confused about what had just happened. I looked over to Scott, and I could plainly see that he was feeling much of the same way that I was.

"What was that thing?" I asked the agent quietly as if I was afraid to hear the answer.

"Again, even if I could tell you, you would not believe me." It was pretty much what I figured he would say; God forbid him to have divulged any secrets to the likes of an unemployed writer and a New York City cop.

"We need to go! Forget whatever it was. It got rid of the problem, and that's good enough for me!" Scott shouted as he unbarred the side door. I just looked at the agent with a sort of disbelief as I walked over to the door, and he returned my expression with an emotionless and stoic face. When we walked outside, the scene was much more bizarre than I could have ever guessed; there was a deep crater where the thing had gone off, and there were glowing purple-blue shards resembling glass or crystal scattered about all over the place and even imbedded into the walls and doors of the carriage house. All the robed figures that were only minutes before trying like hell to get into our keep just laid there lifeless and still on the ground before us. I knew that further inquiry of the agent would be frivolous; if he hadn't told us anything by then, he wasn't going to. So I adopted Scott's way of thinking and figured that it didn't matter as long as it got us the hell out of there—any means to an end.

We got through the gate that was mentioned before, and we followed the agent to his car. It was the first time since the start of all of it that I was actually happy and relieved to see that Rolls Royce. I got in on the passenger's side, and Scott jumped into the backseat; I was actually very surprised that the interior was not full of strange and alien-looking devices. It actually seemed like it was all original.

"So, can this thing fly or some crazy shit?" Scott asked the agent. I couldn't tell if he was joking, being sarcastic, or if he really thought that to be a possibility.

"No, it is just a car, chosen simply because of its elegance, reliability, and our hand in its company's creation," the agent said it almost as if he had been asked it before, and it had grown to a point of annoyance with him. I looked over to him and then back at Scott and had to laugh.

"It's just a car says the guy who just threw a thermal detonator out of the goddamn window," I said as I started laughing maniacally. Scott erupted into laughter just after I said it, and even the agent gave some resemblance of a half-cocked smile as he started the car and put it in gear. Our laughter, as much as we needed it, subsided as the agent sped out of the clearing and out onto the road. The car slid to the side a bit on the wet asphalt, but he pulled it back and straightened it out onto the road. There wasn't much that was left between us and safety; we just had to get out of the town. I slumped back into the seat and put on my seatbelt, letting out a big sigh of relief. I really wasn't sure that we were going to make it through that craziness back at the bed-and-breakfast, and if it weren't for that agent, we probably wouldn't have. I knew that by the end of our drive, the agent would be demanding the disk from me, and I would gladly hand the nightmare over to him.

We finally made it down the long, winding, narrow road leading up to the inn, and the car was just making the turn back onto the main road. As we came to the center of town, something came into view of the headlights—something that no one in that car ever wanted to see again. It was another group of black-cloaked figures standing right in the middle of the road in front of us. Time itself seemed to slow down as I helplessly watched the agent crank the steering wheel for a hard right in what I could have only imagined to be done in all hopes of missing the crowd that was blocking the way. The car did, in fact, miss the group of people; my guess is that the agent knew that the car wouldn't have survived hitting all of them. However, in turning off onto the street to our right, inertia had taken over, and combined with the wet road, there was nothing that could be done at the speed we were going to stop the car from rolling. Everything seemed to be in slow motion from the first point of impact on the driver's side to the two complete rolls that followed; when it was all said and done after a great deal of pain and extremely loud noises, the car was upside down with me dazed and still strapped into the passenger's seat.

I looked over to my left, and I could see that the agent was hurting but still alive. I put one of my hands out against the roof for support as I unbuckled myself, but I fell down hard on the roof anyway. By some miracle, my satchel was still intact and still hanging onto me, for that much I was thankful.

"Are . . . are you okay?" I asked the agent weakly. He squirmed a bit and turned to look at me.

"I think so. I am hurt but not badly." His voice sounded just as pained as my own did. I looked into the back of the car, but there was no sign of Scott. Everything was such a blur that I had no idea what happened to him, or even how long we had been sitting there like that. There was a warm and tingling sensation on my forehead, and I reached up to find out why. I could feel a pretty good-sized gash that traced vertically down the right side of my forehead, and it was bleeding quite a bit. I at least knew enough to realize that it wasn't fatal, or anything to be terribly alarmed with really. I was more concerned with what happened to Scott. Looking back over to the agent, I was about to ask if he knew anything that I didn't, but before I could terror gripped me once more as I watched the robed people pull the agent from the car followed immediately by me.

CHAPTER 13

Every Story Has an Ending, Be it for Better or for Worse

They dragged both of us from the car and out onto the cold and wet street. I couldn't think clearly enough to venture to the thoughts of what was going to happen to us: either that or I really didn't want to know. A sick and putrid stench of gangrenous sorts strongly filled the air around us. Although I wasn't sure of the exact cause, I knew enough to come to the conclusion that whatever prolonged exposure to the rituals involving the disks was, the state of those people was the direct result. They picked me up off the street with their cold and clammy hands and started walking me in the direction of whatever destination they had in mind, and the only thought on my mind was a hope that they would just simply kill me rather than leave me to the immeasurably cruel fate that Nathaniel was subjected to for so incredibly long. As they forced my steps down the road, my more recent fear had been realized when we passed by Scott's body lying lifeless on the side of the road. I felt sick as I stared at the man who was just laughing with me not more than a short time ago, who survived the onslaught of the evil bastards back at the carriage house, only to have met a savage end such as that. I could only guess that at some point during the rollover, he was ejected from the car. All that remained of the man who quickly became my friend was a twisted and bloody mess on the side of the street. It wasn't far at all down that very street that I saw the location to which we were being taken; it was the church.

The sight of the building was not the sole indication of where we were being taken; the disk in my coat's pocket was turgid with activity, not to mention so were my head and ears because of it. I looked over to the agent, and I could easily tell that he was in much worse shape than I was in. The fedora he was wearing was gone and so was his long black overcoat; his white dress shirt under his unbuttoned black suit jacket was bloodstained in various locations that were visible. As for me, my head was still bleeding like crazy, I wasn't exactly sure of the cause for the pain in my left leg and a multitude of various other cuts and scrapes everywhere. Part of me wanted to call out to the agent and maybe concoct some insane plan of escape that would somehow deliver us to safety, but deep inside I knew that there was no way out of it and that my words would be a waste at that point; we were fucked.

For the first time, I had seen since my arrival in that hellish town, the huge front doors of the church opened wide. It was as if the structure itself wished to welcome us to damnation. Though the outside looked like any other early New England house of worship, the interior told a much more vile and gruesome story. Upon entry, the first thing that I noticed was a tall, wide, black altar in the middle of the room surrounded by six other smaller altars with the rest of the disks, like the one that I carried, all perched on top of them. It was behind those, however, that the most upsetting feature was hanging; high up on the wall and wrapped tightly to a post with wire was a brutalized body of an NYPD officer. I could have assumed him only to have been Scott's missing partner. Those were not the only features that made the antichapel so unnerving; there were quite a few paintings of horrific images mostly depicting human sacrifice and various other ritualistic atrocities, the stained glass windows that were littered with words and symbols from their language, and burning candles set out on just about every surface that the place had to offer. They walked us to the middle of the room and stopped. Still holding onto us, all the robed beings started their dark and unholy chanting. I looked over to the agent who was clearly unhappy with our situation and looking pretty pale, or at least more so than he did previously.

"Well, son of Uncle Sam . . . I think we're fucked . . ." *Why not*, I thought, *joke at a time like that.* There was little more than either of us could look forward to in our future. He gave a faint grin as if it were more in disbelief rather than thinking I was funny.

"I suppose we are . . . I didn't have to kill you after all . . ." My own faint smile quickly faded with that comment; I couldn't tell if he was trying to joke with me there in the end or if he was actually serious, so I just opted to believe the prior.

The chanting, which was at first intimidating, had grown to a point of outright annoying as it went on, and on, and on. The jocular thought came to my mind that it would be nicer if they would kill me sooner rather than later, just so I didn't have to listen to that rubbish any longer. Then all at once the voices stopped, and a door on the left side of the room slowly opened. Somehow, I kind of knew what to expect, and damn it if I wasn't dead on. Into the room and through the crowd of cloaked idiots walked the old innkeeper. She wore a much more elaborate and ornate variation of the robes that the mindless followers wore, and in her hands, she held a very old and disturbing looking mask. The face of the mask was one of an expressionless pewter, and there were intricate copper wreaths all about it with a bright green jewel in the center of its forehead.

"We have waited a very long time for this, Mr. Clarke." She stood right in front of me just as stern and properly postured as I had seen her before.

"I'm sure you have." I was pissed at the thought that my ending would be at the mercy of some stick-up-the-ass old hag, so I kept my words short.

"You see, Mr. Clarke, because of your predecessor Nathaniel, we have not been in possession of the seventh piece for quite a long time. He did a very good job of hiding it through his bloodline but failed to realize that the seals all long for each other, and they call out to each other when they are separated. They always find a way to come back together." She seemed quite pleased with herself as she explained it to me and was probably not even the slightest bit aware of how little I cared.

"That's fantastic. It really is." I laid the sarcasm so thick that you would need an axe to cut it. There was no real reason for her to explain any of it to me that I could see; I figured that it was going to be the end of me, so I didn't want to be troubled with hearing any of it.

"Oh, but you don't understand, Mr. Clark. Our lives, our very essences, have been tethered to these seals. We have been waiting a long, long time for them to come back together. Once the act of ascension has begun, it cannot be halted, only completed. We have only been able to sample a taste of our world to come, and it had been skewed and perverted from its true beauty because we lack the last piece, the piece that you have brought to us. We should be thanking you, Mr. Clarke, at least those of us that you and you fellow savages did not murder." The old woman relished in the sound of her own twisted words, and it was to my understanding that they had no idea what they were in for on the "other side" that they so desperately sought after.

"So that's what you think? That some kind of paradise awaits you bunch of murdering fanatics? That really is great! Good for you!" I was practically yelling in her face, and I enjoyed every moment of it. I glanced over to the agent who was wearing the faintest of smiles, and I could only assume that he knew what I knew. If what was waiting for them on that "other side" was one in the same as the nightmarish world teeming with vile and hellish demons that I had suffered encountering, they deserved to be there.

"Bask in your sarcasm while you can, Mr. Clarke, as you will soon find the true purpose behind your being here. Our ritual started with your blood, and it will be completed with the same. You will finish what we started with the death of Nathaniel's beloved Dorothy. She cannot save you now." Then she crossed all boundaries when she reached her cold and wrinkled hand down the front of my shirt, pulled out the necklace, and tore it off me. She studied it for only a second, looked back up and me with a hideous grin, and then cast the piece of jewelry off to somewhere behind her. Her twisted and sinister smile had me pissed off in an instant, and I wanted nothing more than to punch the old broad directly in the face.

Although I somehow knew that Dorothy had come to some ill fate at the hands of those lunatics, to hear it said still came as a shock to me.

"I should have figured as much," I said as I stared her coldly in the eyes.

"The time is now, and the ritual must be complete! Bring forth the light of our passage!" The old woman yelled to her minions and two of them drew the curtains from a large window above the door. The unexplained light from the belfry of the inn was in direct view from the window. No sooner than it coming into sight, the room filled with the light that was coming from the inn, and all the seals began to "sing" loudly, including the one in my pocket. She reached her withered hand into my coat and drew out the seventh piece, placed it on the center altar, and all the gems in the center of the disks started glowing brilliantly; their lights pulsated in rhythm of the energy harmonic song that emitted from them. I was getting antsy and restless, and I couldn't think of any way to stop the madness before it was too late. Sure I thought that they all deserved to burn in hell, but I didn't, nor did I want to end up in any place like it with all those cretins as my company for God knew how long. It was about then, as I was impatiently shifting my weight from side to side, that I felt something in the small of my back—eight ways to make a difference. By some amazing stroke of luck or another miracle of divine intervention, even after everything that had happened, my beautiful, wonderful Colt .45 was still tucked snugly in the back of my jeans. I couldn't keep the smile from my face, and even knowing that I would probably not make it out alive, I was more than comfortable with the idea of taking out that old bitch, and anything beyond that was just a bonus. Fortunately, in my nervous wiggling, not only did I notice my gun still there, but I also noticed that the corpse-like hands that constrained me had weak and breakable grips.

"Even in the face of your demise you still smile, Mr. Clarke. You really must wish to die. In the ancient version of this ritual, the sacrifice of a woman who is pure of heart was thought necessary, but in more modern times, we found that either man or woman would suffice, just as long as they are sacrificed. I know that you will do, Mr. Clarke. The simple fact that you are of the very bloodline that robbed us of our transcendence makes this the most fitting end that I could ever hope for." As much as I detested the very thought of admitting it to myself, I knew that she was very much right in her last words—I was the direct descendant.

"Yes, I'm sure that anything that requires killing someone, especially one of pure heart, is something that will lead you to the best possible outcome a good person could hope for. Listen to yourself, you fucking idiot!" I knew that there was no reasoning when faced with such reckless fanaticism, but my outburst could not be contained.

"That is what the ascension calls for, Mr. Clarke. When one makes the ultimate sacrifice, they will ascend to a level beyond a simple human creature and become something so much more. Your time is now, Mr. Clarke." She put on the horrendous mask and then reached into her black robe and pulled out a very decorative-looking ceremonial dagger. As the evil woman raised it up over her head and chanted some gibberish that I figured was the closest I was going to get for my last rites, my calculating for the right time had come to that very moment. Everything that is about to be written can only be described as the best moment of clarity and adrenaline that I had ever experienced—one of those moments that happens so perfectly that you know that you could never repeat again, even with a century's worth of practice.

Swiftly, she brought the dagger down to meet my heart, but instead, it met the heart of the robed jerk to my right as I lunged left and put him directly in harm's way. Once the dagger was imbedded deep within his chest, he immediately let go of my right arm, which I used to elbow the one holding my left arm square in the nose, freeing me completely. Then, finally able to move without worry, I reached to the small of my back, grabbed the Colt and pulled back the hammer. The woman was still in the midst of figuring out what had just happened as I pressed the barrel of the gun firmly up under her jaw.

"Lady, you are going to hell, and I am more than happy to be the one to send you there." All I could see through the eye slits of the devilishly stoic-faced mask was the look of sheer despair in her eyes, and with that, I pulled the trigger.

The bullet did not go through the helmet-like portion of the mask, but there was a very noticeable bump right at the top where it tried. Still teeming with adrenaline and rage, my moment of perfect execution continued. I did not notice at that time that when she plunged the dagger into her unfortunate follower, the blade had also cut my arm, giving the blood tribute needed for the gate to be opened, either that or it was the death of her follower. Points of light-like lasers shot from the surrounding six seals and into the central gem of the seventh in the middle. As they did, a black opening formed at the ceiling and began to consume the room entirely. The crowd of black-robed people was in disarray the second after I had blasted their leader, and they were moving wildly and aimlessly about the room. They had let go of the agent who I saw take off out of the front door from the corner of my eye. I had seven rounds left in my gun, and since none of the robe-wearing fellows seemed to hold much interest in me anymore, I had seven other ideas of how to spend the shots wisely. One by one, I took aim on the seals sitting on their alters bringing about who knew what hell to our world. Every time I shot one directly in the gem inset in the center, the entire piece shattered with a high-pitched shriek followed by little more than silence. With each one that I hit, those in the black cloaks writhed in agony, screamed, and yelled; it seemed that they truly were bound to the seals. There was but one left, the seventh disk, the piece that had started my messed-up journey to begin with.

"And the horse I rode in on . . ." I thought to myself as I gave one last squeeze on the trigger. The shot rang out, and the disk burst into countless pieces. And as it did, all the people in the black robes cried out and moaned in unison before falling down dead on the floor. The one bit that I found to be troubling was the all-consuming blackness that was still taking the room. I turned and ran for the door as fast as I possibly could, but all at once I was knocked down as if something had fallen down on top of me. I didn't know how right I was.

When I picked myself up from the floor, I knew the instant that I had gotten to my feet that something horrible had happened. The antichapel still was much of the same in its appearance. It was the lighting, the temperature, and the general ambiance of my surroundings that had changed, and all those factors were chillingly familiar. There were no bodies of the followers strewn about the floor, not even the cadaver of the old woman remained, yet somehow or another my satchel was lying there on the floor next to where I had fallen. I sat down on the floor and waived my proverbial white flag as I lit up a cigarette. I figured that it was only a matter of time before whatever creatures inhabited that realm found and gave me the Nathaniel Clarke treatment. As sat there with my smoke as my only company, I remembered that I had stowed away something in the satchel that I just couldn't leave behind in my room; so I reached in pulled out the books and the bottle of scotch and found contentment in at least having something to read in that horrific place. So I opened the journal of Nathaniel and started to read.

To be perfectly honest, there wasn't much past the last entry that I had read just before he was leaving to get Dorothy. According to what he wrote, the followers had captured him and given him profession as a mason and forced him to build the Norcrest Sanitarium so that they could practice their rituals without scrutiny. He helped them build it on the promise of reuniting him with his wife, but they backstabbed Nathaniel after the place was built and used Dorothy and her love for him as a sacrifice in their depraved unholy rites. He broke free of his cell and had tried to save her but, alas, was too late. But before the demented incantations could be completed, Nathaniel stole the seventh piece and gave it to one of the Indian trackers that brought him there in the first place, telling him to take it back to Salem and give it to his son, Alexander, not knowing the curse that thing would bring to the generations that followed. They recaptured Nathaniel after that and subjected him to many experiments that eventually landed him in that realm of agony and sorrow—a place of the most bitter lament. In the last few entries that he was able to write while in that cell, he described that even though not all the seals were present, they were still able to function at a minimal level. Using them as they did, they managed to send Nathaniel to that other place permanently. Interestingly enough, he made a short remark about how exposure to that other world and retuning to ours left those who took practice in it more like rancid corpses than living beings. That explained the rotten smell of them and the dead look as well; whatever it was they were doing slowly poisoned the soul, in turn, corrupting the body. All that was how the seal made its way through my family and traveled along the bloodline, eventually ending up with me. And oddly enough, it explains the staggering rates of suicide and madness in my family history. It wasn't until after the last entry in the journal that I noticed that there were a great many blank pages left to be filled in.

Before I started in on that, I took another drink of the scotch and lit another cigarette for confidence enough to read the rest of the notes written by the agent. Most of them seemed like simple observations of the curious happenings and strange events that surrounded the disks, most of which I had experienced firsthand. Disturbingly enough, there was quite a bit of observations of that other Evan Clark and myself. There were detailed pages about his observations of the other Evan's degeneration and proof that he had been watching me from a distance ever since the disk came into my possession. An odd read, I thought, as all the pages were the third-party perspective on my travels as he witnessed them. It wasn't until toward the end of his scribbles that the information got interesting. According to what he had written, he and his organization had traced the history of the disks back to ancient Irish pagans who truly believed that the disks were meant for human ascension. The notes confirmed that they did not know the real origin of the seals, nor did they know if there were in fact only seven. All that they really seemed to know was that through some means of light spectrum combination and frequencies in harmonic resonance, the seals were able to open a door to other places of existence.

"Well, no shit," I said aloud as I read the notes.

It wasn't clear how they ended up in tribal Ireland, but the notes speculated that it had something to do with Nordic explorers or even an even-more ancient and yet-to-be-discovered civilization. I'd had enough of the history lesson and decided to move on to something much more important—the blank pages in the journal. So I grabbed a pen out of the inside pocket of my coat, picked up the journal, and then sat down at one of the altars to use as a desk and started to write.

That brings the story to now. I have been sitting here for what seems like forever, writing away and pretending to ignore the demonic things taunting me from outside of the windows. I was quick to discover why they didn't come sooner, and that was the discovery that they do not like light, either that or fire. It seems that the more candles burn out, more of them appear at the glass, scratching and whispering, calling for my surrender. The creatures, much like the one Dorothy saved me from back in Pennsylvania, look almost human, save for the black void that is their eyes, and the more sinister and twisted look. Ever since I sat down to write this all down, there has been a growing blue light across the room from me, and it looks as if it grows brighter with each candle that goes out. I figure that as soon as I have finished writing the rest of this, I may go over and see what fresh hell that light will bring me; may it be for better or worse.

The things that have happened, the things I have seen, I have tried to keep accurately the way it all transpired. Even now I can see and hear them scratching at the windows and jostling the doors, just waiting for the moment when the lights go out and all that is left is the dark. There's still so much that I don't understand, and probably never will; I don't think anything or anyone short of God could explain this. I was looking for a story, and I got one. At least I found one last cigarette hiding in the satchel only moments ago, and doubly lucky that there was a .45 round there keeping it company. I have come a long way since leaving Colorado, and none of it was anything I could have ever in my life seen coming. I don't know if anyone will ever find this, these pages upon pages that to anyone else would seem like the ramblings of a madman. If it ever is found, let it end like this: I will not succumb to these monsters, and whatever torment that they have planned for me, I will not give them the pleasure.

There is only one thing left to do now, and it's the only thing I can think to do. I put that last round in the chamber just before I wrote this sentence. All that can be done is to walk toward that pulsating blue light across the room from me and pull back the hammer. They did not win.

Sincerely,
Evan Clarke

Epilogue

The room was black and silent. There was only one source of light, and that was coming from a small lamp perched upon the desk. To his knowledge, that was the only thing in the room; he had been in there many times before, but the lighting had always been the same. A pale white hand with a white cuff scarcely visible from beneath the black suit jacket sleeve appeared under the light holding a manila folder.

"Agent Jefferson . . . I took into consideration your lack of tenure in our organization. This is why I have chosen to be lenient. Now explain to me the events that transpired in the Adirondack village." The voice that came from behind the light was drawn out, deep, and monotone. There was something in his very manner of speech that commanded respect and imposed great intimidation. Agent Jefferson made a hard swallow out of sheer nerves; he knew the steep price paid for failure, especially when it is a mistake on the part of the operating agent.

"The seals were reunited. It was the journalist who carried the bloodline not the police officer. The journalist had the seventh piece, and to my best knowledge, they were activated." Agent Jefferson looked down at the floor, embarrassed in even the simple speaking of the words. He could only speculate what it could have sounded like to his commanding operative when it was put like that. There was a long silence before the room was filled with the deep and powerful voice that seemed disembodied in the dark, almost omnipotent.

"What were the fates of the two, the policeman and the journalist?" Though it was quite the simple question, the answer that Agent Jefferson had for the journalist was no so cut and dry.

"The officer is dead, confirmed. The journalist is presumed to be dead. The followers' church collapsed as he destroyed the seventh seal and the rest of them before that. I managed to escape, and he never came out." He knew even as he said it, that there was far too much assumption in the death of the journalist.

"As you well know, the dead are only as dead as they are confirmed to be. You disappoint me, Agent Jefferson. I will remind you once more, and only this once more. Because you are relatively new to our organization, I grant you pardon for just this once. Now, leave my office." As the door opened behind Agent Jefferson by an unseen force, he couldn't help but wonder what really had happened to the journalist. He quickly dismissed the thought and took his quick leave from the office, the door closing slowly behind him. As he walked down long hallway outside of the office, he knew that the journalist may very well have survived. There was no body recovered in any of the follow-up investigations, nor was there any trace of the belongings that he had carried with him. In the back of his mind, he knew there were many questions concerning the true outcome of that last event.

A year had come and gone since Evan's disappearance, and all hope of finding him had faded when it became a cold case. Savannah couldn't help but feel guilty in many ways, especially because of that last time she had heard from him. The message that he left on her answering machine would leave a scar for the rest of her days. It pleads for her forgiveness and was very ambiguous concerning whatever danger he had found himself in. Though the time had passed, it was a constant thought of her that he probably did not survive the trouble that he was in, no matter how badly she wanted to believe otherwise.

All those same guilt-ridden and punishing thoughts and emotions ran strong in her on the way home from work. With the car parked and the day coming to closure, she got out and walked to the house. There, on the doorstep, was a sight that stopped her dead in her tracks. Wrapped up in a familiar brown and white pinstriped button-up shirt was an unknown item placed for her to find. She carefully walked over to where it was, slowly looking all around as she did. She picked it up from the concrete and cautiously unraveled the shirt from whatever it was. The view for her to see paused her pulse and caused for a tear to fall down her cheek. There on top of what looked to be a very old and tattered leather-bound book was the wedding ring that Evan had worn for years. She rapidly looked in all directions, hoping to see some sign that Evan had been there, but there was nothing. With a sniffle and wiping the tears from her face, she took the items into the house with her.

THE END

The World in Ruins and the Aftermath

Air rapidly and almost violently filled Evan's lungs; it was as if it was his first breath of life. His eyes opened quickly, and he sat up as though he had just awoken from a terrible dream. All around, his eyes darted, hoping to see something, anything, that would make sense. As he did, everything slowly started to come back to him. He picked himself up from the debris and rubble from the collapsed antichapel and started to analyze all that happened just before he found himself in the middle of a fallen building.

He remembered walking toward the ever-growing blue light at the other end of the room from him, fully prepared to do what he needed to do. As he stood just before it, he put the gun to his head and was ready for whatever happened next, or so he thought. When he stepped into the light, he was surrounded by a pristine peace, and every fear and feeling of hopelessness melted away. It was then that he saw Dorothy, and she appeared out of nowhere. She explained a great many things to him—things that he previously did not understand.

All that had happened to him, more or less, was presented to everyone along the line of those who held the seals. They failed, whereas Evan had succeeded. They all gave in to the power of the seal and were broken by its ill will. He was the only one who met the challenge and completed it to shining glory. Evan, with Dorothy's guidance, had brought that nightmare to an end. She had protected him from the hells of that other realm and shielded him from its terrors ever since the beginning of his misfortunes. Yet there was something else she had not told him until then, something that would alter the course of his life as he knew it.

Evan stood there in the ruins contemplating everything that had been told to him. She didn't only tell him of things that he had done, but also of things that he will and should do. In the light, when she appeared to him, she asked him to do only one thing—to make sure that no one else would ever befall the tragedy that was her and Nathaniel's. By that, she meant stopping those who would try to hide and cover-up such paranormal and unexplainable events and tragedies. A gift was given to him, there in the light, and it was something that he could not himself fully understand. Before she returned him to our world, she once again gave him the necklace that he thought he had lost prior to that. Along with the necklace, she put her hands on his cheeks, leaned in slowly, and kissed him on his forehead. As her lips met his skin, a rush of energy coursed through his body to the likes he had never before experienced. He felt that in that very instant, something in him had changed, and he was right.

Stepping out onto the street and into the beautiful glow of the sunrise, though he couldn't explain it or understand it, he could feel the world around him as he never had before. Each and every breath that he took was filled with the energy and life of all things around him, and he had an unspoken harmony life itself. His eyes could see the movement and flow of that very life force and all energies from every point around him and all at once understood how everything was connected. Evan did not fully know why he was experiencing that or how such a gift had come into his possession. But it was in that very thought that the last words Dorothy had told him before she disappeared back into the light:

"Evan, I give you illumination—the truest that the light can offer. It is a gift of divinity, only for you. With it, you can save those who need to be saved and stop those who found the light of divinity by false means. Go now, Evan, return to serve your purpose . . ."

It was after she said that, that Evan woke up in the rubble and ruins only moments before.

He took another deep breath as he stood there bathed in the soft orange light of the rising sun, somehow feeling its every beam. There was something else that he began to feel, and it was something that he had never felt so strongly before—a sense of purpose. As he slowly walked down the street, the thoughts of where to go and what to do next circled around in his head. It was then that his foot found something lying on the ground. He looked down to see that it was a side-view mirror of an old Rolls Royce; the thought occurred to him that it must have broken off during the wreck. When he picked it up for further examination, the reflection of himself that it showed him made Evan lose care for the mirror altogether. The reflection looking back at him from the mirror was in fact him but very different. His light brown hair was as white as snow, and his blue eyes seemed to have some sort of soft glow in them. It was then, with that vision of his new image, that brought great meaning to the last words Dorothy had said to him. She had given him the light, she had illuminated him, and his purpose was to stop those who had attained the same by false means, and he knew the ones that she spoke of. He dropped the mirror to the ground and looked up to the sky; somehow, he knew that there was something up there in the light, something great and unexplainable. Whatever had given him his gift had specific intentions for him, and he would meet the expectations. Evan looked to the road before him that led out of that town and understood what it was that he needed to do. Armed with only that understanding and an uncountable number of unanswered questions, he set forth into the unknown.